BLOOD FEUD

A TOM ROLLINS THRILLER

PAUL HEATLEY

INKUBATOR
BOOKS

Published by Inkubator Books
www.inkubatorbooks.com

Copyright © 2023 by Paul Heatley

Paul Heatley has asserted his right to be identified as the author of this work.

ISBN (eBook): 978-1-83756-198-8
ISBN (Paperback): 978-1-83756-199-5

For Aidan

PROLOGUE

It's late in the stash house. The lights are off. The only glow comes from the television. It's playing a baseball game.

Anthony Rollins sits slumped in a chair. He sips a beer. He's barely watching the game. His eyelids feel heavy. He nods off momentarily, but then jolts back awake. He runs a hand down his face and then back through his hair, trying to wake himself up.

Connor Sharpe sits in the chair across from him. He seems more engrossed in the game. "It's a repeat," Anthony says. "You think they're gonna play a live game at this time of night?"

Connor waves a hand. "I don't give a shit," he says. "It's the Cubs. And I haven't seen it before. I don't know who wins."

Anthony doesn't know who wins either, but he doesn't mention this. He's never been a big sports fan. He takes another drink and realizes the can is almost empty. He forces himself up out of the chair and goes through to the kitchen.

Dylan is there already, smoking a cigarette by the open window. His Springfield XD is on the table. He looks back as Anthony enters and tilts his chin in greeting. "How's it going?"

Anthony shakes his empty can. "Need a refill." He crushes the can and dumps it in the trash, then goes into the refrigerator and brings out a fresh one. "You thirsty?"

Dylan shakes his head and flicks the cigarette out the window. He pulls it closed and turns around.

"How's it look out there?" Anthony says.

"Quiet," Dylan says. He takes a seat at the table and starts disassembling his gun.

"Jesus Christ," Anthony says, cracking open the can and leaning against the refrigerator. He takes a drink and shakes his head, watching Dylan work.

"What?" Dylan says.

"Nothing," Anthony says. He tilts the bottom of the can toward him. "Just when you're working like that, you remind me of someone."

Dylan doesn't answer. He focuses on what he's doing.

"You coming through to watch the game?" Anthony says.

"I know who wins it," Dylan says.

"Connor's enjoying it."

"Connor's a simpleton."

Anthony frowns. "That's harsh. Connor's all right."

Dylan glances at him with an eyebrow raised. "He's your friend," he says. "Not mine. You ain't my buddy either, so you don't have to hang around in here. I'm not looking for company."

"Ezra had me believe we were all brothers," Anthony says. "You telling me that's not the case?"

Dylan stares at him.

Anthony pushes off the refrigerator and returns to the living room. "Asshole," he mutters, dropping back into the chair.

"What was that?" Connor says.

"Nothing. Don't worry about it."

Anthony and Connor have their own guns, but they're not carrying them. They're in the kitchen with Dylan. Dylan is the muscle. Anthony and Connor are just here to make up the numbers. An extra set of eyes and hands. Extra security, just in case. There shouldn't be any trouble. There hasn't been anything serious happen for a while. Just regular stuff – you see a rival gang member before they see you, you either keep your head down or you run. If you're feeling particularly tough, you get the drop on them and stomp their face into the sidewalk. Anthony never feels particularly tough. He's a firm believer in strength in numbers. He keeps his head down. Stays out of trouble.

Or at least out of *more* trouble. He already has enough on his plate. He thinks about Harlan. Thinks about how that son of a bitch has backed him up into a corner and –

There's a knock at the door. It's hard and firm and demands attention. Anthony and Connor look at each other. The knock comes again.

They hear Dylan's chair scrape back from the table in the kitchen. He appears in the doorway, his gun down by his side. He looks in on them. "You want me to get that?" he says, jerking a thumb back toward the door, unimpressed.

"I mean, I'll go get it if you want," Connor says. "But I'm not expecting anyone."

Dylan and Connor aren't expecting anyone, either. No one has called ahead. No one should be at the door.

Dylan waves him away and turns, heading for the front.

He calls through the door as he gets closer. "*Yo*. What you want?"

Anthony can hear someone respond from the other side, but it's muffled, and he can't make out what they say.

Dylan evidently does, and it must satisfy him. He goes to the door and looks out through the spy hole, then unlocks the door.

Anthony can't see, but he listens. Connor has settled and returned his attention to the baseball replay. Anthony remains alert. Hears Dylan turn the last lock. The door swings open. Dylan's voice, "What you looking for?"

And then three gunshots, and the sound of Dylan's body hitting the ground. Anthony jumps to attention. He knows it's Dylan. The gunshots came from outside. The sound of the body landing was inside the house. Too close to be anyone else.

The door swings open wider, hitting against the wall. The shooter steps in. Three more gunshots, making sure Dylan is dead.

Connor is frozen in his chair. He looks up. "What do we do?" His eyes are wide, and he's no doubt wishing he had his gun. The kitchen feels like it's a mile away right now.

"Out the window," Anthony says, grabbing Connor and hauling him to his feet. He listens behind them, by the door. He can hear footsteps now. One pair, by the sound of it. Coming down the hall, toward where they are in the living room. Anthony throws open the window. There's no point trying to be quiet. They need to be *fast*. He throws Connor out ahead of him. "*Go!*"

As Connor's feet disappear through the open window, Anthony jumps out after him. A gunshot rings out behind him, tearing into the wall to his right, and then another smashes the window. He grabs Connor and they start running, jumping over the fence and into the next yard, and then continuing, over fences and through yards, staying away from the road, breathing hard and waiting for the sound of another gunshot chasing them down. It doesn't come. The shooter isn't interested in them. The shooter wants what's inside the stash house.

Anthony and Connor don't think about all they've left behind. They think about saving their own skins. They keep running, even when they feel like their lungs are about to explode and their legs are going to give out. They run, and they disappear into the cold, dark Chicago night.

1

Tom Rollins has been in Hopper Creek for a year.

He lives with Hayley Teller. They have their routines. Every Sunday, so long as Hayley isn't on shift at the hospital, they visit Del Nowak's grave together. If she's working, Tom goes alone. On Wednesday nights, neither of them works. They make time for each other. They go on dates, or they go for a walk, or they just stay in and watch a movie. They have breakfast together most mornings, either before Hayley goes to work or just after she returns from night shift. Sometimes, when Tom is off, he meets her at the hospital for lunch.

Tom does not allow himself to grow soft, however. Every morning, he wakes early and goes for a run. A new gym has opened in town, and this is his destination. For thirty to sixty minutes he lifts weights and strikes a punching bag, and then he runs home.

Tom has found a job in town. He works as a bartender. It's not the first time he's tended bar. Del's hardware store closed down after his death. He was murdered inside the store. The family didn't want to keep it. Didn't want to go into it. Tom closed it down for them. Helped with the selling of it. He refused to take any of the money they offered him as thanks. He couldn't take it, not after everything that had happened. He felt responsible. Not just for what happened to Del, but for what almost happened to Hayley.

But that was a year ago. Tom has settled in. He has a job, a home, and a girlfriend. He's happy.

He's bored.

But he won't admit it to himself. Or, at least, he *tries* not to admit it to himself. Tries not to think about it at all. The truth is, though, he misses the action. Misses travelling. Misses living by his wits. It makes him think back to what people have said to him in the past – some accusatorily, and some with concern. That he's addicted. Addicted to the action. To the danger.

Addicted to war.

At first, the bar provided some semblance of excitement. There were some rowdy regulars who needed to be calmed down. Some of them were determined to test themselves against the new bartender, the one they knew was ex-Army. Tom allowed them to test themselves, but they were fast learners. They don't hassle him anymore. They come, and they have a quiet drink, and everyone enjoys a pleasant evening.

It's been a long, long time since there was last any real trouble. Seven months, he thinks. Seven months of nothing but pulling and pouring drinks.

It's another quiet night. Tom wipes down the bar and looks around. A few booths are occupied. An older married couple in one. A couple of young women in another. A couple of the regular guys who used to give Tom trouble when he first started working here, but now couldn't be any nicer to him.

The lighting in the bar isn't bright, but it's not the dimmest Tom's ever seen, either. It's enough. The walls are decorated with black-and-white posters of bands and singers the owner likes – The Doors, The Beatles, Led Zeppelin, Lynyrd Skynyrd, Jimi Hendrix, Allman Brothers – the list goes on. There's an old-fashioned jukebox full of seven-inch vinyl records, mostly consisting of the bands and singers on the walls. One of the regulars dropped some coins in it earlier, and the bar has been treated to an evening of Johnny Cash, Dolly Parton, Waylon Jennings, and Willie Nelson.

It's not long until closing time. Tom checks his watch. Just another hour. The younger ladies are the first to leave. They bring him their glasses, and Tom thanks them, and they all say goodbye before they leave.

Not long after they've gone, the door opens again. A couple of young guys come in – late twenties, early thirties, Tom would guess. They stride straight to the bar. Their eyes are on him the whole while.

Tom steps closer to them, just the counter between them. The two men don't sit. "What can I get for you both?" he says.

The two guys aren't tall, but they're squat and broad. Firm men with lower centers of gravity. Not easy to knock down. Tom can see from the looks on their faces that they're not here for drinks and some quiet chatter. They look like they're after trouble, and Tom perks up at this. Feels something stirring within himself.

Both men are glaring at him. They haven't spoken yet. They're trying to intimidate him. Tom doesn't back down. He smiles at them. One of them is bearded, and the other has a mustache. The bearded one is first to speak.

"You the one they call Rollins?"

"That's me," Tom says.

"Figured," the bearded guy says, looking him over. "You match the description."

"Help you both with something?" Tom says. He can feel the eyes of the people still in the bar looking over, intrigued. They can sense what is coming just as well as Tom can.

"You remember our cousin?" Mustache says. "What you did to him?"

Tom shrugs. "You're not giving me much to go off."

"You broke his arm," bearded says. "About six months ago now."

"Broke his arm, huh?" Tom says. "Yeah, I think I remember him now. Six months? I thought it was longer."

"Yeah, well, he's all healed up now, but you put some fucking fear in him. He won't come back near this place."

"Good," Tom says. "He tell you *why* I broke his arm?"

"He was just having a good time," Bearded says.

"Tell that to the women he was groping," Tom says. "I catch him grabbing an ass, I give him a warning. He calmed himself down for all of five minutes, then I catch him over there by the jukebox, and he's touching up another female patron. Ass and chest this time. I was all ready to throw him out, but she told me not to. She said she didn't want any trouble." Tom looks both men in the eye. "I did as she asked, but she left soon after. That was her night ruined. But I didn't do anything to your needle-dick cousin then because she'd asked me not to. He tell you any of this? No? That figures.

"He was looking pleased with himself by that point. He'd

had a couple of drinks, but he wasn't drunk. He knew what he was doing. He knew everything he was doing. He knew when he sat down next to the young lady in that booth right there" – Tom tilts his head to the right – "he knew she'd had too much to drink. It was a busy night, a Saturday, and once it got quiet, I was going to call her a taxi. But he slid into that booth next to her before I could do that. He made sure to slide in next to her while I was distracted. Then, next time I look up, he's got his hand up her skirt, and she looked like she didn't have a clue where she was, let alone what was happening. When I pulled him off, he took a swing at me. And *then* I broke his arm. Did your asshole rapist cousin tell you all of that?"

Mustache wavers a little, but Bearded looks like he doesn't give a shit. "Why should I believe a word you say? You're just trying to justify what you did, cover up for yourself."

"I was here." One of the regulars speaks up from his booth. "I saw what happened, and it was exactly how Rollins says it went."

"We ain't talking to you, old man," Bearded barks across the room. "Sit your ass down and mind your business."

"Don't talk to my customers that way," Tom says. He keeps his voice level.

"Fuck you," Bearded says. He slaps Mustache – Tom thinks they're brothers – in the chest with the back of his hand. "Let's deal with this asshole and get outta here."

Tom shakes his head. "I'm gonna give you a chance to walk out," he says. "It sounds like your cousin might have learned a lesson. Am I going to have to teach it to you, or will you follow his example?"

Bearded lunges forward, reaching for Tom over the bar.

Tom watches him, unimpressed. It was a stupid move to make. Tom is too far out of reach, and Bearded has left himself wide open. Tom grabs him by his reaching wrist with his left hand, then wraps his right around the back of his head and slams his face down into the counter. Bearded's nose bursts and leaves a butterfly-shaped splat of blood on the hardwood. He stumbles back, spitting blood and holding his face, but he doesn't go down. He's clearly dazed, though, and isn't any immediate danger.

Tom turns to Mustache. "How about you?" he says. "You gonna listen to reason?"

Mustache looks at Tom, then at his brother, and then turns back to Tom. He's conflicted. He bites his lip and shakes his head. "Oh, man – I gotta," he says, sounding regretful.

He makes a grab for Tom, and much like his brother, he leaves himself undefended. Tom swings his right hand around and hits him with an open-handed strike across the jaw. The sound is so loud it's like a gun going off. Mustache's head rolls around on his shoulders, and he falls back limp, dropping to the ground.

Bearded is shaking himself loose, wiping blood from his top lip. He sees his brother fall. He snorts and comes forward. Tom jumps up onto the bar as he gets close and kicks him in the face. If his nose wasn't already broken from its introduction to the hardwood bar, it is now.

Tom hops down from the bar and punches him in the stomach, doubling him up. He gives him a shot to the kidneys, too, to keep him subdued, and then grabs him by the back of his jacket and marches him to the door. He throws him out, and Bearded stumbles and falls and lands on his back. He groans and gingerly touches his nose, but he doesn't try to get up. Out of the corner of his eye, Tom sees someone coming down the sidewalk, but they're small and female, and he doubts they're with these two.

He returns to the bar to retrieve Mustache and carries him out, dumping him on top of his brother, who coughs as the weight is dropped onto him. "Two of you get out of here now," Tom says. He kneels down closer so the conscious brother can hear him better. "And forget about trying to avenge your cousin. If he's got any sense, he's learned from what he did wrong. If he's got any smarts, he knows he's lucky I didn't break both arms."

Bearded whimpers, but all the fight has gone out of him. He's not interested in getting hit again.

Tom stands, but before he can turn and go back into the bar, he hears a voice behind him. A female voice, and familiar.

"Throwing out a couple of troublemakers?" she says.

Tom spins. It's Cindy Vaughan.

She raises an eyebrow and grins. "Y'know, last time we met up after some time apart, you were doing the exact same thing."

Tom starts to smile, but then he freezes and looks up and down the street. "What are you doing here?" he says. "Has something happened? Are you in trouble?"

Cindy laughs. "It's not always bad news, Tom," she says. "I came to see you."

He doesn't know why she would come all the way here just to see him, or even how she knows where he is, but for the moment, he doesn't care. He steps closer and wraps her in his arms, and she laughs again and hugs him back.

2

_____

Inside the bar, Tom pours Cindy a drink. The patrons who were remaining have paid up and filed out after witnessing the night's action. "You came all this way just to see me?" Tom says, pushing the glass toward Cindy.

She takes a sip and then glances toward the door. "I think I might be early," she says.

Tom frowns. "Early for what? I was about to close."

Cindy looks at him and bites her lip. "I feel bad," she says. "I thought I was running late, so I rushed here, but now I'm starting to think that I've come too early and ruined the surprise."

"Surprise?" Tom says. And then it occurs to Tom what she might mean – today is the twenty-fourth of April. It's his birthday. He's thirty-three years old. He looks at Cindy and cocks his head.

"Happy birthday," she says.

As if on cue, the door opens, and Hayley steps into the bar. She sees them both and does a double take. "Cindy?" she says.

"Sorry," Cindy says. "I thought I was late, so I came straight here."

Hayley doesn't seem to mind. She laughs. She turns to Tom. "Happy birthday!" she says, and then Tom sees that she's not alone. Behind her, filing into the bar, he sees Zeke Green with his family – his wife, Naomi, and their children, Tre and Tamika – and then after them comes Taylor Hendricks, with her brother, Josh, and his wife, Tilly. Then, at the rear, he sees his father – Jeffrey Rollins – and by his side is Tom's stepmother, Sylvia.

Tom blinks, caught off guard. "What," he says, coming around the bar to get closer to everyone, "what's all this?"

Hayley steps up to him and cups his face. "I wanted to surprise you," she says. "And plus, this way I get to meet all the people you've told me so much about." She kisses him and then lets him go so he can greet the friends he hasn't seen in a long time. He reaches Zeke first, and they embrace.

"It's late," Tom says, looking at the children. "When did you get in?"

"We got here yesterday," Zeke says, laughing. "I did a little surveillance on you, man – I watched you get here at the start of your shift, and you never suspected a thing."

"Oh," Tom says, grinning, "it's like that, is it?"

"Yeah, it's like that, and don't try to come at me now saying something like, *I felt eyes on me at all times*, because I know it's not true."

Naomi steps forward, shaking her head. "He was so proud of himself," she says, embracing Tom. "You should have heard him – *I got him, Naomi, he never knew I was there!* It's good to see you again, Tom."

Tom hugs her back, then gets down to embrace Tre and

Tamika. "The two of you have got *big*!" he says. "I know I've missed a few birthdays – how old are you now?"

"Eight," Tre says.

"Six," Tamika says. They're both shy. It's been a long time since they last saw him.

"Oh, wow, that really has been a lot of birthdays. Do the two of you even remember who I am?"

"We remember you, Uncle Rollins," Tamika says. Tre nods along.

"I'm glad to hear that," Tom says. "Well, since you've made it all the way out here, we're gonna have to make sure we get all caught up. I wanna hear everything the two of you have been up to. Although, it's pretty late for you both – you're not tired?"

Tamika grins and shakes her head. Tre laughs behind his hand, like he and his sister are admitting to something they shouldn't.

"I made sure they had a nap before we came here," Naomi says. "They protested, but I insisted on it. Otherwise, they were either gonna be real grumpy right about now, or they'd be falling asleep on their feet – maybe both." To her children she says, "Have you both said happy birthday to Uncle Rollins?"

They dutifully do, and Tom straightens up. He notices Zeke has gone over to Cindy. They know each other already, from when they helped Tom out in Mexico and Arizona. That was a long time ago, now. Or, at least, it feels like a long time. Naomi and the children head over to join Zeke, and he introduces them to Cindy.

Hayley steps close to Tom. "How come they were calling you by your last name?"

"How do you mean?"

"Why were they calling you Uncle Rollins?" Hayley says. "Instead of Uncle – never mind. I just heard it in my head. I get it now."

Tom turns to Taylor. She's sixteen now. Though they've kept in touch via letters, they haven't been exchanging pictures. Tom hasn't seen her since he left her in the security of her brother and his wife's home in Portland. She looks taller, and healthier. Happier, for sure.

"Tom," she says, smiling. "It's nice to see you again."

"It's good to see you too," Tom says. "Isn't tonight a school night? And you're all the way out here in New Mexico, partying? This is not the impression of yourself that you gave me in your letters. You make yourself sound so studious."

"I'm so studious I can afford to miss a few days," she says. She steps forward for a tentative hug.

"You're looking well, Taylor," Tom says.

"Thanks," she says, smiling shyly. She's been through a lot already in her short life, but Tom sees she still possesses the same inner strength she always did. There's a firmness about her. A resilience. A defiance. He's glad to see it's still there.

He spots her necklace. The Santa Muerte pendant. He gave it to her. He reaches out and holds it briefly in his palm, remembering the woman who gave it to *him*.

"I wear it all the time," Taylor says.

He smiles at Taylor, then shakes hands with her brother and his wife and lets them move into the bar to get settled. Jeffrey and Sylvia have already come through and taken seats at the bar. Tom will catch up with them soon. He turns back to Hayley. "So," he says, "a surprise party?"

"I know it's not your kind of thing," Hayley says, "but, I

dunno, it's your birthday, and I just wanted to do something nice for you. So I reached out to all the people I know you're friendly with and invited them here."

"I appreciate it," Tom says. "But am I expected to work this?"

Hayley laughs. "I spoke to the owner, he said we could help ourselves so long as we don't break anything or make too much mess. But I also let him know there'd be kids and minors present, so it wasn't like things are going to get too wild."

"I dunno, Zeke's kids are real party animals. They could be kicking over tables by night's end."

"They have that look about them," Hayley says, grinning. "Oh, by the way, as you can see, I got in touch with your dad and your stepmother, but I couldn't get through to your brother."

Tom nods. "How did you get everyone's details?"

"I – look, I'm not proud of this, but I went through your things to get details. You've told me so much about Zeke and Cindy and Taylor, I wanted to be able to invite them here to see you. Also, it gave me a chance to finally thank Cindy for when she helped you find me before that psycho surgeon could cut my kidney out." She strokes his arm. "Did you hear what I said about your brother?"

"Yeah," Tom says. "It's fine, don't worry about it."

"He wouldn't answer when I called, and he didn't answer when I messaged."

"It's fine," Tom says. "I doubt I have his up-to-date number. Even if you'd got through, I don't think he'd have agreed to come."

"You never talk about him, Tom. Are you ever going to tell me what happened between the two of you?"

"Sometimes brothers fall out," Tom says. "Listen, I'd better go and mingle." He holds Hayley by the shoulders and kisses her on the forehead. "Thank you for this. This is – it's very unexpected."

Hayley smiles. "You're welcome."

From the bar, Zeke calls over, "We gonna get some music playing in here, or what?"

Tom waves. "I'll deal with it. Tre, Tamika, you wanna come help me pick something?" He motions them over, and they each take a hand as Tom leads them toward the jukebox. He passes his father and Sylvia on the way. "Hey," he says. "I'll catch you both in a minute."

Jeffrey chuckles. "Take your time," he says.

"Enjoy your party, Tom," Sylvia says. "We're not going anywhere."

3

It's been a week since Dylan was shot dead. A week since Anthony and Connor fled from the stash house. When they finally stopped running, they agreed to split and lie low while they figured out what to do. Anthony said he'd be in touch with Connor, but so far he hasn't had any ideas other than to keep out of Ezra's way and the way of any other of the South Side Street Kings. Ezra is not known for being reasonable. No doubt the stash house was stripped of all the drugs in it, which would have just thrown salt on the open wound of losing Dylan.

Anthony knows Ezra would have preferred it was either he or Connor who were killed. Dylan was a good soldier. The two of them, though, they're just bodies. He knows this. Knows how he's viewed within the gang. Knows his place in the pecking order.

Connor is hiding out at his sister's. Anthony stressed to him that it was important not to go home. That would be the first place the Street Kings would come looking for them.

Anthony, for his part, is staying with Stacey Shapiro, his girl-friend. Her eight-year-old son, Billy, is also present. Billy's father is not on the scene. Stacey got pregnant with him when she was seventeen. The father was twenty-three. By the time Billy was born and she was eighteen, the father had split town. Stacey doesn't know where he went. Doesn't know if he's still in Chicago, even.

Stacey's apartment is not big. It's cramped, having the three of them all together. Most of the time, though, Stacey is out working. Mostly she's out at night, and Anthony takes care of Billy. Stacey is a stripper. Her schedule keeps her free enough to take Billy to and from school. Anthony doesn't accompany her. He doesn't go out. The closest he gets to outside is the window.

He watches the street, looking out for familiar faces. Street King faces. If he sees them, he needs to run. He hasn't seen them yet.

He sits back on the sofa and runs his hands back through his hair. It's late. He put Billy to bed a couple of hours ago. He sits in the dark. Not even the television is on. If anyone comes to the door, he's not planning on answering it. When Stacey gets back, and she's due soon, she has her key.

This is no way to live, but Anthony isn't sure how to go about getting his life back. He knows what he *needs* to do, of course. What he and Connor need to do to appease Ezra. They need to find out who ripped them off and killed Dylan, and they need to get their goods back. Or, at least, they need the monetary equivalent of what was stolen to pay Ezra back. To make it up to him.

Anthony isn't sure how to go about accomplishing any of those things. It's been a week, and he doesn't have any ideas.

He hasn't heard anything from Connor. He takes that to mean Connor hasn't had any great ideas, either.

Anthony has not been sleeping well. He's too on edge. Too much time obsessively checking the window, watching the street, studying every vehicle passing by and all the ones parked up and down the road. It's not just an assumption that the Street Kings are looking for him – he knows they are. The night after the stash house was raided, after he'd already spent a tense day hiding out at Stacey's, she came home from her shift and told him a couple of Street Kings had come by looking for him. Anthony knew this would happen. The Street Kings are silent partners in the strip club. They have the majority shareholding, not that their names show up on any paperwork. It's how Anthony and Stacey met. He'd been sent to keep an eye on the place one night. It was a quiet night, and Stacey looked bored. They got to talking.

So Anthony knew they would look for him there. Knew they would question Stacey – but he also knew they wouldn't get too rough with her, because she's one of their best earners. Stacey kept her cool. She didn't back down to them. Didn't give anything away. When she told them she didn't know where Anthony was, she made it believable.

No matter how believable she may have been, Anthony knows there's still a risk they could be watching her building. They'd be stupid not to. Just because he hasn't seen any of them doesn't mean they're not out there somewhere.

Unable to sit still, writhing with pent-up energy that has nowhere to go, he checks in on Billy. He's sleeping soundly, his mouth puckered in his cherub face. Stacey will be home soon. Anthony returns to the sofa and awaits her.

She gets back twenty minutes later, bag slung over her shoulder, hair scraped back. She looks tired. Anthony waits until the door is closed before he says, "Long night?"

"*Busy* night," Stacey says. She collapses onto the sofa beside him. She's showered before leaving the club, but Anthony can still smell remnants of hair spray clinging to her scalp, and see tiny bits of glitter that shimmer on her cheeks and her chest. "How'd Billy go down?"

"Fine," Anthony says. "He's never any trouble."

She nods. Billy's a good kid.

"Anyone come by looking for me?" Anthony says.

Stacey nods. "Every night. Always the same two guys – Stewie Norton and Ethan Hardy. Guess they're the two who've been assigned to find you. I wonder if they're looking for Connor, too, or if he got his own designated team."

Anthony grits his teeth. Stewie and Ethan are heavy hitters. If they find him, he's not sure if they'll give him a chance to talk before they start hitting him. Hell, he's not even sure if they'll just hit him.

"Anyway, I told them the same thing I have every other time – I haven't seen you since last week."

"They're not gonna buy it for long," Anthony says. "If they even buy it now."

Stacey stifles a yawn. "What're you gonna do?"

"I don't know yet. I'm trying to think."

"You've had a long time to do that."

"It's not coming easy."

She nods. She doesn't push him.

"Do they follow you back?" Anthony says.

"Not that I've seen, and I'm careful. I check. If they do, they're sneaky about it." Another yawn creeps up on her, and this time, she doesn't try to fight it. "I'm gonna get to bed. You gonna join me, or are you gonna sit by the window all night?"

Before Anthony can answer, there's a knock at the door. They both freeze and turn toward the sound. A *knock*. It's not the buzzer. Not someone asking if they can be let into the building to come on up. A *knock*. Someone is right outside the door, physically out in the hallway.

Neither of them says a word. They look at each other. Anthony can see the worry in Stacey's eyes, and he knows she can see the fear in his.

They don't move. Don't make any effort to get up and go to the door. There's another knock. It's not any louder than before. The same impact. Same rhythm. Then there's a voice, calling through. "Don't keep me waiting, Anthony," it says. "I know you're in there."

Anthony knows the voice. It doesn't belong to a Street King, but that doesn't make him feel any better. He stands. Grits his teeth. He needs to answer the door.

"What are you doing?" Stacey whispers.

"It's Harlan," Anthony says.

He goes and unlocks the door and looks into the grinning face of Harlan Ross. He's leaning against the frame. "Thought you were gonna keep me standing out here all night," he says, then steps into the apartment without waiting for an invite. He looks around the room. Stacey has sat up on the sofa and is staring hard at the new arrival. She doesn't look so tired anymore.

Harlan looks right back at her, smiling. Anthony sees him run his tongue around the inside of his mouth, over his teeth. "Well, well, well," Harlan says. "Miss Shapiro. It's wonderful to finally meet you in person."

Stacey's eyes flicker toward Anthony. She knows who Harlan is, but only by reputation. Only from what Anthony has told her about him. About how he's a cop. A detective, in fact. About how about a year back he picked Anthony up, but rather than book him, started extorting him for protection money under threat of violence and arrest. About how he's currently on forced leave because he was caught on camera beating a black man so bad he went blind in one eye.

Harlan stares at Stacey for longer than is comfortable. Anthony can see she's creeped out. That he's making her skin crawl. He makes Anthony's skin crawl, and Anthony never gets the feeling Harlan wants to fuck him. He knows that's exactly what he's thinking about when he looks at Stacey.

"What're you doing here, Harlan?" Anthony says, hoping to draw his attention.

"Came looking for you, buddy," he says, finally turning back to Anthony. "Heard you're lying low."

"Supposed to be. How'd you find me?"

Harlan winks at him. "I can always find you, Anthony. I always know where you are."

Anthony knows he's being purposefully cryptic, just trying to get under his skin, but sometimes it feels like this is the truth. He's never been able to avoid Harlan for long. Anthony bites his tongue, then forces himself to ask the question he fears most. "Have you told the Street Kings I'm here?"

"Now why'd I wanna go and do a thing like that?" Harlan says, showing all of his teeth when he smiles. He reminds Anthony of a shark, and Anthony feels like the unwitting prey.

"What can I do for you?"

"You know what you can do for me, Anthony."

He's here for money. He nods, then looks past Harlan. "Stacey, maybe you should wait in the bedroom while we talk –"

"No, no," Harlan says, holding up a hand to Stacey, motioning for her to stay right where she is. "I like her right there. She gives me something good to look at." He winks at her.

Stacey suppresses a shudder.

Anthony takes a deep breath. "Harlan, listen – I'm not working right now. You know that. I'm broke. I've just gotta deal with everything that's happened, and then I can pay you back, I swear. With interest, I promise."

"Uh-huh." Harlan isn't smiling anymore. "Thing is, Anthony, you know that *I'm* not working right now, either. I've gotta keep the money coming in, buddy. I gotta *eat*. You ain't trying to starve me now, are you?"

"Harlan, I swear to you –"

"I'm not interested in excuses, Anthony." Harlan has a hard stare. His whole face is hard. His shoulders are broad. He's built like a football player, except for in the middle, where he's gone soft. Anthony knows he's dangerous. Knows he's fast, and knows he's strong, and he doesn't want to upset him here, in Stacey's home, with her present and Billy just in the next room.

Harlan holds out his hand, palm up. He flicks the fingers in a *gimme* motion. "Money," he says.

"I don't have any," Anthony says, swallowing.

"Then you're gonna have to find it."

"It's not – it's not here. There's nothing. I don't have anything –"

Before Anthony can blink, Harlan is on him. The hand that was out is now wrapped around his throat, and he's slammed up against the wall hard enough to shake the whole apartment. Stacey is on her feet, but Anthony waves for her to stay back. If she gets too close, Harlan won't hesitate to hurt her, too.

The grip is tight, and Anthony feels the air slipping out of his lungs. His eyes begin to roll back. Harlan eases up a little, lets him get some breath. "Don't fuck with me, Anthony," Harlan says. "Do not *fuck* with me. We have an arrangement. I expect you to hold up your end, no matter what."

"Let go of him!" Stacey says, glancing back toward Billy's bedroom door, hoping he's not disturbed by the noise and won't come to investigate.

Harlan shakes his head. "I'm not letting go until I get what I came here for."

"*Please*," Stacey says. "Listen, listen – I have money, okay? I can pay – I can pay, just let him go."

Harlan looks at her, considering. Anthony remains pressed up against the wall, air passing thinly through his constricted throat. Then he can breathe again, and he gulps it down, filling his lungs. He rubs his bruised neck, coughing.

"All right," Harlan says, to Stacey. He gives her the same *gimme* gesture he earlier gave Anthony.

Stacey goes to her handbag and pulls out her purse. "It's mostly in ones," she says, pulling out crumpled notes.

"Don't worry," Harlan says. "I know how you make your money. How much have you got? And don't hold out on me, girl. I'm still standing pretty close to your man here. It's not gonna take much for us to pick up where we just left off."

Stacey empties the contents of her purse. She counts out the notes. "I've got four hundred dollars."

"Four hundred dollars, huh? That much, even after covering your tip out and your house fee? You been busy tonight, girl. You've been popular. How's that make you feel, Anthony, knowing that so many men have seen your girl dancing in her birthday suit?"

"It's not all from tonight," Stacey says.

"It's gonna be a lot of ones."

"It's not *all* ones." Stacey stands and hands the notes out to him.

Harlan takes it from her and counts it. "You said four hundred," he says. "This is three-fifty."

"We need groceries," Stacey says. "Please, I need to keep something."

Harlan doesn't say anything. He just keeps his hand out.

Stacey understands. She gives him the remaining fifty. Harlan counts this up, too.

"You ought to be ashamed, Anthony," Harlan says. "Sending your girl out, working her fingers to the bone to keep you afloat, and you're just sitting around all day, not bringing in a damn dime."

Anthony doesn't answer. There's nothing he can say.

Stacey speaks for him. "Just get out," she says. "You've got your money. Just leave."

Harlen stuffs the notes into his wallet and puts the wallet back in his pocket. He takes his time, smiling all the while. He steps up close to Anthony before he leaves. Anthony flinches. "I'll see you again soon, buddy," he says. "Don't go wandering too far. You know I'll be able to find you anywhere you go."

Anthony grits his teeth and turns away. He doesn't watch

as Harlan leaves. He hears the door close. He closes his eyes and takes a deep breath. His throat hurts.

Stacey comes to him. She doesn't say a word. He's thankful for that. Instead, she wraps her arms around him and squeezes him tight, and he holds her and buries his face in her neck and tries not to shake all over.

4

A fter the party, most of the attendees have come to Tom and Hayley's. Naomi took the kids back to the motel to get them to bed, but Zeke has come along. Everyone's inside the house apart from Tom and Jeffrey, who sit out on the porch. They haven't had a chance to talk yet, just the two of them.

Tom looks out over the neighbourhood. It's late, and it's dark, and everything is calm and quiet. Behind him, from inside the house, he can hear laughter. He turns to his father, who is looking down the road, a faraway expression on his face. He holds a beer bottle in both hands, the bottom of it resting in his lap.

"I feel like you've got something on your mind," Tom says. "I've been getting that impression all night."

Jeffrey chews the inside of his lip, still looking down the road. "Wanted to let you enjoy your party," he says. "That girl of yours, she's a good one, ain't she? I like her. Sylvia does, too. Hell, I always liked her. When she got in touch, it was good to hear from her again. A real pleasant surprise to find out that the two of you have got back together. She was good for you back then. She still is now. But back when the two of you were teenagers, I was real disappointed when you broke up."

"You're changing the subject."

Jeffrey smiles, then finally turns to him. "That's not what I'm doing," he says. "I'm just letting you know what we think of her. She's a sweet girl. She always has been."

"I already know that," Tom says. "I wouldn't live with just anyone. Now, why don't you tell me something I don't know, like what it is that's on your mind."

Jeffrey opens his mouth to speak, but before he can, he coughs. He covers his mouth with his fist, then sits forward, still coughing. Tom frowns, then reaches over and pats him on the back. Jeffrey waves him off, the fit ending, then sits back and catches his breath.

"You all right?" Tom says.

Jeffrey holds up the bottle. "Must've gone down the wrong way."

"You weren't drinking."

"It was nothing," Jeffrey says. He takes a drink now. "Just something in the back of my throat." He takes another deep breath, then swallows. He clears his throat. "I need to talk to you about Anthony."

In a way, Tom isn't surprised. He sits back and folds his arms. "What's he done this time?"

"I'm worried about him."

"That's nothing I haven't heard before."

"I know," Jeffrey says. He chews his bottom lip, rolls it back and forth between his teeth. He coughs at the back of his throat and looks like he's trying to suppress another fit.

"Do you have a cold or something?" Tom says.

"Yeah, maybe something like that." He holds back another cough, then takes a drink. "I got some messages from Anthony, a couple of weeks ago now. He made it sound like he was in trouble."

Tom grits his teeth. "He's always in trouble."

"But he doesn't always ask for help."

"Is that what he was doing in the messages?"

"Not directly. I think he's too proud to come right out and say he needs help, but these felt like the closest he'll get."

Against his better judgment, Tom asks, "What did he say?"

"You can read them." Jeffrey reaches into his pocket for his phone, but Tom holds up a hand to stop him.

"Just give me the CliffsNotes."

Jeffrey leaves his phone where it is. He takes another drink, then says, "He's in Chicago, and he's gotten involved with a gang. Or maybe a few gangs; he wasn't clear. But I got the impression it's something he's fallen into, and he's struggling to get out."

"Is he *in* a gang, or just involved with them?" Tom says.

"Like I said, I don't know. He wasn't clear. But he made out like he owes money, and he's struggling to pay it back, and he's worried about what's going to happen to him if he can't."

Tom sits back. "Well. That sucks for him."

"He's your brother, Tom."

"I know he is. I know exactly who he is." He turns his head to look his father in the eye.

Jeffrey sighs. "Tom," he says, haltingly, hesitantly, "will you go and speak to him?"

Tom turns away. He doesn't answer.

"Tom?" Jeffrey prompts.

"I'm not going to Chicago."

"He's your brother, and if he's asking for help I figure this has got to be some real trouble he's in."

"He made it very clear the last time we spoke that he doesn't want my help."

"You still gave it to him."

"I didn't do that for *him*," Tom says, turning to his father, knowing his words are coming out harsher than he intends, that his eyes are blazing, but he doesn't care. "I did that for Alejandra."

Jeffrey doesn't flinch. Doesn't back down or get defensive. He just nods sadly. "I know you loved her, Tom, but so did Anthony. And she was carrying *his* child. He's been hurting bad ever since she died. And Tom, listen, I'm not picking sides, you understand? I'm sure you had your reasons for what you did, and I'm sure they made sense to you, but you took her ashes away from him. You took *their* ashes away."

"I took her back to Mexico," Tom says. "It's what she wanted. She told me. I took her home."

"Anthony figures that's probably where you went. But Mexico's a big place, and he knew he wouldn't be able to catch up to you, even if he knew exactly where you were going. That tore him up, right along with everything else. You didn't see how he was after you were gone, Tom."

Tom clenches his jaw. "Look, I...I regret how it happened. But I was grieving, too. I was angry. I wasn't thinking straight."

"I told you, I'm not taking sides. You don't have to explain yourself to me."

Tom nods. "I know. But...I... If there's one thing I'm sorry for, it's that. It's been a few years now, and there's a lot of distance between what happened then and right now, and I can see what I did a little clearer. I did what I thought was right. But I understand those ashes weren't just Alejandra. They were their child, too – Anthony's child. And I get that I took that away from him." Tom falls silent and stares out into the dark. "How...how was he, after I'd gone?"

"He tried going after you, at first," Jeffrey says. "He got as far as the border and then realized how impossible it was going to be to find you. He came back. After that, I think he stayed in bed for about three days. And then, one morning, me and Sylvia went to look in on him, and he was gone. He'd left through the window in the middle of the night. No one else in the commune had seen him go. I didn't hear from him. For years, we didn't know where he was, until he sent me those messages."

"You heard from him since?"

Jeffrey shakes his head. "No, nothing. I responded, of course, but I didn't get any reply. Tried calling him, too, but no answer. Last time I called, it said the number didn't exist anymore."

"I'm sure that alarms you."

"It does. Last time I tried him was yesterday. That was when it said it didn't exist. Hayley had already invited us here to see you. I figured I'd tell you and hoped you'd do right by your brother. That you'd find him and get him out of there."

"I've done right by him for a long time," Tom says. "I've done right by him too many times. He said he doesn't want my help. Even if I were to go, what difference would it make? He'd just fuck up again somewhere down the line, get himself in a new kind of trouble. He's not going to learn if I'm always there to clear up for him."

Jeffrey bites his lip. "So it's a no."

"I'm sorry," Tom says, "but it's a no. I'm not going to Chicago. I'm not going out of my way to help someone who has made it clear they don't want it. It's time for Anthony to stand on his own two feet."

Jeffrey purses his lips. He nods. It's clear he's disappointed, but he doesn't press the matter.

They sit in silence for a moment, then Tom stands and says he's going back inside. "You coming?"

"I'll be in soon," Jeffrey says, forcing himself to smile. "Just give me a minute. I won't be long."

People don't stay for much longer. They file out into the night, embracing and handshaking and saying their goodbyes as they go. Zeke holds Tom tight and squeezes his shoulder before they part. "It's been too long," he says. "Don't make your next birthday the next time I see you."

"It's your birthday before then," Tom says. "Invite me to it."

"Well, now that you're not roaming to and fro and you seem to have settled down, maybe I'll actually be able to, for a change."

Jeffrey and Sylvia are last out the door, and Jeffrey doesn't give any indication that he's upset about Tom's refusing to go to Chicago and find Anthony. "We'll see you again soon, Tom," Sylvia says, kissing him on the cheek. "I've told Hayley here to ensure it."

After they're gone, Tom and Hayley are left alone, and the house feels emptier and quieter in their absence. Tom can't remember them ever having so many people around at one time before. Usually they entertain Hayley's friends from work, and they only come in either twos or threes.

"Let's go to bed," Hayley says. "It's late, and I'm tired. I'll deal with this mess tomorrow."

They head upstairs together and get into bed. Hayley props herself up on an elbow and smiles at him. "You and your father were outside talking for a while," she says. "Was everything all right?"

"We were just catching up," Tom says. "It'd been a long time since we saw each other last."

"Did you enjoy your party?" she says.

"You know, considering I've never been much of a party person, *yes*, I did. Thank you. It was good to see everyone."

"It took a *lot* of planning," Hayley says, laughing. "And I know what you're like, so it was very difficult to get all the numbers – I had to make sure I put everything back *exactly* how I found it. You're very OCD about security. If anything's out of place, you always notice it. So I had to be careful about that. I'm shocked you never called me out on anything."

"I assumed you'd been cleaning."

She laughs again. She strokes his arm. "I'd just noticed that you'd seemed kind of...*distant*, lately. Distracted. I just wanted to do something for you."

"I appreciate that."

"Are you okay, Tom?"

He smiles at her. "I'm fine. Thanks for caring."

She nods. "I like Cindy. The two of you have spent a lot of time together, haven't you?"

"We've helped each other out."

"She's very pretty."

"I suppose she is."

"Has anything ever happened between you?"

Tom raises an eyebrow. "No," he says. "We're friends. What, are you jealous all of a sudden?"

"No, just curious. Of all the women here tonight, well,

Sylvia is your stepmother, and Naomi is married to Zeke, and Taylor is a child – Cindy is an attractive single lady, and like I said, the two of you have spent a lot of time together. So I was just wondering is all."

"Now you know."

"Now I know." Hayley leans in and kisses him. "I know it's way after midnight, but neither of us has been to sleep yet, so I guess this technically still counts as your birthday." She kisses him again, then slides a hand down his body. "Are you up for celebrating a little longer?"

Tom wraps his arms around her. "I'm sure I can be persuaded."

5

H arlan sits in his car and counts out the money Stacey gave him, feeling satisfied with the haul. It's not as much as he would have liked, but it was clearly as much as they had. He grins to himself and drives north through the city, toward New Eastside. His night is just beginning.

He may not have got as much as he wanted from Anthony on this trip, but that's fine. Anthony is an investment. He's paid out so far, for as long as they've known each other. Harlan is planning to make a lot more from him, and hopefully very soon. He has plans.

Harlan parks down the block from where he's going and continues on foot. He walks alongside the elevated El line and follows it to the Eastside City Tower Apartment building. There isn't a train passing by right now, but he knows that when they do, they pass slowly here, approaching a station just a little further down.

Harlan doesn't need to be buzzed into the building. He knows the code. He lets himself in and heads up to the twelfth floor. What he said to Anthony earlier wasn't entirely true – just because he's been benched from the force doesn't mean he doesn't have *any* money coming in. He *does*. Harlan keeps his fingers in a lot of pies. This is one of the many. Anthony doesn't need to know about this until he has to.

On the twelfth floor, he's let into Matt Rossi's apartment. It's late, and Matt Rossi isn't the one who answers the door. Matt Rossi will be tucked up in bed, knocking on z's. Leo DeLuca lets him in. "You're late," he says.

"Not by much," Harlan says, stepping past him. "Ten minutes, what's that?"

"What's your excuse?" Leo says, checking the hallway and then closing and locking the door. He folds his arms and waits.

"Just had some business I needed to take care of," Harlan says. "Ran a little longer than I was expecting."

They don't need to lower their voices despite Matt being asleep. His bedroom is at the other end of the apartment, and the walls here are thick.

Leo grunts, then unfolds his arms and starts heading through to the office where they'll spend the night.

"Who was on before us?" Harlan says, following.

"Ray and Peter," Leo says without turning. Ray Palladino and Peter Fanelli. "They hung around a little when they saw you weren't here. Surprised you didn't pass them on your way in."

"Like ships in the night," Harlan says. In the office, he takes a seat in a swivel chair and leans back with his feet up on the table. There's a deck of cards already out, and he can imagine how Ray and Peter were killing time on their shift. Card games are a regular occurrence in here. Harlan has won and lost more than his fair share.

Leo glances at him, then takes a seat in front of the bank of monitors fixed up to the wall. Harlan looks at them too, but there's nothing to see. They cover every room in the apartment, apart from Matt's bedroom and the bathrooms. They also cover outside in the hall and the stairwell, and one points directly at the elevator to see everyone who comes and goes. There's another in the lobby pointing at the entrance, and another outside, covering the front of the building. Right now, there's no one to see on the inside cameras. He spots someone on the outside camera, shuffling past the front of the building, swaying from side to side. A guy in a suit, clearly suffering the effects of too much alcohol.

Harlan stares at the screen in the middle. Matt's office. It's in darkness, but the cameras have night vision, and he sees everything with a greenish glow. This office is mostly for show. Matt rarely uses it. He conducts most of his business outside the building, usually in an office he keeps elsewhere in the city.

Officially, Matt Rossi is an accountant. Truthfully, he's a moneyman for the Mob. Hence all the security. Hence Harlan and Leo working the night shift to keep an eye on everything. Someone is always here working security. It's not for Matt. He has Al Bruno for that. It's *his* job to take care of Matt, especially if he's carrying money. The rest of them are here for what's inside Matt's office. On the other side of his desk, behind the painting of a ship on stormy waters up on the wall. *That's* what's important.

The apartment is mostly guarded by Mob guys, but not always. Harlan isn't the only crooked cop on the payroll. It's a good way to make some extra cash. It's an *easy* way to make extra cash. Nothing ever happens. No one is stupid enough to try to rip off the Mob.

Harlan grins to himself. He turns away from the camera looking into Matt's office and picks up the deck of cards, starts shuffling them. "Is Al still here?"

"No, he's gone home," Leo says. "But you know he'll be back early in the morning."

"It's hard to imagine Matt without Al somewhere near."

Leo grunts. He gets to his feet. "Everything looks quiet. I'm gonna make a coffee. You want one?"

"Sure," Harlan says, still shuffling the deck.

"How d'you like it?"

"Same way I like my collars – black."

Leo chuckles at this. He pauses on his way out of the room. "How's that going for you, by the way? I heard what happened. Hell, I've seen the video."

"You like it?" Harlan says, wriggling his eyebrows. "Some of my best work."

Leo chuckles again. "The city don't think so."

"Fuck the city."

"You're lucky it didn't cause a riot."

Harlan waves a dismissive hand.

"How deep's the water you're in?"

"The standard. They gotta do all this shit to make it look good, y'know? They'll go through all the motions, get it done, and then I'll be back out closing cases before you know it."

"He looked kinda young. What'd he done?"

"You care?"

"No. Just curious."

Harlan shrugs. "Damned if I know. I was just nearby and answering a call. As a detective, ordinarily I wouldn't have bothered, but I felt like the exercise. I don't know what he was supposed to have done, and I don't care."

Leo doesn't chuckle this time. He laughs. "You're cold, man."

"You gotta be. It's a cold world."

"One black coffee, coming up," Leo says, and leaves the office.

It's not true. Harlan knows what the kid was supposed to have done. The call he was answering was in response to shoplifting. Problem was, the kid he tackled didn't have anything to do with it. The kid had seen cops running down the street toward him, and he'd taken off in the other direction. Wasn't planning on hanging around to turn into another statistic. Unfortunately for him, he bumped into Harlan coming the other way.

Not that Harlan feels like he needs to defend himself, *but* if he *did* need to say anything in his defense, he'd point out that the other two cops who'd been running the kid down in the first place never thought to point out to him that he was beating on the wrong guy.

Whatever. It was done now.

The other thing he wasn't entirely truthful about, though, is getting back out on the streets. This time, he's not so sure it's going to happen. This could be one disciplinary too far. Hell, because of that goddamn footage that every motherfucker seems to have seen, it could be even worse – it could be a sentence. The best he could hope for is he just loses his job, but his lawyer has levelled with him. The department could look to make an example of him, to prove a point, and he could end up serving time.

Leo wasn't wrong when he said he was lucky there wasn't a riot. The whole city was lucky.

Harlan sucks on his teeth, thinking about all of this. He tries not to think about it often. It's out of his control. Instead, he prefers to think about things he *does* have control over.

He puts the deck of cards back on the table and gets to his feet. He steps closer to the monitors. Gets up close to the one in the centre. Matt's office. The desk. The painting.

This he can control. Soon, hopefully. Soon he won't need to worry about losing his job or getting locked up. Soon, he'll be long gone, and no one will ever find him.

nthony wakes on the sofa, sunlight streaming in across his face. It hurts his eyes, and he twists away from it.

Then he realizes the light isn't what has woken him. It's the sound of knocking on the door. *Hard* knocking.

Anthony freezes. He looks up as Stacey appears in the living room, pulling her dressing gown tight around herself. Her hair is wild. Her legs and feet are bare. She's been woken by the sound, too. She looks at Anthony. He scrambles to the window and looks down, half expecting to see the building surrounded by Street Kings, but there's no one there.

Stacey clears her throat. "Who is it?" she says.

"We just wanna take a look around, Stacey," a familiar voice calls through. Anthony knows it. Ethan Hardy. From what Stacey has said about them calling by the strip club looking for him, Stewie Norton is probably out there with him, too. "We just wanna see the place for ourselves, that's all. Let us in. If he ain't here, you don't have anything to worry about."

"Mom?" Billy appears in his bedroom doorway, rubbing his eyes.

Stacey waves for him to stay where he is. "Listen," she says, calling back through the door, "you've woke my kid up. Let me put him back in his room, and then I'll let you in." She motions frantically for Anthony to go out the window, down the fire escape.

Ethan, or Stewie, tries the door handle, shaking it hard. The door rattles in its frame. "Come on and let us in right now, Stacey," Ethan calls. "None of us wants this to be any more difficult than it is."

Anthony, as quickly and as quietly as he can, opens the window and slides out onto the fire escape. Looking back, he sees Stacey hurry to Billy and scoop him up in her arms. As that happens, Ethan and Stewie kick the door open.

"Shit, he's there!" Stewie says, pointing, and they both bolt toward him and the open window.

Anthony descends the fire escape as quick as he can, but he stumbles as he reaches the bottom and falls six feet, landing hard on the concrete below. It knocks the wind out of him, but Anthony can't feel anything serious – no broken bones, no busted nose or fractured skull – so he scrambles back to his feet and starts running.

Already he can hear Stewie and Ethan coming down the fire escape after him. They're coming so fast it sounds like they've just thrown themselves out the window. He doubts this is the case, but he doesn't dare turn back. He needs to look ahead and keep running.

His left knee hurts. He knocked it hard on landing. It's not broken, but it's slowing him down. He feels like he's running in a dream, where he's in slow motion, but everything around him is regular speed. He can hear Stewie and

Ethan gaining on him, their feet pounding the ground hard.

Anthony limps down the block and takes a sharp left, his shoulder hitting the wall as he turns, spinning him and almost sending him off balance.

Everything hurts. His head is pounding. His lungs are burning. He doesn't feel like he can get into a good rhythm. He can't speed up. All the while, Stewie and Ethan are getting closer.

Desperate, Anthony throws himself into traffic, running across the road. Vehicles hit their brakes to avoid him, screeching across lanes. Horns blare. Only one of them comes close to taking him out, a van that clips his right hip. It spins him and this time knocks him down, but Anthony is quick to his feet. He spares a glance back over his shoulder and sees Stewie and Ethan struggling to maneuver their way through the halted, angry traffic. Their eyes are on him, though. Anthony locks eyes with Ethan, just for a second, but he can see he's not happy. Neither of them are. They're not happy that Anthony has hidden from them, and they're not happy that they're having to chase him.

Anthony gets to the other side of the street and keeps going, down to the next corner and over the road where the traffic is thinner, because the lights are on red. He flees toward an unused and overgrown parking lot, aiming for the trees at the end of it. If he gets there, he can disappear out the other side. There's barbed wire atop the fence, but he'd rather take his chances with that than the Street Kings.

He doesn't look back. He avoids tripping in the parking lot's potholes. Stomps down the weeds as he goes, finally feeling like he's able to block out the various pains from his fall, and is picking up speed. When the chain-link fence is close enough, he dives for it, finding finger and toeholds. He starts to climb. Branches and leaves poke through the links, making it difficult.

But then, just as he begins his ascent, he feels a weight slam into him from behind, almost driving him through the fence. Hands grab him and throw him down onto his back, driving the air out of him yet again. A foot is placed on his chest, pinning him.

Ethan leans close into Anthony's face. "You shouldn't've run, man."

Anthony laughs, which causes him to cough, convulsing his whole body. "Shit," he says, "did I have a choice?"

7

The morning after the party, people come around to the house to say goodbye.

Zeke, Naomi and the kids left early. Zeke called ahead to make sure Tom was up. "I'll be in touch," Zeke said. "It's been so busy, we've never had a real chance to talk. I'll give you a call, and we can talk properly."

It was another hour before Taylor and her family showed up.

"I've been in your house, and now I know you've got a computer," she says. "So maybe it's time to switch to email when you write me?"

Tom grins. "What, you don't like my letters? I thought they were more personal."

"*You* write the letters, I'll respond via email. It's far more convenient."

"Teenage girls have very busy lives, Tom," Hayley says, nodding. "You really need to take that into account."

"See? Hayley gets it," Taylor says. "Two against one."

"All right, all right," Tom says, holding up his hands. "I'll take all of this into consideration."

Cindy turns up as Tom and Taylor are embracing, and then he's shaking hands with her brother and his wife. Cindy holds back until Taylor and her family have gone. She steps forward, hands in pockets. "Imagine this," she says, "a visit where neither one of us is in trouble. I wasn't sure I'd ever see the day."

"It's a hell of a thing," Tom says.

"At least I got to see you throwing those two guys out of the bar," Cindy says. "Or else this visit just wouldn't have felt complete."

They hug. "How's your new place?" Tom says as they break.

"It's all right," Cindy says. "Not too different from the last. You'll have to come visit next time you find yourself in Texas. Bring Hayley with you. I'm sure she'll love it."

"I'm sure I will," Hayley says, embracing Cindy in turn.

Before they can complete their goodbyes, Hayley's phone begins to ring. She slips it out of her pocket and checks the screen. "It's Sylvia," she says before answering.

At the mention of her name, Tom instinctively reaches for his pocket, wondering why Sylvia is calling Hayley instead of him, or if he's missed a call from her, only to find he doesn't have his phone on him. "Hey, Sylvia, how's every-thing – *what?*" Hayley falls silent, her brow furrowing. Tom and Cindy pick up on her tone and her silence, and both turn to look at her. "Hold on. I'll put Tom on." She holds the phone out to him. "Sylvia's upset," she says. "Your dad, he's –"

Tom takes the phone from her. "Sylvia? It's me. What's happened?"

"I woke up, and your father has gone, Tom," Sylvia says. She sounds breathless, like she's close to tears. "He's taken the truck."

"Are you sure he isn't just at the store?"

"He's been gone too long. I've tried calling him, but it just keeps going to voicemail. I think he might be going to Chicago – for Anthony. Did he tell you about the messages?"

Tom takes a deep breath. "Yeah, he told me."

"Tom, I'm worried," she says, and now she *is* crying. "He's going to get himself hurt."

"My dad can take care of himself, Sylvia. You don't need to be upset. He'll be back before you know it. He'll go there and see whatever nonsense Anthony has got himself involved in, and then he'll come home."

"Tom, you don't understand – you need to go after him, to help him, make sure he's all right –"

"Sylvia, trust me, my dad doesn't need my help." He can see Hayley and Cindy both watching him. Hayley is concerned, but Cindy looks confused. "If my dad could hear you say that he needs me, he'd laugh. He's more than capable of –"

"Tom, no, listen to me." She takes a deep breath. There's something in her tone that Tom doesn't like. Something that makes him clamp up and expect the worst. "Your father...he didn't want me to tell you, he doesn't want anyone to know, not yet, but your father has cancer, Tom. Lung cancer. He's not well."

Tom feels his stomach sink. The world almost drops out beneath him, but he manages to stay standing. He clenches his jaw. His left fist balls. His right presses the phone hard against his ear.

"Tom, are you still there? *Tom?*"

"I'm here." His voice comes out quieter than he expects it to. He takes a deep breath and forces himself to loosen up. "I'll go and get him, Sylvia. I'll make sure he doesn't get hurt."

He hangs up the phone and hands it back to Hayley. "How much did you hear?" he says.

She looks sad. "I'm so sorry, Tom."

He nods. "I need to go and get him."

"I'll go and pick Sylvia up," Hayley says. "I'll keep her here until you get back."

"I'll just go and grab some things," Tom says.

"You're going to Chicago?" Cindy says.

"Unless I can cut him off before he gets there," Tom says. "We don't know how long ago he set off. He could've left as soon as Sylvia fell asleep, which would mean he's already hours on the road." Tom runs a hand back through his hair. "It's unlikely I'm going to be able to cut him off."

"You want some company?" Cindy says.

"You don't have to do that," Tom says.

Cindy shrugs. "I don't have anything else going on. I'm free as a bird."

Tom looks at Hayley. "Cindy's helped you find people before, right?" she says. "Take her. I'll get Sylvia and make sure she's all right."

Tom looks back at Cindy. "You sure?"

"Wouldn't offer if I weren't."

Tom nods. "All right. I've gotta grab some things. You need anything?"

"Got everything out in my car already."

"Grab it – we'll be taking mine."

8

To Anthony's surprise, Stewie and Ethan don't lay any kind of beating on him. Nothing beyond how bumped up and bruised he already is from the chase. They each took an arm and hauled him to their car, bundling him into the back. Ethan drove, and Stewie sat in the back with him, jabbing a Glock into his ribs.

He knows where they're taking him. They go to the South Side, and sure enough, Ethan pulls the car to a stop in front of The Cauldron. The South Side Street Kings own The Cauldron. It's a bar. They operate out of the back room. No doubt Ezra is in there right now, waiting for him. Waiting to speak to him. Waiting to tell him all the things he's unhappy about.

"Don't try to run again," Stewie says, sticking the Glock into his jaw. "You try to run, I'll put five in your back."

"Gotcha," Anthony says, holding up his hands. "No running."

The three of them go into the bar, Stewie staying close to Anthony's side. The bar isn't open. It's empty save for the bartender behind the counter, going over inventory with a clipboard. He glances up as the three men pass by, but he doesn't say anything and promptly gets back to what he's doing. He works here, but he's not a Street King. This isn't any of his business.

They go through into the back room. It's a wide space almost as big as the front of the bar. Ezra lounges in a leather chair pushed up against the rear wall, one leg draped over its arm. Ezra has a lean, hard face. His body is the same. He's always frowning. Always looks angry. There's a scar running down the left side of his face from his eyebrow to his jaw that he picked up in a knife fight when he was fifteen. A few other Street Kings are standing around, keeping guard. Cross-legged on the floor, near to Ezra's chair, is Connor. He's not tied up, but he sits with his fingers laced atop his head.

"Well, well, well," Ezra says, looking Anthony over. "You weren't as easy to find as he was." He nods toward Connor. "Though from what I hear, we're gonna have to have a talk with Stacey."

"It's not Stacey's fault," Anthony says. "I asked her not to say anything."

"Uh-huh." Ezra runs a fingernail down his front teeth, picking at his gums like there's something lodged there. "Why didn't you come see us, Anthony?"

Stewie pushes Anthony roughly forward, closer to Ezra. Anthony manages to keep his balance. He looks at his boss. Ezra raises an eyebrow, awaiting a response. "We were trying to find out who was responsible," Anthony says. "Who it was that raided the stash house. We were trying to find them, rather than come to you empty-handed."

"Doesn't seem to me like you were trying too hard," Ezra

says. "Seems more to me like you were hiding out, not doing much of shit."

"We knew we needed to get back what was stolen from you."

"I don't see how you can bring back Dylan."

Anthony doesn't have an answer to this.

Ezra doesn't say anything for a while. He watches Anthony. "You didn't see who it was?" he says finally.

Anthony shakes his head.

Ezra nods. "That's what he said." He indicates Connor. "But, you know, it doesn't hurt to get a second opinion." He claps his hands together and lowers his leg from the chair's arm, sitting forward. "So what are we looking at here? We don't know who we're dealing with. I don't like that, Anthony. You gotta know I don't. It could be anyone. We're vulnerable from all sides right now – it could be the blacks, Latinos, Nazis, and we don't have a fucking clue, and neither of you have got anything to give me to help us work it out."

Ezra stands, and Anthony tries not to flinch. Ezra points at Connor and speaks to someone over Anthony's shoulder. "Stand him up and get him over next to his buddy."

One of the Street Kings hauls Connor up to his feet and pushes him toward Anthony. Anthony has to catch him to keep him from falling.

Ezra paces the floor in front of them. He runs a finger down his long scar while he thinks. He shakes his head and stops, turns to them both. He talks mostly to Anthony. "You know how much product was in that house?"

Anthony nods. "Yeah."

Ezra tells him anyway. "There was twenty thousand dollars' worth of product that *you* were supposed to be protecting. That would have brought us in roughly eighty thousand dollars of profit. *That's* how much you owe me. You understand that?"

Anthony's spine stiffens at the number, but he manages to nod. Out of the corner of his eye, he sees that Connor is nodding too.

"Uh-huh," Ezra says. "But let's not forget the fact that Dylan was killed. One of ours. A good soldier. One of the best. Because of that, I'm gonna round the total up to one hundred thousand dollars. That's what the two of you are gonna pay me back. And you'd both better think yourselves damn lucky, because Dylan was worth a hell of a lot more than twenty thousand." He glares at them each in turn. "You got that? We clear?"

"We're clear," Anthony says.

Connor mumbles something that sounds like an affirmation.

"You got one week," Ezra says, stepping back and returning to his chair. "One week from today to pay me back. You don't, I'm gonna make an example of you both. I'm gonna make sure a rip like that never has the chance of happening again through negligence like what you displayed. I'm gonna make it so you wish you'd gone down with Dylan."

Anthony clenches his jaw until it aches. He can imagine what kind of example Ezra is planning to make. He's heard stories about the tortures that go on back here. The bone breakings. The skinnings. He sees how Connor sways beside him, like he's about to pass out, and he knows he's heard all about them, too.

"We're Street *Kings* for a goddamn reason, boys," Ezra says. "High time for the two of you to act like it. Now, go and get my fucking money."

Anthony has to take Connor by the elbow to keep him steady as they head to the front of The Cauldron. Ezra calls to them before they can disappear through the door. "Don't think about skipping town," he says, waving a finger from side to side in the air. "You won't get far. I'm gonna have eyes on you. You even *think* about running, and I'll make it last for *days*."

Anthony tries to stand firm. He nods once. He doesn't know if he looks solid, or if he looks like he's about to fall apart. Inside, he feels like water. He keeps a tight grip on Connor's elbow and leads him through the bar.

9

Tom drives while Cindy tries to get a track on Jeffrey on her laptop. They've been on the road a few hours now. Tom doesn't have the radio on. He isn't playing any music. The only sound is the tapping of Cindy's fingers on the keys. "How long's it gonna take us to get to Chicago?" she says, without looking up.

"Couple of days," Tom says. "We'll get there late tomorrow. You found anything?"

"I'm still scrubbing through," Cindy says. "He's got more than a few hours on us. I highly doubt we're gonna cut him off."

Tom grunts. He'd expected this was the case.

"You don't wanna put some music on or something?" Cindy says, still without looking up. "I don't mind if you want some background noise. It's not gonna distract me."

"I'm not in the mood for music."

"Yeah. It's feeling real intense in this car, Tom. What're you thinking?"

Tom doesn't answer.

Cindy raises her head now and looks at him. She takes a deep breath. "You're thinking about your dad."

Tom stares straight ahead, watching the road.

"You wanna talk about it?"

"I don't think so."

Cindy reaches over and squeezes his leg, attempting to comfort him. "I'm not going to push it, but just know that if you *do* want to talk – about anything – I'm right here."

Tom nods. He appreciates it. "I've got a lot on my mind right now."

"Thinking about your brother, too?"

Tom nods toward the laptop. "Anything?" he says. He doesn't want to talk about Anthony.

"I'll tell you when there is," Cindy says, but she turns her attention back to her computer.

Tom focuses on driving. He doesn't want to let his mind wander. If he thinks too much on the bombshell Sylvia dropped earlier – that his father has cancer, that he's dying – he's not sure what this might do to him. He keeps thinking of his mother. Cancer killed her, too. He grits his teeth.

"Hayley's nice," Cindy says, typing.

"Yeah," Tom says.

"When I found out you were settling down, I've gotta admit, I was shocked." She laughs. "But after meeting her, I can see why."

Tom doesn't say anything.

Cindy takes a deep breath. She touches his leg again. "I'm sorry, Tom. It's just...it's hard seeing you this way. You've just had this news, and I dunno, I'm talking to you like I'm expecting you to be the same as you always are. But I get it. You want to be quiet. You want me to be quiet."

"I don't want you to be quiet," Tom says. "You're fine.

You're not doing anything wrong. Like I said, I've just got a lot on my mind."

Cindy nods. She refocuses on her work, on trying to find Jeffrey. Ten minutes go by. "I think he may have taken an alternative route," she says. "I got him leaving Hopper Creek, but then he disappeared soon after that. I think he's avoided cameras."

"That sounds like him," Tom says. "Should've expected that."

"Do you think he did that so we couldn't track him?"

"He'll have done it so *no one* can track him," Tom says. "He's always been this way. If he has to take a two-hour drive to avoid a half-hour route with cameras, he's taking the two hours."

"Well, I have bad news for him when he gets to Chicago..."

"He hates cities," Tom says. "For more reasons than just the cameras. He's never been much of a people person." Tom pulls out his phone. "I'm gonna try him again." He rings his number. Jeffrey's phone is switched off. Tom has tried calling a couple of times already, and this has been the case each time.

"Nothing?" Cindy says as he slides the phone back into his pocket.

"Still off," Tom says.

"You want me to keep searching?" She motions to her laptop.

"Don't bother," Tom says. "If you say you can't find him, I believe you. Don't waste your time. All we can do now is get to Chicago. We'll find him when we're there. By then, he might have turned his phone back on."

Cindy closes the laptop. "It's gonna be a long drive," she says.

"Put some music on."

"*My* music?"

"Sure."

Cindy hooks her phone up to the stereo and starts thumbing through her collection. "You ever heard of Throbbing Gristle?"

"I've heard *of* them," Tom says.

"You're gonna hate them," Cindy says, grinning. "You ready?"

"Uh-huh," Tom says. "I can't wait."

10

Anthony and Connor put distance between themselves and The Cauldron before they stop into a bar. They take a seat at the corner of the counter, nursing their drinks and keeping their heads low and close together.

Neither of them spoke much on the way here, but since they've stopped, Connor has kept repeating the same phrase over and over: "This is bad, man, this is bad." He leaves a pause, glances around over his shoulder, occasionally takes a drink, then repeats, "This is bad." He shakes his head.

"I know it's bad," Anthony says, getting tired of the mantra. "But we can't wallow in that. This is a mess, and we're gonna have to try to clean it up. If we don't, you know what the alternative is."

Connor is already pale, but it looks like he goes paler at this. He has to clear his throat before he can speak again. "*H-how* are we gonna clean it up?"

Anthony doesn't answer straight away. He looks down the length of the bar, toward the door, like he expects a

Street King to walk in, making a show of how they're keeping an eye on them both. He watches until someone else walks through, but it's no Street King. An older guy, a midday drinker, like the rest of the bar's current clientele. He's old and haggard, and his potato nose is full of burst blood vessels. Anthony turns back to Connor, who is staring at him eagerly.

Anthony sighs. He takes a drink. "We're not gonna be able to find out who it was ripped us off and killed Dylan, so let's just forget about that. Put it to one side. Whoever they are, they'll probably show themselves eventually. Let Ezra deal with that. So if we cut that problem out of *our* particular set of problems, we need to think about how we're gonna make the money we need."

"Whatever you're thinking, it's easier said than done."

"I know that. Because what I'm thinking is, we're gonna have to do what was done to us." Anthony makes sure the bartender is out of earshot. He's at the other end of the counter, wiping glasses and watching the news. He's not paying them any attention. "We're gonna have to rip and run. We're gonna have to hit rival gangs. We're gonna have to take their money and their drugs. It's our only option."

Connor looks like he might be sick.

"I think...I think that Ezra knows this," Anthony says. "I think he knows this is our only option. I think it's what he *wants*. Someone struck at him, so he wants us to strike back at others regardless of whether they were involved or not."

Connor swallows and then nods. "You're probably right," he says. He's steeling himself. He doesn't like the danger they're about to put themselves in, but he knows they don't have any other choice. Connor can be a wild card. Anthony knows this. He's seen it firsthand. Some of the other Street

Kings dismiss him as weak, as not smart enough, and he knows that some of them think he's simple, but Anthony knows when push comes to shove, Connor is likely the one to be pushing back hardest. "We've got guns," he says, "but we're gonna need bigger ones if we're gonna do this. Peashooters ain't gonna do us any good." He runs his hands down his face. "If we're going to war, we wanna make sure we're armed for it."

Anthony is nodding at this when the door to the bar opens again. On instinct, Anthony glances toward it. He sees a familiar face. It's not a Street King.

It's Harlan.

Anthony feels his blood run cold. Harlan looks right at him and smiles. He comes over. "Well, well," he says. Connor looks back to see who it is. He frowns. He doesn't know who Harlan is. No doubt Anthony is going to have to explain their arrangement to him later. "Imagine finding you here."

"I'm sure it's a real surprise," Anthony says. After Harlan turned up at Stacey's last night, Anthony is starting to believe Harlan when he says he knows where he is at all times. Anthony doesn't like it. He's going to have to be more careful. Keep wide eyes and be always aware of his surroundings.

Harlan takes a seat next to Anthony and motions to the bartender for a beer. "Day drinking, huh?" Harlan says. "Don't mind if I join you."

Connor shoots Anthony an inquiring look. Anthony shakes his head and mouths that he'll tell him later, but Harlan sees it. He reaches out a hand toward Connor to shake. "Harlan Ross," he says. "Detective, Chicago PD. I extort your buddy here. You must be one of his fellow Street Kings."

Connor blinks. He looks from Harlan to Anthony and

back again. Harlan makes it clear he's waiting to shake. Connor reluctantly takes his hand.

The bartender arrives with Harlan's beer. Harlan pays for it, and the bartender retreats down to the other end again, returning to the news. Harlan takes a long drink, watching them both all the while. "So what's got the two of you looking so down?"

Neither of them answers.

"Come on now, Anthony. You can tell your old buddy Harlan."

"It's not your concern," Anthony says.

"Maybe I'm looking to make it my concern."

"Why would you want to go and do a thing like that?" Connor says.

"Isn't that what friends do for each other?" Harlan says.

"We're not friends," Anthony says. "You terrified Stacey last night. I didn't appreciate that."

"And I don't appreciate having to come and find you when you're overdue," Harlan says, getting close. Their shoulders are touching. "So why don't you cut the shit and tell me why the two of you are sitting here drinking in the middle of the day and looking like your grandmother's just died."

"You follow us here?" Anthony says.

"I was just passing by," Harlan says.

"You follow us *to* The Cauldron? You see me get run down this morning?"

"Careful, Anthony," Connor says.

"He knows what The Cauldron is," Anthony says. "And he knows who's inside it, too."

Harlan rests his head on his hands, propping himself up on the bar. He smiles.

"So why don't *you* cut the shit," Anthony says, "and tell me why you followed us here."

Harlan takes a drink. He looks around the bar, eyeing up the older day drinkers huddled in the corner. "Shit," he says, sucking his teeth. "Imagine if your whole life comes down to that. You even bear thinking about it? Your whole life, and you end it in some shitty South Side bar, just waiting for the end. Depressing, huh?"

Anthony doesn't look back at them. He's seen them already. Connor doesn't, either. Their eyes are focused on Harlan.

"Yeah, I know what goes on in The Cauldron," Harlan says, turning back to them. "I know all about it. Know exactly who it was you were talking to in there, too. And judging from the looks on your faces, I'm guessing you're in trouble with your boss, am I right?"

Anthony stares at him.

Harlan chuckles. "What'd the two of you do to upset him?"

"What's it matter to you?" Connor says.

"I already told you why it matters to me," Harlan says. "I'm just sitting here making conversation, asking why the two of you are looking so sour. Now maybe you both can stop asking me the same damn questions over and over, and start answering some."

Anthony knows Harlan won't stop until he gets the answers he wants. He sighs and says, "We owe money."

"There, was that so difficult?" Harlan says. "How much?"

"A lot," Anthony says.

"A *lot* isn't a number," Harlan says.

"Enough that we're gonna struggle to pay it back."

"That so? You got a deadline?"

"It's flexible," Anthony says, not wanting to tell Harlan the truth. He's already told him too much.

Harlan grunts like he knows this is a lie, but he doesn't push it. "I'm sure it is," is all he says to this. He takes a slow drink. Anthony can sense something is coming. He knows how Harlan works. Is accustomed to his body language. He braces himself. Harlan is either about to say something or hit him. That's how it usually goes.

"What if I was to tell you," Harlan says, using his words rather than his fists, though Anthony remains tense, "that I could maybe help the two of you out with your jam?"

"Not interested," Anthony says.

"You don't even know what I'm offering yet."

"I know we don't want any part of it."

Connor watches the two of them speak, his eyes moving back and forth between them.

Harlan chuckles. He finishes his drink. Anthony stays on edge, watching him, unblinking, all the while.

"It's an offer," Harlan says, putting his empty bottle down on the counter. "I never said it was a demand. Not yet, anyway." He nudges Anthony with his elbow like this is a joke. "I'll give the two of you some time to think. I'm sure when you start approaching your 'flexible' deadline, you might start to get desperate, and then you might be willing to hear me out." Harlan stands. "I'll talk to the two of you again soon."

He leaves the bar. Anthony and Connor watch him go. Anthony feels like he's been holding his breath the whole time Harlan has been present. His hands are shaking, and he balls them into fists to hide it.

"What the hell was that all about?" Connor says.

Anthony stares at the closed door. "Whatever it is, we

don't wanna know, I'm sure. I don't trust him. And I don't like how easy he took us turning him down. That's not like Harlan, uh-uh."

Harlan is up to something. It's clear he wants Anthony in on it, or else he wouldn't have approached him at all. Anthony gnaws at his bottom lip. He can taste blood. He takes a drink, hoping to calm his nerves, but it doesn't work. His nerves have too much to be worked up about – Ezra's money; the Street Kings most likely following and watching them; the fact they're going to have to put their lives on the line to pull off some big rip and runs; and now whatever Harlan is up to.

Anthony turns back to Connor. "You're right," he says. "We need bigger guns."

11

I
t's late. Tom and Cindy have checked into a motel for the night and gone to a nearby diner to eat. They still haven't heard back from Jeffrey. At this point, Tom isn't sure they will until Jeffrey has reached Chicago.

They take a booth by the window to sit and eat. Tom checks the time. "We'll eat and then get some sleep. I wanna get an early start tomorrow."

"Sure," Cindy says. They've both ordered burgers. It doesn't take long for the waitress to bring them over.

Tom sits in the corner with his back to the wall and a clear view of the rest of the diner, as well as out the window and into the parking lot. Their motel is just a little way down the road, and he can see its neon sign announcing vacancy. They walked here. It only took five minutes.

The diner is busier than Tom expected it to be so late in the day, but it's quiet. It's calm. The only noise comes from a booth with three truckers on the opposite end of the building. They talk and joke loudly, and laugh even louder. They try to flirt with the waitress, and she smiles and laughs along, but Tom thinks they're making her uncomfortable. He noticed them turn in their seats when Tom and Cindy entered. They looked Tom over, but they paid the most attention to Cindy. The way she's dressed and how she looks, no doubt. They frowned at her Godflesh T-shirt, likely not knowing they're a band.

Tom ignored their eyes, but he's kept them in mind and within view. He knows they could be trouble if they don't feel up to minding their own business.

"How you doing?" Cindy says.

Tom looks back at her.

"You've barely eaten," she says, nodding toward his plate.

"I'm fine," he says, picking up his burger.

"You seem distracted."

"I *am* distracted."

Cindy nods. She chews thoughtfully, then says, "I took a walk around Hopper Creek yesterday, when I first got there. It looks like a nice place. It felt strange to see where you grew up."

"I grew up outside of it, mostly," Tom says. "In my father's fortress."

"Well, it's a nice place. I imagine it was probably nicer when you were young. I've always been a city girl. I wonder sometimes how I'd cope in a small town like that."

"I wonder that myself," Tom says, his eyes drifting toward the window, watching the streaking headlights of cars passing by.

"What does that mean?" Cindy says. "You aren't happy there?"

Tom turns back. "That's not what I said." He takes another bite of burger.

Cindy watches him, but she doesn't say anything. She mulls over his words, considering their meaning.

Tom watches the other people in the diner, scanning the room. He shouldn't have said anything. He shouldn't tell Cindy that he's bored, that he's unsatisfied, that something is missing from his life – but at the same time he wants to. He almost did. It's a struggle to keep his mouth shut.

He puts the burger down. Cindy notices. She looks at him expectantly. He looks back at her, into her eyes. He thinks of how long they've known each other. Everything they've done together.

"Truth is," he begins, and then his phone begins to ring.

Tom pulls it from his pocket and looks down at it, expecting it to be Hayley checking in, but it's not. It's his father. "I'll take this outside," he says, getting to his feet and heading out of the diner, answering the call as he goes.

"You've been trying to call me," Jeffrey says.

Tom feels the cool night air on his face. The air is fresh. "I'm sure you can guess why," he says.

"I'm going to help my youngest son," Jeffrey says. "I asked you to do it, and you refused, so I'm going to get him myself."

"Sylvia told us about the cancer."

Jeffrey falls silent at this.

Tom doesn't push him. Their mutual silence stretches. Tom watches the road.

"Yeah, well. There it is," Jeffrey says. "Now you know. Nothing any of us can do about it."

"Are you getting treatment?"

"Start it in a couple of weeks, but I'm under no illusions, Tom. I'm going to die. All the treatment is going to do is prolong things a little. Buy me a few more years at max."

"You need to come home, Dad."

"I will."

"You need to come back right now," Tom says. "You're not well. You can't do this."

Jeffrey laughs. "You trying to tell me what I can't do?"

"Where are you right now?" Tom says.

"You sound like you're outdoors, Tom," Jeffrey says. "You coming after me?"

"Tell me where you are. If you're not going to turn around and come home, I'm going to bring you home."

"Yeah? And how are you gonna do that? You gonna beat me into submission, Tom? You gonna beat me down and drag me back with you?" Jeffrey laughs again. "I know you could, Tom. The days of me being stronger than my oldest son are long behind me. I don't have any illusions about *that* either, and I'm not too proud to admit the truth. You're stronger than me. So is that what you're gonna do?"

Tom grits his teeth. "I'm hoping to appeal to your common sense. Tell me where you are."

"I already told you, I'm going to get my youngest son," Jeffrey says. "He's in trouble, and I'm not going to let him down. I feel like I've let him down – I've let *both* of you down – too much already. I'm not going to tell you where I am, Tom, but I don't think you're going to stop following. I'll see you in Chicago." Jeffrey hangs up.

Tom sighs and lets the phone fall from his ear and dangle by his side. He breathes out hard and watches the cars pass by. He focuses on the motel's neon sign, then lifts the phone again and calls Hayley. She answers quick, like she's been expecting his call. "Hey," she says. "I was about to call you. I wasn't sure if you'd still be driving."

"No, we've stopped for the night. Just getting something to eat right now."

"Have you managed to find your dad?"

"Not yet," Tom says. "But he had a big head start on us. We're not gonna catch up to him until Chicago."

"Have you managed to get in touch with him at least?"

"Yeah, we just spoke. He wouldn't tell me where he is. I'm not surprised at that, though. How's Sylvia?"

"She's worried about her husband," Hayley says. "And she's worried about you and Anthony. I've given her a sedative, and she's sleeping in the spare room right now. She'll probably sleep through until morning. Should I tell her you've spoken to Jeffrey?"

"Tell her he's fine," Tom says. "And we'll bring him back soon."

"If you follow him all the way to Chicago, what then? Are you going to talk to Anthony?"

"The real question is if Anthony will talk to me."

"And if he does, what then? Are you going to help your father?"

"I'll have to cross that bridge when I come to it."

Hayley pauses a moment, then says, "Okay. You be careful, all right? I'll be thinking of you."

"Will do. I'll check in when I get the chance." Tom hangs up and puts the phone back into his pocket. He turns and looks into the diner and notices a minor commotion.

The booth of truckers has emptied out, and the three men are now at the other end of the diner. They're by Tom and Cindy's booth. They're leaning over Cindy. It looks like they're giving her a hard time. A few other patrons are looking over, as well as a couple of waitresses.

Tom enters the diner and approaches the booth. As he gets closer, he sees that Cindy isn't backing down from the truckers. This is pissing them off. He gets close enough to overhear what's being said.

"I get it, I do," she says. "You're on the road, and you're all lonely, and your only real company is your own right hand, but fellas, I'm not interested. I mean, I'm not even *flattered,* if I'm honest. You can come over here with all your bravado and your posturing, but, guys, I'm just not gonna fuck you."

"That ain't what we said," one of the truckers says, pressing a hand on the table and leaning over her.

"Oh, I heard what you said, but I also read between the lines. I see a couple of you are wearing wedding bands, and I just won't commit to being your piece of strange."

"Damn it," another of the truckers says from the shoulder of his buddy leaning over her. "That ain't what we said. We want you out."

"Why d'you want her out?" Tom says.

The three truckers stiffen and turn at the sound. It's clear they weren't expecting him to be back yet. They turn to him fully, straightening up, puffing out their chests.

"We want you and your girlfriend out," the one who was leaning over Cindy says.

"And why's that?"

"We don't like how she looks," the trucker says. "We don't like what she stands for. And the two of you are a package deal so far as we're concerned, so you can get out with her."

"We don't want any trouble in here," one of the waitresses calls out from behind the counter. "They're not hurting anyone, guys. Just leave them be."

The truckers ignore her.

"Guys, seriously," Cindy says, grinning, "just go back to your booth, or your trucks, now. You hang around, you're just gonna get yourselves hurt."

"Shut your mouth, bit–"

"Don't finish that," Tom says. "I'm gonna pretend you weren't even *thinking* about what you were about to call her." Tom inhales through his nose. "I've had a really long day. And this really long day started with some really bad news. So believe me when I say I'm not in the fucking mood for your bullshit."

The truckers look into his eyes. They see he's not messing around. They falter. Two of them back down a little, but the one at the fore, the one who leaned over Cindy, doesn't want to lose face. He swallows and clears his throat. He starts to jab a finger into Tom's chest. He opens his mouth to speak, but Tom cuts him off.

"Get that finger out of my chest, or I'll break it."

The trucker wavers.

Tom looks into his face, and he doesn't want him to waver. He wants him to keep the finger exactly where it is. Wants him to double down. Wants him to continue acting tough. Tom thinks about his father and his cancer. He thinks about his mother and the cancer that killed her when he was just a boy, when she was still young. He thinks of Anthony, and he thinks of Alejandra. He thinks of Hayley and of Cindy, and he thinks of how this man was about to call Cindy a bitch. He thinks of all these things, this whirlwind in his brain that has plagued him since this morning, and he thinks how he wants this trucker to give him an excuse to break his finger, and then he wants to beat him down. Beat him until his face is broken and Tom's own fists hurt from hitting him.

The trucker doesn't give him an excuse. He takes his hand back. He even mumbles an apology and then gestures to his two buddies to follow him. They don't go back to their booth. They go straight out of the diner. Tom stands and watches until they're completely gone. He slides back into the booth opposite Cindy.

"Soon as you were gone, they came over here," she says. "I think they'd been waiting for an opportunity to come and say something."

"Are you all right?" Tom says.

"I'm fine. I've dealt with assholes like that before. I mean, what were they gonna do? *Hit* me? They weren't gonna win themselves many supporters if they did that." She tilts her head, looking at him, studying him. "Tom, are you okay?" She reaches across the table and places a hand over his, and Tom realizes his hands are still balled into fists. He forces them to open. "How was the call? What did your dad say?"

"He said we'll see him in Chicago."

12

Anthony and Connor are being proactive.

They've spent the day driving around town, looking out for active corners, making a note of where they are. They've been sitting for a few hours down the block from one that looks promising. It's stayed busy all the while they've been here.

Yesterday, they were not proactive. Yesterday they were foolish. They wasted time. After Harlan left them in the bar, they proceeded to get drunk. Looking back, it was a regrettable decision. Though it was also understandable. They'd had bad news. They couldn't think straight. They needed to decompress. And to top it all off, Anthony was aching from his various falls when he was chased.

Anthony didn't go back to Stacey's last night, and he's realized he hasn't been in touch with her since he was chased out of her apartment by Stewie and Ethan. He stayed at Connor's place, too drunk to go much further, but also wanting to get an early start on today's work. He doesn't have his phone on him. It got left behind in the chase. Then, at

Connor's, he was so drained after everything that happened yesterday that he fell straight to sleep on the sofa. Finding a way to get in touch and let Stacey know he was all right completely slipped his mind.

Sitting in the car, watching the corner, he knows she's going to be pissed. She's more than likely half out of her mind with worry right now. She'll probably be relieved when she first sees him, but then she'll be angry, and Anthony won't blame her.

Anthony tries not to think about this too much. About how she'll react when he walks back into her apartment with its now-busted door. He'll fix it as penance. It won't be enough to make it up to her, but it's a start. He focuses instead on watching the corner. Seeing how they operate. Watching the bodies that come and go. Getting an idea of what kind of routines the corner boys keep. Spotting their lookouts, and noting where they all are. He knows this is the kind of thing his brother would do. All this preparation. He shakes the thought out of his head. In moments of danger and moments of preparation, he finds himself thinking of his brother often. He'd rather he didn't. He'd rather Tom wasn't anywhere near his thoughts and memories.

"I think we've seen as much as we need to," Anthony says. "You agree?"

Connor nods. "Yeah, I reckon so. When we coming back?"

"Later. When it's dark. We need to make a move. We can't waste any more time."

"Got it."

"Right now, I need to go and see Stacey," Anthony says. "I need to tell her what's happened."

"Last night, you kept saying she was going to kill you."

"I did?"

"Yeah. You were drunk. Maybe you don't remember. I told you I'm sure she'll understand. It's a tense situation. You weren't so convinced."

Anthony takes a deep breath. "I guess I'll find out soon enough. Drop me off?"

Connor starts up the engine. "Sure." He checks the time before he pulls away. "While you're making up with her, I'll go see if I can find us some heavier firepower."

Connor drops Anthony off at the sidewalk in front of Stacey's building. They arrange their meet-up for later on, and then Anthony steels himself and goes inside.

The door to the apartment isn't as bad as Anthony expected. It's going to need a new lock, and he assumes there's probably something lodged up against it from the other side to keep it shut right now. The door itself looks all right save for a few boot prints. Anthony knocks.

"Who is it?" Stacey calls.

"It's me."

Sure enough, he hears something being dragged aside before the door opens. Stacey flings the door open, eyes blazing, and then wraps her arms around him fiercely. She pulls him close and holds him tight. "You asshole," she says into his ear. She lets go enough so she can look into his face. "Where the hell have you been?" She sniffs, smells the residual alcohol clinging to his clothes, and raises an eyebrow.

"Yesterday was a really long day," Anthony says. "I'll tell you all about it." He looks at the broken door. "But first, I'll fix the lock."

"First you'll come and see Billy," she says. "He's been missing you."

They step into the apartment, and Anthony sees the foot-locker that was serving as the door's makeshift lock. Billy is in his room, on the floor playing with action figures. He jumps up when he notices Anthony and rushes to him. Anthony drops to a knee and catches him in his arms.

"It's a good thing you've come back when you have," Stacey says, stroking the back of his head. "I'm supposed to go to work in a couple of hours, and I wasn't sure if I was going to be able to make it. I couldn't find any care for Billy, and even if I could, I'm not sure I could expect a sitter to come here with a busted door."

Anthony keeps hold of Billy and hugs him tight, his eyes closed. He breathes in the soapy clean smell of him. "It's all right," he says, but he's not sure if he's speaking to Stacey or Billy. "I'm here now." He takes in another deep breath and lets go of Billy, lets him return to his toys. He turns back to Stacey as he stands. "You're gonna have to call someone anyway," he says. He raises his hands to calm her before she can protest and says, "I'll fix the door. It's fine, they can come here. But I've gotta go out."

Stacey folds her arms. "Let's go to the bedroom," she says, tilting her head. "It's time to tell me what's going on, and I don't think we want Billy to hear it."

13

Harlan rolls around the city. It's getting late. He's visited a few drug dealers he leans on to extort money. He had to slap a couple of them around. One of them was in front of his girlfriend and children. They cried, but they didn't try to intervene. They knew it would just make things worse if they did. Harlan slapped the dealer bloody, until he finally started coughing up cash that he had stashed around his house – wrapped in plastic in the toilet tank, in the bottom of his mattress, and in an outside pipe.

Harlan isn't hurting for cash. Not yet, anyway. But being suspended is a dry business. No income. It's also boring. Harlan has found himself getting his kicks where he can.

He's got something big in the pipeline, and he knows it's coming soon. He waits for this. Soon, the suspension won't be an issue anymore. He won't be so bored. He won't have to think about Chicago ever again.

But he needs to kill time until this plan is in play.

He goes to the strip club where Stacey Shapiro works. Anthony's delightful girlfriend. She's far too good-looking for an asshole like Anthony. She looks like she needs a real man. A man like Harlan.

Inside the club, he goes to the bar and takes a look around. He spots Stacey up on the stage, swinging around a pole. She's not naked yet, but Harlan doesn't think it'll take long. She's in a bikini that doesn't leave much to the imagination. He watches her face. She's smiling, putting the effort in, but Harlan thinks she looks distracted. Every so often her mask will falter and slip. Her eyes glaze over. He wonders what's running through her mind. Wonders if it has anything to do with the visit he paid them the night before last.

Harlan is in shadows, and she doesn't notice him. He wonders how many faces she sees in the crowd, or if she ignores them all and works through. Her smiles and come-ons are all fake, plastered on purely for extra tips. He doubts the rest of her audience notices how she seems distracted. She seems to be doing well enough for herself. The guys in the front row are throwing her plenty of bills. Stacey flips her hair and bites her lip, and the men hoot and holler.

Harlan orders a beer and books a private dance for when she's done onstage. The bartender tells him she'll be available in a half hour. Harlan can wait. He nurses his drink and watches her. He likes how she moves. She takes off her top and swings it around her head. She doesn't have the biggest breasts, but Harlan doesn't mind. They look natural. He glances at some of the other girls and sees that this is a rarity.

Another girl comes by and offers him a dance, but Harlan tells her some other time. He's already got one booked. Tonight, he only has eyes for Stacey.

Her routine ends, and she leaves the stage, and Harlan is

quietly disappointed she never took off her bottoms. He guesses she doesn't go that far. Still, he got to see more than enough. He checks the time – twenty more minutes to wait. Twenty minutes, and then he'll get to see her up close.

Harlan gets another drink, and he's still nursing it when the twenty minutes are up. He sees Stacey appear, and Harlan is pointed out to her. She doesn't realize it's him yet. She comes over smiling. She's in her bikini again and a frayed vest. She wears thigh-high boots with a heel so tall it's amazing she can keep her balance. She gets closer, closer, and she's still smiling. Another come-on. Another *tips ahoy* smile. Then she gets so close, and she looks up, and she sees who he is. Her smile fades. Her face drops.

"I assume there's somewhere private for us to go?" Harlan says, grinning. "This is my first time here. You're gonna have to lead the way." He holds his hand out to her.

Stacey looks around, but there's no help for her. She deliberates, biting her lip, trying to find a way out. She doesn't want to make a scene. She doesn't want to cause any trouble. Reluctantly, she takes his hand and guides him from the stool. They go into a back room together. It's a small room, and instead of a door, it has a red velvet curtain that hangs all the way down to the floor. The back wall is a plush curving sofa. Harlan takes a seat.

"What do you want?" Stacey says, folding her arms, trying to cover herself.

"You've got nothing to hide from me, girl," Harlan says. "I've been here a while. I saw you up onstage. I've seen it all already." He looks her up and down, and his tongue flickers out over his lips.

Stacey shudders. "What do you *want*?" she says again.

"I want what I paid for. I want a dance."

"Are you...are you serious?"

"My money spends just as well as everyone else's."

Stacey hesitates. She doesn't move.

Harlan claps his hands together, hard, and she jumps. "I said *dance*," he says.

Stacey does as he says. She doesn't have any other choice. She closes her eyes and starts slow. She pretends she's somewhere else while she rolls her hips, running her hands back through her hair. She slips out of the frilled vest.

"I paid for a *lap* dance," Harlan says. "You're nowhere near my lap."

She swallows. She keeps her eyes closed. She moves closer, in motion all the while. When she's within touching distance, Harlan reaches out and strokes her thigh.

Stacey opens her eyes and snatches her leg back from him. "No touching," she says.

"Not usually," Harlan says. "But you're gonna make an exception for me, aren't you?"

Stacey is struggling to control her breathing. Harlan thinks he can see the way her heart is hammering, the way the skin flutters and pounds between her breasts. She swallows. She looks uncomfortable.

Harlan smiles. He sits back. "Dance," he says.

Stacey does. Harlan keeps his hands to himself. He admires the view.

Stacey keeps her back to him. She dances and tries to get through this. After a while, she turns her head. Forces her eyes open. Looks back at him over her shoulder. "How – how did you find Anthony?" she says. "How did you know where I live?"

Harlan smiles. "Turn around."

She does. She keeps dancing. Gyrating. Her eyes are open now. She looks at him, waiting for his response.

Harlan stares at her bikini top. "Take it off."

Again, Stacey hesitates, but she understands her situation. She glances back toward the curtain and then slips out of it.

Harlan grins, staring brazenly. "Anthony can't go anywhere that I won't know," he says. "I know his routes and his hangouts. And I'm especially going to remember if there's a beautiful lady there."

She doesn't look flattered.

"You shouldn't worry about Anthony," Harlan says. "Not from me, at least. Me and him, we're old pals. I'm good to him. Hell, I've taken him drinking in the past, and I paid, because that's the kind of guy I am. Of course, it didn't cost me too much – he's a real lightweight. You ever noticed that? You must have. Doesn't take much to get him drunk. You get him drunk, and he'll tell you his whole life story. He'll answer any question you ask him."

Stacey doesn't have anything to say to this.

"I'll take care of him, don't you worry none. And I'll take care of you, too, Stacey. All you have to do is say the word. I'll take good care of little Billy, too."

"What are you – what are you saying?" Stacey says. "What did you come here for? What do you want?"

"Just letting you know," Harlan says, "if ever you're looking for a real man, I'm just a call away."

Stacey has stopped dancing. "You're not my type."

"Do I look like a little bit of disinterest is going to put me off?"

Stacey is horrified. She steps back and retrieves her vest. "We're done here," she says. "The dance is over."

"That's fine," Harlan says. "I got my money's worth."

Stacey storms out of the room, covering her chest and throwing aside the curtain as she goes. Harlan watches her leave. He runs his tongue over his front teeth. She's an attractive woman. She stirs things in Harlan. Desires. He wants to do bad things to her.

Anthony is a very lucky man.

14

It's late when Tom and Cindy finally roll into Chicago. Tom pulls to the side of the road and calls his father. Beside him, Cindy stifles a yawn. She stretches in her seat, twisting her body from side to side. Tom hears pops coming from her spine.

Jeffrey answers. He coughs a couple of times and sounds groggy. "Tom," he says, then coughs again. "You woke me up."

"I'm in Chicago."

"Uh-huh, and I'm trying to sleep. We'll meet in the morning."

"Are you kidding me?" Tom says. "I'm not planning on hanging around. Tell me where you are."

"Y'know, Tom, you catch more flies with honey than with vinegar. You should keep that in mind when we catch up to Anthony. I'll see you in the morning." Jeffrey hangs up.

"What do we do now?" Cindy says as he puts his phone away. "Find somewhere to spend the night?"

"Yeah," Tom says, though he's not happy about it. "I guess we don't have any other choice."

"We're gonna spring for a decent hotel, though," Cindy says. It's not a request. "We're not cheaping out, I'll tell you that right now. We've been on the road for the better part of two days, and my body is *stiff*. You're gonna have to treat a lady tonight, Tom."

"That sounds reasonable," Tom says, and then pulls away and starts driving again while Cindy pulls out her phone and finds them a hotel.

15

Anthony drives to Connor's place to prepare. He hung around Stacey's apartment until the babysitter turned up, then headed out into the night. Connor comes to the living room window and waves him inside when he pulls to a stop in front of the house.

"I didn't have much time to work with, so you're gonna have to bear with me," Connor says. He's in the bedroom. Anthony goes through to him. There's something on the bed. It's small, like a rock. Connor motions to it. "I got a grenade."

"What the *fuck*?" Anthony says, the object becoming clear in his eyes.

"Like I said, I didn't have much time. This was all I could get before we needed to meet up again."

Anthony stares at the grenade. He doesn't know anything about grenades. Tom would. He pushes this thought aside. Of course Tom would. Tom was in the fucking Army. The grenade is green, with a round, smooth body. It doesn't look like the pineapple-style ones Anthony has seen in old war movies. He sees its pull-pin and its safety clip. Being so close to it makes him uncomfortable. "Are you sure it's active?"

"I don't see why it wouldn't be," Connor says.

Anthony looks at him and raises an eyebrow. "Probably because the same people who would *sell* a grenade, of all fucking things, probably think that if someone is stupid enough to buy one, then they can get away with selling a dud. Jesus Christ, Connor, what were you thinking?"

"I was thinking it was better to turn up with something rather than nothing at all."

Anthony shakes his head. "Well, you were wrong. You need to hide this away somewhere safe for now, and get rid of it as soon as you can. We're not taking that with us."

"So, what? We just take our Glocks?"

"It looks like that's the only option we've got."

Connor grumbles as he picks up the grenade and takes it to his closet, putting it into a shoebox and tucking it to one side. "Whatever, man," he says, turning back.

They head out, taking Anthony's car. They go back to the corner they watched earlier in the day. They're both dressed all in black. They have balaclavas in the glove compartment. Connor pulls them out and rests them in his lap. They watch the corner. There's some activity there right now. They see the two guys guarding it. They're both black. One is skinny, but the other looks like he hits the weights regularly. They wait until the corner clears, and then Anthony pulls out his Glock. Connor does the same.

"Follow my lead," Anthony says. "I'll do all the talking. Got it?"

"Not a word," Connor says. He's focused. Intense. He hands a mask to Anthony.

They leave the car and stick to the shadows as they

make their way up the block. The two corner boys don't see them. Their lookouts don't see them. Anthony knows it's important they don't get seen until they want to be. They need the element of surprise. They want this to be quick and clean. They don't want a gunfight. They can't risk one.

Anthony is in the lead. He reaches the corner of the building opposite and looks the area over. There's no one else around. Just the two corner boys talking between themselves. Anthony opens and closes his empty left fist, balling it tight. He squeezes the handle of the Glock in his right hand. Grits his teeth. Reaches behind him and pats Connor, letting him know he's about to make a move.

They race over the road, Glocks raised. "Hands up, hands fucking *up!*" Anthony says.

The corner boys turn, startled, but they're smart, and they do as he says.

"Weapons over here, right now! Come on, let's go, move it!"

The skinny guy has a revolver, and the bigger has a Magnum. They toss them over to Anthony.

"You ain't wanna do this," the bigger guy says. "You're gonna get yourself in trouble."

"Shut up," Anthony says. "We didn't come here for conversation. Hand over everything you've got – cash and drugs. *Now.*"

Connor steps forward, keeping his Glock raised. The skinny guy looks to the bigger guy. The bigger guy nods. The skinny guy hands over the cash in his pockets, then retrieves their stash from where it's concealed in a hole low down in the wall. It's not much, Anthony notices. None of it is, the cash or the drugs, especially for how busy they've looked both tonight and earlier in the day. Connor is able to pocket it all.

"That all of it?" Anthony says. He waves his gun like he means business. "You're *sure*?"

The bigger guy laughs. "We've just had a pickup, dumbass. You came an hour ago, maybe this would've been worth it."

Anthony grits his teeth. He steps back and kicks their weapons down a storm drain. He flicks his head at Connor, and Connor turns and runs. Anthony backs up, keeping the Glock trained on both corner boys, and then when he reaches the building on the opposite side of the road, he turns and bolts after Connor. Last he saw, the bigger guy was still laughing at them. Anthony dives into the car, behind the steering wheel, and spins the car around and speeds off. He hits the wheel as they go. "*Fuck!*"

Connor checks over what they got. Anthony is already prepared for disappointment. "Shit..." Connor says.

Anthony takes a deep breath. "Tell me."

"A bag of weed, a bag of pills, and three hundred fucking dollars in cash." He hits the window with the side of his fist. "God*damn!*"

It's not enough. It's nowhere near enough.

They're far enough away from the corner. Anthony pulls over. They've both removed their masks. They're back in the glove compartment.

"If this is the haul," Connor says, "how many fucking corners are we gonna have to hit? Even if they haven't just had a collection, is it gonna make enough of a difference?"

Anthony stares at the cash and the drugs in Connor's lap. Even if they hit a few more corners tonight, and whether it's a similar, better, or worse take, they're barely going to have a grand. He runs his hands down his face. "This is no good," he says. He drums his fingers on top of the steering wheel. "We're gonna have to do something else."

"I'm not robbing a bank," Connor says. "Ripping off corners is one thing, but I'm not going after a bank."

"I never said anything about a bank," Anthony says, glaring at him. "No, what we need to do is go after exactly what *we* lost."

"What do you mean?"

"Stash houses. That's what we've gotta hit. We find stash houses, and we hit *them*. That's our only hope. Even if we can't get enough cash, we can at least get enough product to pay Ezra back."

"You think he'll accept that in lieu?"

"I think he will," Anthony says. He sighs and shakes his head and stares off down the road. "We're gonna have to fucking hope so."

16

Tom and Cindy wake early. After Tom has showered and dressed, and while Cindy is showering, Tom calls his father. Jeffrey sounds wide awake. He says he needs breakfast. Tells Tom he'll meet him at a diner close to where he's staying and gives him details of where that is.

"Breakfast sounds good to me," Cindy says, drying her hair.

They reach the diner, and Jeffrey is already there. He spots them as they enter. Tom sees the way he looks at Cindy. He's frowning, wondering what she's doing here. They join him at his table. He's sitting at a booth in the rear, his back to the wall. Tom and Cindy slide in opposite him, and Tom feels uncomfortable with his back to the room. He knows, however, that Jeffrey will be watching the space. Jeffrey is observant. He taught Tom a lot. This, at least, eases some of Tom's discomfort. Not all of it, though.

A waitress comes over before they can say anything to

each other. Cindy orders pancakes. Tom gets eggs. After she's gone, Jeffrey nods toward Cindy. "I'm surprised you brought a friend."

"We're good at tracking people in the wild," Tom says. "Cindy is good at tracking them in cities. I brought her to help find you. I didn't know if you were ever going to answer your phone."

Jeffrey smiles at her now. "That's good. Now you can help us find Anthony."

Tom doesn't say anything to this, but Jeffrey looks at him like he can read his mind.

"I made myself clear when we spoke on the phone," Jeffrey says. "I'm not leaving without your brother. I'm worried about him, Tom. I can't get in touch with him, and that's tearing me up. I'm not going to lie – I'm struggling to keep it together right now. The closer I got to Chicago, the more worried I got. I don't think I slept more than a couple of hours last night. Now I'm here, I just want to find him, to see him, to make sure he's not hurt." He sits back and takes a deep breath, scratching at his forehead.

Now that he knows his father is ill, that he's dying, Tom can see it much clearer. He looks thinner. His skin is pallid. He looks older, as if Tom's learning of his sickness has suddenly aged him in his eyes.

Jeffrey looks back at him. He stifles a cough. "I know what you're thinking, Tom. It shows on your face."

Tom realizes he hasn't said a word to his father since they sat down with him. Cindy holds his hand under the table, and he wonders what the look on his face is like. He squeezes her hand and then takes a deep breath. "I know Cindy has her heart set on breakfast," he says. "But once we're done eating, let's find Anthony."

Jeffrey's face lightens. "You've come around?"

"You haven't left me much choice." Tom pauses while the waitress brings over their food. "Let's find him, and then let's go home."

17

After they're finished eating, Tom, Cindy, and Jeffrey leave the diner and go to Jeffrey's hotel room. Cindy has her laptop. She gets to work, searching out Anthony and where he might be.

Tom and Jeffrey stand to one side and let her work. "What's she doing?" Jeffrey says.

"Searching his name," Tom says. "Trying to get a lead – a job listing, an address, some kind of record on him that could give us an idea of where to go."

Jeffrey nods, watching Cindy, seeing how her fingers fly over the keys while her face never leaves the screen, her eyes constantly scanning. Jeffrey shakes his head and looks away. "That's too fast for me."

"She only ever gets faster." Tom studies his father. "How are you feeling?"

"I feel fine," Jeffrey says, a little too quick, not meeting his eyes.

"You know I need you to be clear with me," Tom says, staring at him until he finally does look back.

Jeffrey sighs. "All right," he says, knowing Tom is right. "I don't feel one hundred percent, but I feel good. I've got this cough I can't shake, and I get tired easier than I used to, but that's about it right now."

"If Anthony is in trouble, are you up to dealing with that? I want the truth. I need it, you know that."

Jeffrey considers this. Tom doesn't prompt him. Jeffrey is appraising himself. "Yes," Jeffrey says, looking him straight in the eye. "I'm up to it."

Tom nods. He believes his father. Jeffrey understands that if there is trouble, Tom needs to be able to rely on him. He can't lie. Lying puts all of their lives at risk.

They stand in silence for a while, the only sound the tapping of Cindy's fingers racing over the keys. She stops long enough to pop her knuckles, and then continues.

"What was it Anthony said to you?" Tom says. "What brought you up here?"

"I think he was drunk," Jeffrey says. "Having a dark night of the soul, it seemed. Lamenting his life choices. Saying he'd got in trouble with drugs and gangs." Jeffrey purses his lips. The concern is apparent on his face. His features are pinched, and Tom thinks this is the worry more than the cancer.

Cindy sits back and turns to them. "He worked in an electrical goods store for about six months a year ago," she says. "They had an address for him listed on file. It might be out of date now, but it's probably worth going by. I can't find anything else for where he might be living."

"You've checked he's not anywhere else?" Jeffrey says.

"Of course I've checked," Cindy says, jerking a thumb back at her laptop. "What do you think I was doing all that time?"

Tom grins. "Let's go check the address."

18

A nthony and Connor have split up. They need to find a stash house. Separate, they can cover more ground.

In his rearview mirror, Anthony notices he's being followed. He recognizes the car. Adjusting his mirror, he can see the driver. He's not surprised. It's Harlan.

Anthony continues on for a few blocks, keeping an eye on the mirror. Harlan doesn't tailgate him. He keeps a safe distance. Doesn't speed up or slow down. Doesn't lose him, either. Anthony finds a place to pull over. Harlan parks right behind him. Anthony waits for him to get out of his car, but he doesn't. Anthony sighs and rolls his eyes and gets out. He goes to Harlan and leans in at his open window.

"Anthony," Harlan says. "Fancy seeing you here."

"Why are you following me, Harlan?" Anthony says.

Harlan winks. "Just checking in. Making sure my buddy is okay."

"Uh-huh. I'm real busy, Harlan. I've got a lot I need to do." Anthony looks down the road, wondering if Harlan is the only person following him right now. There could be Street Kings out there too, watching him, and maybe they know who Harlan is. Maybe they know that Anthony is talking to a cop.

"I heard about a street corner rip and run last night," Harlan says.

"You *heard* about that, huh? I thought you were suspended. Who's gonna tell you about such a minor thing?"

"I'm still a cop, Anthony. That never goes away, not really. I've got contacts. They speak to me."

"Sure. Why you telling me about this?"

"You have anything to do with it?"

"Not sure why you would jump to that conclusion. But, y'know, I heard about a rip and run, too, but it sounded *real* quiet. Like, no one got hurt. There wasn't a bullet fired. Not the kind of thing that would get the attention of any cop."

Harlan grins. "We keep our ears to the ground for all kinds. You'd be surprised."

"Uh-huh. Or maybe you were there. Maybe I'm not the only person you follow around at all hours of the fucking day and night."

Harlan waves a hand. "Ah, this is fun, Anthony, but let's not beat around the bush any longer. Get in the car."

Anthony doesn't move. He grits his teeth and stares at Harlan.

"I'm not gonna ask again."

Anthony heads around the other side of the car and gets in.

"You've been giving me some real attitude lately, Anthony," Harlan says, turning to him.

"I guess that'll happen when you choke me in front of my girlfriend while her son sleeps in the next fucking room."

Harlan runs his tongue around his mouth. "Yeah, I did do that. But they're not here right now, Anthony, so what do you think I might do to you when it's just the two of us?" Harlan leans in close. "So why don't you watch your fucking mouth?"

Anthony forces himself not to flinch. Forces himself not to back off.

Harlan stays close to him for a moment longer, then pulls back to his side of the car. "Sure, there weren't any gunshots last night," he says. "No one got hurt. But what about next time? And I'll be honest with you, buddy, if you get into a firefight, I see it going one of two ways. You get killed, or you get caught. Either way, whether you end up in the ground or in a jail cell, you're no good to me. And with that friend of yours, I don't have the highest of hopes. Is it just the two of you?"

"I don't understand why you care so much."

Harlan stares at him. He's not smiling. His face is hard. "Is it just the two of you?"

Anthony nods.

"That's not enough. I got a good look at that kid, Anthony. He ain't built for what you got to do – neither of you are."

"You offering to help?"

"Matter of fact –"

"I already told you, I'm not interested in whatever it is you got planned."

"There's that attitude again."

"Damn it, Harlan, you're stalking me."

"I got a job in mind. A big-money job. I need bodies. You help out, you get a cut. Whatever you owe, I'm sure it's enough to pay off your debt."

"How much are we talking?"

"You haven't agreed to anything."

Anthony doesn't want to get involved with Harlan any more than he already is, but the offer, as vague as it is, is tempting. After last night, their rip and run on the corner and their meager earnings from it, Anthony is desperate. He knows Connor is, too. Time is running out.

They still have the hope of finding a stash house, though. It's a slim hope, but it's worth clinging to. They don't have anything else.

"I can see you're thinking real hard, buddy," Harlan says. "You keep thinking. I'm not gonna press you for an answer right now. I just want you to know that the offer is there. Keep that in mind. Once you start feeling like you've got no other hope, you get in touch with me. I have a feeling you might get there real soon."

Anthony doesn't say anything. He gets out of Harlan's car, and Harlan surprises him by driving away. Anthony wipes a hand across the back of his mouth. He feels sick, knowing how close he came to agreeing to help. He can't trust Harlan. Whatever he's planning, there's a double-cross in there somewhere.

Anthony goes back to his own car on unsteady legs. He doesn't pull out straight away. He takes deep breaths. Steadies himself. Tries to get Harlan's words out of his head. He needs to focus. He needs to find a stash house. Once he's done that, he can forget all about Harlan's offer. He won't need that money anymore.

19

Tom, Jeffrey, and Cindy reach Anthony's house. Or, at least, the house he was registered as living at back when he worked at the electrical goods store.

Jeffrey goes to the door. Tom and Cindy stay in the car and watch. Tom sits in the driver's seat. Jeffrey was in the passenger seat beside him. Cindy leans forward between the two front seats, watching Jeffrey go. "So," she says. "Are you going to tell me what the problem is between you and your brother?"

Tom doesn't answer. He sees his father knocking on the door and waiting.

Cindy turns to Tom. "Well? Tom? What is it?" She frowns, concerned. "You don't want to tell me?"

Tom clears his throat. "I'm concerned that if I tell you, it'll change your opinion of me."

"What, really? Shit, Tom, what did you *do*?"

Tom continues to watch his father. There's no answer at the door. He sees how Jeffrey moves away, goes down the side of the house, exploring further. While he watches, he tells Cindy what happened between himself and his brother. Tells her about Alejandra's ashes.

Cindy listens without interrupting. When he's done, she absorbs what he's said. "Well, shit, Tom," she says, turning to him. "I mean, I was there with you when you went up against those Nazis. I know what they did to Alejandra, and I know what she meant to you." She purses her lips. "I think taking her ashes was wrong. I mean, I get why you needed to do it for *you*, but for Anthony – that wasn't just Alejandra, that was his child, too."

"I know that," Tom says.

Cindy turns to him. Her face is sympathetic. She surprises him by what she does next. She doesn't say anything. She leans closer and wraps her arms around him. Tom is caught off guard, but after a moment, he tentatively hugs her back.

"I don't think any less of you," she says into his ear before letting go of him. She pulls away, adding, "But I get now why Anthony probably doesn't want to see you."

Jeffrey returns to the car. He opens the passenger door but doesn't get inside. He leans down to talk to them. "No answer," he says. "But I took a look around, looked in some windows – it's Anthony's place, all right."

"How are you sure?" Tom says.

"Saw a picture of your mom pinned on the wall in the bedroom."

Tom nods.

"What now?" Cindy says. "We wait here until he turns back up?"

"We can't guarantee he's going to come back," Tom says. "We'll go inside, take a look around. See if we can find anything that might give us some kind of idea as to where he might be."

Tom and Cindy get out of the car, and the three of them go up to the house. "I'm gonna pick the lock," Jeffrey says. "Cindy, maybe take a step back. Tom, you got my six?"

Tom nods.

"What's wrong?" Cindy says.

"He might've set traps," Tom says.

Cindy frowns. "Why do you think that?"

"It's what we would do," Tom says, watching as his father gets down to a knee.

Jeffrey checks the door before he does anything, pressing the edges, ducking down and looking at the bottom of it. He presses an ear to the wood, then reaches into his pocket and pulls out a lock-picking kit.

Tom grins. "Always prepared."

"That's nothing," Jeffrey says, getting to work. "You should see the trunk of my car."

"What's in the trunk of your car?" Cindy says.

Tom grins, and Jeffrey says, "Guns."

While Jeffrey picks the lock, Tom looks down the side of the house. "I assume you've checked the windows already."

"What do you think took me so long?" Jeffrey says. The lock clicks, but Jeffrey doesn't push the door wide. He glances back at Tom.

Tom looks back at Cindy, makes sure she's at a safe distance, then nods at his father. Careful, cautious, Jeffrey pushes the door open. He stays on his knees. Tom knows what he's doing. He's waiting for any kind of resistance against the door, something like a tripwire. Maintaining the same slow speed, he gets the door open all the way. No tripwire. Jeffrey looks into the hall. Tom peers over the top of him. Neither of them can see anything.

Tom can smell something in the air. Something sweet and strong and familiar. Rotten food. "I don't see anything we need to worry about," he says.

Jeffrey stands and takes the first step into the house. "Anthony?" He waits, but there's no answer. "Anthony, it's me. Dad."

"There's no one here," Tom says.

They explore the house, checking for traps, but there are none. Tom shakes his head. His brother should know better. In the kitchen, he finds signs that Anthony hasn't been here in a while. There's half a loaf of bread reduced to potent mold. In the refrigerator, the milk is three weeks out of date. There are some cold cuts that have turned green and shiny. Tom goes back and gets Cindy.

"You can come in," he says. "It's clear."

Jeffrey summons them through to Anthony's bedroom. Pinned to the wall next to the bed, Tom sees the picture of their mother that Jeffrey mentioned. It's not a picture Tom has seen before. She's wearing a long summer dress and smiling over her shoulder, her body turned to the side to show off that she's pregnant. Tom assumes the baby she's carrying is Anthony.

Jeffrey points at another picture just below it. "I don't suppose you know who she is?"

A younger lady, with a child. The boy is holding onto her side. They're both smiling. The woman's head is tilted, and her long hair hangs down, brushed over so it falls over the top of the boy's head.

"I doubt Anthony has a secret family he's never mentioned," Jeffrey says.

"The boy's too old," Tom says, thinking of Alejandra. She was killed three years ago. She was pregnant three years ago. "I'd guess he's about seven or eight." He looks a similar height and build to Tre Greene, Zeke's son, and he's eight.

"I'll see if I can find out who she is," Cindy says, snapping a picture on her phone to later load into her laptop. "If she's easier to find, maybe she can tell us where he is. I doubt he's got her picture on the wall for nothing."

Tom starts to turn away, but then he notices a framed picture on the other side of the bed, standing upright on the bedside table. Tom goes round to it and picks it up, holds it in both hands. Tom swallows and feels a click in his throat. It's Alejandra. Much like the picture of their mother, she's pregnant in this photograph. Tom keeps a picture of Alejandra in his bag. He doesn't look at it all that often, because whenever he does, he feels the same thing he's feeling right now – a knife, twisting in his guts. A hand squeezing around his heart. Without a word, he puts the picture down. He can feel Cindy and Jeffrey watching him. He doesn't say anything. He goes to the window and looks out, looking around. It gives him a view of the road directly out front. He can see his parked car.

Further down the block, something catches his eye. A parked car with two men sitting inside. They're obscured by a tree and other parked vehicles. They've tried to hide themselves from view. Both of them are facing the house. Tom steps back from the window. "The house is being watched."

"I didn't see anyone on the way in," Jeffrey says.

"They've been careful."

"You're sure they're watching the house?" Cindy says.

"Not totally, no," Tom says. "But it looks like they are. I've seen them now, though, and their car. When we leave, we'll check if they follow us."

"Well, it doesn't look like there's anything else here for us," Jeffrey says. "So let's go now and see if they do."

They leave the house and get into the car. None of them look toward the men who Tom thinks could be watching them. They stay casual. Tom pulls away from the front of Anthony's house, keeping an eye on the side mirror as he goes. The car doesn't follow, not straight away. As he reaches the end of the block, the car pulls out.

"Here they come," he says. "They're keeping their distance."

"Who do you think they are?" Cindy says.

"Anthony said he was in trouble with gangs," Jeffrey says. "Could be them. If it is, and if they're looking for him, that's a good sign, I reckon. Means they don't have him yet."

"Then let's make sure we don't lead them to him," Tom says.

20

Connor has found a stash house.

Anthony met up with him an hour ago. The first thing he asked was how he'd managed to find it. Connor said he'd asked around, but made sure to only speak to people he trusted implicitly. "I was careful," he said. "I was *real* careful, don't worry about anything. These aren't guys who'll tell anyone. These are customers, and I made sure to reward them enough they'll keep quiet."

They've been watching the stash house from afar, with binoculars. Reconnaissance again, like when they watched the corners. Except this time, when they're ready to move, it should prove to be a much more rewarding haul.

They lie flat on the roof of a building away from the neighborhood where the stash house is. They're on the garage roof of an abandoned house. The windows of the house are smashed, and the doors are hanging loose. This neighborhood is elevated and looks down on the one with the stash house. Up here, the streets are a casualty of drugs. Very few of the houses are occupied.

The stash house is in a black neighborhood, and Anthony and Connor can't get any closer. They'll stand out. Their presence would raise too much suspicion. And more than that, they'll be in danger.

"Whose stash house is this?" Anthony says. "You know that?"

"Second City Skulls," Connor says.

"Jesus Christ," Anthony says. "I was worried about that." He's aware of the Skulls. Of course he is. Every Street King knows about them, and knows to stay very, very clear of them. For any rival gang to wander into their south-side territory is an instant death sentence.

Anthony's heard the story of how they got their name, too. Their founder, who is currently serving three life sentences and would never step foot outside a prison again, captured three members of a Nazi gang. He skinned their faces so that their skulls were showing through, then dumped their bodies on their own territory. He did the same to two members of a Latin gang. The name stuck after that. They emblazoned T-shirts with the image of a bloodied skull and tattooed it into their flesh. Their territory is marked by the bloodied skull spray-painted on walls, sometimes obvious and sometimes subtle. It's important to be aware of them, especially for the likes of Anthony and Connor and any other Street King.

They watch the house for a while in silence. At first, they needed to be sure it was a stash house. Anthony is sure now. There are people standing guard. Four people in and around the house, patrolling the block. He spots the people inside standing at the windows, looking out. He doesn't have a great idea of what weaponry they're carrying, but he can see they're carrying handguns, at least. There could be heavier equipment inside the house.

"It's what we're looking for, ain't it?" Connor says.

Anthony lowers the binoculars. "Yeah," he says. "I'm pretty sure it is."

They shuffle back off the roof, keeping low and out of view. They've seen and know all that they need to. Now, it's a matter of preparation. It's a matter of action. Anthony grits his teeth and swallows hard. He knows what's coming. Knows what they have to do next. He knows they have to rip off the Second City Skulls.

And he knows, more than anything else, that this could be the death of them both.

21

Harlan isn't following Anthony right now. He's busy. He's at the apartment, working security. He got here early. A few of the other guys are present, and Harlan is playing cards with them. The game was Harlan's idea. A distraction. Leo DeLuca is here again, along with Ray Palladino and Peter Fanelli. They play poker in the guard room. It's supposed to be Harlan and Leo on security again, but Ray and Peter don't seem to be in any rush to leave.

Matt Rossi and Al Bruno are here, but they're going out soon. They call into the guards' office. "Gentlemen," Matt says. He's a thin guy with a high, reedy voice. His hair is slicked back, which makes his clean-shaven face look very thin. He has small round spectacles balanced on the bridge of his nose, and wears a light gray double-breasted pinstripe suit. He stands ramrod straight, like he has a stick up his ass. Harlan has always thought he dresses like he's in an old gangster movie about the glory days of Chicago crime – *The Untouchables*, perhaps, or *Public Enemies*.

"You looking to get dealt in, boss?" Ray says.

"I wish," Matt says. "I don't have the time right now. It's Mrs. D'Amico's birthday party, and we've gotta leave soon to get there. It's all the way across town, and traffic's probably gonna be a bitch."

Harlan has never met the D'Amicos, but he knows Mrs. D'Amico is the wife of a high-ranking capo in the Mob.

Matt turns his attention to Harlan. "How you doing, Officer Ross? How's the suspension?"

"As well as can be expected, Mr. Rossi," Harlan says, putting his cards facedown and turning to the money man. "All things considered."

"Any progress on the investigation?" Matt says.

"It is what it is. Now I just gotta wait. Nothing more I can do."

"You know that we're all rooting for you, right?"

"I appreciate that, Mr. Rossi."

Matt nods once, like he's handing out benedictions, like he thinks he's some kind of bigshot capo. "Shame about the video."

Harlan's aware it's a shame about the goddamn video. That's all he's been hearing since it happened. "You can say that again." He forces a self-deprecating grin and gives a hands-out shrug like *What you gonna do?*

Al Bruno follows his boss into the office and flanks him, standing close. Al is the polar opposite to Matt. He's squat and hulking. His brow is hooded, and Harlan has never seen him crack a smile. He speaks, but mostly he communicates in grunts if he can get away with it. His clothes are not tailored like Matt's. Tonight is one of those rare occasions he's squeezed himself into a suit. Usually he wears jeans, with T-shirts tucked into them. The occasion of Mrs. D'Amico's birthday has necessitated his dressing smartly. Tonight, he wears black dress trousers and a light blue shirt that looks so well-creased Harlan thinks it's likely fresh out of a packet of three. Al looks uncomfortable in these clothes, though. He twists from side to side and rolls his shoulders, and he looks more sullen and miserable than usual. He nudges Matt, and he grunts.

Matt glances at his watch. "Yes," he says, as if Al has said anything at all. "I suppose you're right. Gentlemen, enjoy your game."

They all say goodbye to Mr. Rossi. He and Al leave the office. Harlan plays another round, by then certain that the two of them are out of the apartment and likely out of the building and in their car. "I'm out this round," he says, pushing himself up from the table. "I gotta go take a shit."

"This guy's losing so bad his guts have turned to water," Peter says, busting balls.

"Nah, he's just so low on cash now, he's gotta go search in his underwear, see if he's stashed any in there," Ray says, joining in.

Harlan laughs along, holding up his hands in acknowledgment as he goes. Leo is dealing and doesn't have anything to add, and soon the three men are engrossed in their fresh hand. None of them are watching as Harlan passes by the bank of video screens and subtly kills the feed to Matt's office.

Harlan slips out and makes sure to close the office door after him. The three men playing cards are likely not checking the cameras – this is why Harlan suggested the game in the first place – but just to be careful, he makes sure to stay in view of them on his way to the bathroom. He peels off before he enters the room, though. He makes sure to close the door as if he's inside.

He pins himself up against the wall, staying out of view of the cameras. He moves around the apartment, avoiding their line of sight. He's studied this route a lot over the past couple of months. Has examined it on the cameras and made sure that none of it shows up on the footage. He's committed it to memory.

With his phone out, he snaps pictures as he goes. Chronicles his journey to Matt's office and the safe. He takes more pictures of the layout, zeroing in on the painting behind the desk. He moves fast in here. Goes to the painting and holds it aside, making sure to get pictures of the safe itself. He puts the painting back into place, exactly as it was, and then slips back out into the hall. He sneaks back to the bathroom, then opens the door and steps back into view of the cameras as if he's just exited it. He returns to the office and the poker game.

"Nerves settled?" Peter says, without looking up, when he returns.

Harlan makes a show of patting his stomach. "All better," he says. "Ready for the next round."

"Yeah, well, you've gotta wait," Ray says. "You just stand over in the corner there like a good boy until it's your turn again."

Harlan dutifully complies and takes the opportunity to reconnect the feed to Matt Rossi's office. He stares at the screen hard, making sure nothing is out of place. It's all as it should be.

22

Cindy hasn't found out the boy's name, but they don't really need that. The woman he's with in the picture, however, is called Stacey Shapiro.

"She's not registered as living in the city," Cindy says. She's in the backseat, leaning forward over the top of her laptop. Tom is driving and watching the mirrors, observing the car that is still following them. He's been driving around the city, trying to give them the slip, but they're persistent. They stick to him, keeping a safe distance. At one point, they had to run a red light to keep up, but after they'd made it, they pulled right back again.

"Where does it say she lives?" Jeffrey says.

"Crystal Lake," Cindy says. "With her mom, it looks like. But there's no guarantee that's where Stacey actually lives. She could be in the city and just hasn't changed her address."

"How far is it to Crystal Lake?" Tom says.

"An hour and a half."

"I don't really want to go an hour and a half out of our way if she's not going to be there," Jeffrey says.

"We could speak to her mom," Tom says. "That's better than nothing."

"Providing her mom is there," Jeffrey says. "She might be at work. We could end up hanging around for hours just to ask a question she might not have an answer for."

"We don't have to go to Crystal Lake," Cindy says. "Stacey works here. We can just go to her work."

"What's she do?" Tom says.

"I think she's a stripper."

"You think?"

"Well, she could be a bartender or a waitress – whatever she does, it's at a strip club."

"Where?"

"Not far from here. I'll give you directions. Second right, and then straight on for a few blocks."

23

Anthony and Connor get ready to go out. To go to the stash house. To go deep into the heart of Second City Skulls territory.

They're in Stacey's apartment, in the living room. She's out right now, with Billy. Anthony feels more nervous than he did when they hit the corner. He knows this won't be as quiet and straightforward as that was. It's highly unlikely there will not be a shot fired.

"You all right?" Connor says.

"Of course I'm not all right," Anthony says. "Are *you*?"

"You're breathing pretty heavy."

"That's the least of my problems right now." Anthony sighs and takes a seat, resting his head in his hands.

They're planning on leaving soon. They came back to pick up their weapons and their all-black gear again. Their balaclavas. It's still light, but they want to get there early. Find somewhere to lie low. Scope the place out again. Wait for the right moment for them to strike.

Connor sits down beside Anthony and squeezes his

shoulder. "I'm worried," he says. "Of course I am. I'm just trying not to think about it." Connor takes a deep breath. "I know what people think about me, Anthony. They think I'm stupid. That I'm slow. And maybe I'm not the sharpest tool in the box, but I'm not a total idiot. I'm fucking terrified about what we're going to do tonight. I know what it means. I know what could happen to us, what they could do if they catch us. The reason people think I'm slow is because I like to focus on one thing at a time. I've gotta be careful. I know that if I don't focus on just one thing, then I'm gonna get it wrong. I'm gonna mess it up. It's always been this way for me, from all the way back in school. I was slow, but the work I got done, I always got good grades on. Thing is, though, because a lot of the work *didn't* get done, I was always flunking." He chuckles. "So what I'm saying is, I'm trying not to think about what could happen tonight, because if I do, I'm gonna fixate. That's all I'm gonna be able to think about, nothing else, and I'll just end up focusing on how *not* to get caught instead of what it is we *need* to focus on – getting the money and the drugs. *That's* what's important, so that's all that matters to me right now. Nothing else."

Anthony looks at Connor. "That makes sense," he says. "I get it." He nods. "Let's do it your way. Let's just focus on what needs to be done, and then we can worry about all the other stuff."

"And, y'know," Connor says, "if we're lucky, it'll be as quiet as it was the other night. In and out."

"That's the plan, but we need to be realistic."

"All we need to think about is the plan," Connor says.

Before Anthony can say anything else, the door opens. It's Stacey and Billy. She frowns looking at the two of them. She sees their guns, and her eyes go wide. Anthony hides them before Billy can see, stuffing them into the bottom of the holdall that also holds their balaclavas and dark jackets.

"What's happening here?" Stacey says.

"Hey, Billy," Anthony says, holding out his palm for a high five, which Billy duly delivers. "You remember Connor, right? Go show Connor some of your toys while me and your mom talk. I'm sure he'd love to see them."

"You'd better believe I wanna see them," Connor says, holding out his hand for Billy to take and lead the way. "Show me what you got." They go off together into Billy's bedroom. Connor nods at Anthony, understanding what Anthony needs, and makes sure to close the door so Billy can't hear anything.

Anthony turns to Stacey and holds up his hands. "You're not going to like it," he says.

"Just don't lie to me," Stacey says.

Anthony doesn't. He tells her what they're planning on doing. As he gets further through it, he sees how Stacey's face drops. How her concern grows. She swallows like she feels ill.

When he's done, she's shaking her head. "Anthony," she says. "Anthony, this is...it's crazy." She knows about the Skulls too. "You're going to get yourself killed."

"We're going to get killed if we *don't* do this," he says. "And that's guaranteed. At least this way we've got a fighting chance."

Stacey bites her lip. Her eyes are moist. She wipes them, not allowing herself to cry. "When's this going to be over?"

"Soon," Anthony says. "I promise."

"And what then? What about Harlan?"

Anthony cocks his head, surprised that she would bring

Harlan up. "Don't worry about Harlan," he says. "I'm dealing with him. I'll figure out what to do."

"He came by my work last night," Stacey says.

Anthony feels his throat tighten. "He did *what*? What did he say? What did he do?"

"He didn't say much of anything," Stacey says. "But he wanted a dance."

"From you?"

Stacey nods.

"That mother*fucker*... Did he do anything? Try anything?"

"No."

"Okay. Okay. What did he *say*, though? Why was he there?"

"He said he wanted me to know that he cared about you, and that he would take care of you, and that I didn't have to worry about anything." Stacey shivers, remembering. "But it wasn't so much what he said as the way he said it. You know? It didn't feel at all reassuring. It felt like coming to see me was a message for you. I wasn't sure if I was going to tell you about it or not. Maybe telling you is exactly what he wants."

"I'll...I'll..." Anthony trails off. He thinks about what Connor said. About focusing on one thing at a time. He closes his eyes and takes a deep breath, pushing what Harlan did out of his head. He can't think about that, especially not right now, and especially not tonight when they go after the stash house. He opens his eyes again and looks at Stacey. "I'll deal with it. I can deal with everything, okay? You've just gotta bear with me. I'll get it all done. One thing at a time, but it'll all get done."

Stacey chews her bottom lip. "This is too much, Anthony," she says. "I'm worried about you."

Anthony wraps his arms around her and pulls her close, trying to reassure her with his touch, with his warmth and his closeness. He doesn't say anything further. Words aren't any good now. He's said all he can already. Soon, he and Connor will need to leave. For now, he holds Stacey, knowing that tonight she will be racked with worry, knowing that she will not be able to sleep. Knowing that he needs to make sure he gets back here to her in one piece, with the money to pay off Ezra, and then that's one less thing he has to think about.

24

Tom decides against going straight to the strip club while the two men are following them. He continues on down the road for a couple of blocks, getting clear of the club, putting it behind them. He wants to deal with these men. Get them off the scent. Trying to slip them isn't working.

He pulls over in front of an apartment building. The sidewalks here are quiet. There are other cars around, but not many people on foot. "Wait here," Tom says, checking the mirror. He sees the car behind pull to the side of the road about a block back. "I'm gonna get the drop on them. Make sure they don't follow us to the club."

Jeffrey and Cindy stay in the car while Tom gets out. He walks to the apartment building and goes to the door as if he's going to go inside, but he slips away from the door as he reaches the corner, goes down to the end of the building. He turns left and goes to the far corner of the neighbouring building, then doubles back on this street, parallel to where his father and Cindy are parked, as well as the two men following them. He walks until he's certain he's past the car that was following, and then crosses back to the street where they're all parked. Tom peers out and spots the following car on the opposite side of the road, parked and watching Jeffrey and Cindy.

Tom crosses over the road and gets close to the car. He can see the two heads in the front, watching where he's parked. There's no one in the back. This is good. Tom makes an assumption that the doors are unlocked and pulls open the rear passenger side. In one fluid motion, he gets in and closes the door after him. Before the men in front can turn, he's already on them. He grabs the passenger from behind in a choke hold, his forearm pressing deep into his carotid artery and cutting off the blood flow to his brain. The driver twists and reaches for Tom, but Tom is prepared and jabs him on the bridge of the nose with a left. The driver's reaching arms go instead to his face, clutching at his nose and frantically wiping away the tears from his eyes.

Neither man is carrying a gun that Tom can see. That doesn't mean they don't have any. They could be in the glove compartment or tucked down the back of their jeans. Wherever they are, Tom doesn't give them a chance to grab them. The passenger has gone limp. Tom lets go of him and grabs the driver with both hands, pulling him close and spinning him around and applying the same choke hold. The driver, despite his busted nose, has a little more fight in him. He scratches at Tom's face with one hand while his other stretches, reaching for the glove compartment. As Tom suspected.

Tom pulls on him, almost yanks him into the backseat of the car with him, getting his reaching fingers further from the glove compartment. His arms flop. Tom drops him back into his seat and arranges both men as if they're having a nap. They won't be unconscious long, so he moves fast. He pulls the keys out of the ignition and leaves the car.

Tom could have questioned these men, but there was no need. It's apparent what their purpose is. Like Tom and his father, they're looking for Anthony. They wouldn't have any information to give. It was apparent, too, from their casual dress and their tattoos that they are likely members of at least one of the gangs Anthony had told his father he was in trouble with. Better to just incapacitate them and move on. Tom heads back to his car, dropping their keys down a drain as he goes.

"They're out for now," he says, getting back behind the wheel. He turns the car around and goes back to the strip club.

It's still too early for the club to be busy. There are men around, watching the stage, and a couple drinking at the bar, but Tom imagines that in a couple of hours the place will be packed. It'll be hard to move.

"She's not one of the stage girls," Cindy says, checking the performers.

A girl walks past them in leather thigh-highs, wearing a thong and a stars-and-stripes bra that barely covers her nipples. She looks at Tom, and her eyes narrow, like she's maybe seen him before.

"You know her?" Cindy says, nudging him.

"No," Tom says, "but she looked like she recognized me." He steps after her, saying, "Excuse me?"

She stops, forces herself to smile, but Tom can see behind her eyes that her mind is racing, still trying to figure out why he looks familiar. "You looking for a dance, honey?"

She looks beyond him, to Cindy and his father. "We do group specials."

"We're not looking for a dance," Tom says. "We're looking for someone who works here. We think she might be a dancer. Her name's Stacey Shapiro."

Some recognition comes into the girl's eyes, and she studies Tom closer. But she looks like she has doubts. She shrugs and says, "What's she to you?"

"We think she's a friend of my brother's," Tom says. "Maybe more than a friend, we're not sure. But we're hoping she can help us find him."

"Your brother?" the girl says, and her face lights up now, but she doesn't let herself get too carried away. She's cautious. The girls here likely deal with men spinning all kinds of stories just to get closer to the dancers. "What's your brother's name?"

"Anthony," Tom says. "Anthony Rollins."

"*That's* why you looked so damn familiar!" the girl says, laughing and patting him on the arm. "As soon as I saw you, I thought I knew you."

"You know my brother."

"Sure, I know Anthony. Of course I do." She looks Tom over, shaking her head with relief that she's finally worked it out. "You look a lot like each other. Except you look older, and bigger. And kind of meaner – don't take that the wrong way. You're intense, man. But yeah, that's what was throwing me. I saw you, I thought of Anthony, but then I looked again, and I wasn't so sure."

"Is Stacey here?" Tom says.

"No, sorry – she's not working tonight."

"What is she to Anthony?"

The girl looks surprised. "Well, she's his *girlfriend*. He's never told you?"

"We haven't seen each other in a while. It's nothing against Stacey, I'm sure. Am I right in thinking she has a kid?"

"Billy, yeah. He ain't Anthony's, though. The biological dad's just some bum Stacey knew back where she came from. He ain't in the picture."

"I don't suppose you would tell us where we could find Stacey, would you?"

The girl sucks her teeth. "We're not supposed to give out personal information."

"I understand that," Tom says. "I'm sorry to have to ask, but we really need to find my brother."

She's considering. She's already on the fence, Tom can tell. She glances around the club. "Listen, I'll tell you on account of I can *see* with my own two eyes that you're Anthony's brother. *But* – you didn't hear this from me, you understand?"

"I understand," Tom says. "I don't even know your name to tell it."

She nods at this. "Yeah, that's true." She gives Tom Stacey's address and swears him to secrecy once again.

Tom goes back to Cindy and Jeffrey and tells them he has the address. They leave the club and get back in the car. Before they leave, Tom checks the area, makes sure the two men he knocked unconscious haven't revived and tracked them back down. There's no sign of them. There's no sign that anyone is watching them or following them anymore.

25

Harlan goes to a bar when he's finished at the apartment. He looks through the pictures on his phone while he nurses a beer.

The bar is busy. Music is playing loud, but Harlan doesn't hear it. He's engrossed in the images and the promise they hold for the future – for *his* future. Bodies bustle against him as they pass by, but he doesn't feel them. What he *does* feel is the smile that starts to slowly spread across his face.

It takes a while before Harlan realizes that someone is looking right at him. That they're trying to get his attention. Harlan doesn't look straight up. Doesn't turn his head. Out of the corner of his eye, he can see them. Two young black guys down the opposite end of the bar, both of them leaning forward, studying him. Harlan's hearing comes back, aware of everything going on around him now. The music is some rap song that he doesn't know. The voices around him are a blur apart from the two that are directed at him and cutting through the din of everything else.

"Hey – hey, you, over here."

"Hey, man, *hey*, we're talking to you."

Slowly, Harlan looks their way. He doesn't recognize either of them, but that doesn't mean he hasn't picked them up at some point. If they're looking to hassle him, give him some trouble, then they're barking up the wrong tree.

One of the guys is chunkier than the other. He nudges his thinner friend and says, "It is, man, it *is* him."

"I think you're right, man," his thinner friend says, starting to grin.

Harlan leans toward them, though there are plenty of bodies separating them around the bar. "Do I know the two of you?"

The thinner guy shakes his head. "Nah, man, you don't know *us*."

"You're him, ain't you?" the chunkier guy says.

Harlan feels his smile starting to falter. These aren't a couple of past collars. He's never had anything to do with them.

"You're the cop, aren't you?" the chunky guy says. "The one who beat a brother so bad you blinded him."

Harlan is aware that some of the other people around the bar, the ones close enough to hear, are starting to listen in. They're paying attention. They're starting to turn and look at Harlan, and he thinks some of them are realizing he's exactly who the two black guys think he is.

"That's you, ain't it?" the skinny guy says.

There's too many people around. Harlan can't address these two men the way he'd like to. He grits his teeth and pushes himself up from his stool, draining the last of his beer. "I think you've got the wrong guy," he says, loud enough for everyone within earshot to hear. "I don't know what you're talking about."

"Nah, man, nah – you're *him*. You know exactly what we're talking about."

Harlan is walking away from them, and he isn't sure which of them is calling after him.

"Where you going, man? You don't gotta run away, we're just talking to you!"

Harlan can't help but notice that their voices aren't getting distant. They're keeping up with him. Following him out of the bar. Other people are looking over to see what the commotion is. They're watching Harlan as he goes. Harlan lowers his face and gets out of the bar. No one tries to block his way or stop him from leaving. No one else seems to be following him.

Harlan doesn't look back. He gets outside into the night air and peels off to the side. He hears the bar door swing open and shut behind him, but it's not for long, and soon enough he hears the same two voices from inside the bar.

"Come on, man, slow down!"

"We just wanna talk with you!"

Harlan grits his teeth. He's clear of the bar now. They all are. The streets are quiet here. There's no one else around to see them. Harlan doesn't turn back to the two men. He slips down an alley. He knows they can see him. Knows they're going to follow.

In the alley, he presses himself up against the wall and waits for them to follow. He reaches into his waistband and pulls out his 9mm Luger.

The thin guy leads the way, and he has his phone out. He's holding it out at arm's length in front of him, turned on its side to record. Harlan is sick of the sight of camera phones. He grabs the skinny guy's wrist and brings the handle of his gun down on his forearm. The bone breaks. It takes the skinny guy a moment to realize what has happened. His eyes widen, but before he can scream, Harlan strikes him across the face with the gun's barrel. It tears his cheek open and knocks out one of his teeth.

The chunkier guy watches wide-eyed. "Holy shit, man – the fuck are you doing?"

Harlan shuts him up with a fist to his ample stomach. The chunkier guy drops to his knees. Harlan goes to the dropped phone and picks it up. He hurls it back to the ground, smashing it. The skinny guy is whimpering. Harlan kicks him in the kidneys, then moves on to the chunkier guy.

He hauls him up to his feet and pins him to the wall by the throat, his Luger jammed into his cheek. "You listening to me?" Harlan says, shoving his face in close. The chunky guy nods. "That *was* me from the news. I blinded the *brother*. And you know what? I didn't know him. I didn't know what he'd done when I caught him, and I didn't care either." Harlan presses the gun in hard, drilling it into the chunky guy's cheekbone. "So if I did that to him, what do you think I'd do to someone who's actually pissed me off, huh? Someone like *you*?"

The chunky guy can't answer. Harlan doesn't give him a chance. Holding him by the throat still, he strikes him in the temple with the handle of his gun, dazing and bloodying him. Harlan doesn't let go. He hits him again and again and again, until the guy's legs give out under him, and Harlan lets him drop.

The two men are lying in a heap on the ground. Harlan tucks his gun away, breathing hard. He snorts hard and spits to the side, then rolls his head to pop the tendons in his neck. He leaves them where they lie.

26

When they reach Stacey's building, Tom and Cindy wait behind in the car again. Jeffrey goes up to the building, remembering the door number the stripper gave to Tom. He reaches the intercom and hits the buzzer to her apartment.

Jeffrey has to wait a moment before she answers. It takes so long he starts to worry she's not home. If she isn't, that doesn't necessarily put them back to square one. It does mean they're losing more time, however. They'll have to sit in the car and watch the building until she returns – or perhaps until Anthony turns up, whoever comes first.

He doesn't have to worry about this for too long. A woman's voice comes over the intercom. "Yes?" Her tone is curt, but she also sounds worried about who might be on the other end.

Jeffrey has to stifle a cough before he says anything. "Hello there," he says. He swallows. "You don't know me, but you might know who I am – my name is Jeffrey Rollins. I'm Anthony's father. I believe you know my son?

I'm in Chicago looking for him, and I was told you might
–"

She cuts him off. "You're Anthony's dad?" She sounds
hopeful for a moment, but he can tell she's staying cautious.
"When's his birthday?"

Jeffrey tells her. Even tells her the time of day he was
born.

"Okay, okay – what's his mother's name?" Stacey says.

"His mother's name was Mary, and his stepmother is
called Sylvia."

"All right, okay," Stacey says, almost excitedly, Jeffrey
thinks. She's heard enough. She believes he's who he says he
is. "I'm going to buzz you in – come straight up to my apartment, and don't waste any time!"

Jeffrey picks up on the urgency in her voice, and as soon
as she buzzes the door open, he does as she says. He takes
the elevator up to her floor. In the past, he would have
sprinted up the stairs, but he has to be realistic. The cancer
is slowing him down. He *could* still sprint up them, but not
the way he used to. He wouldn't be going as fast as Stacey
has requested. His lungs can't take it, not the way they used
to. He can still push himself when he needs to, but right now
isn't one of those times. Jeffrey feels a depression attempting
to descend at this realization – soon, his lungs will never be
able to take anything as strenuous as that ever again. They're
not going to get better.

He shakes the pall off as the elevator reaches Stacey's
floor, and he steps out to find her waiting at the end of the
hall for him. He recognizes her from the picture in Anthony's room.

"Jeffrey?" she says.

"That's me," he says.

She runs to him, and Jeffrey thinks she's going to throw herself into his arms, but she pulls herself short and grabs at his jacket. "He needs you," she says, her eyes wide and earnest. "He needs you *right now* – he's going to get himself killed!"

"What do you mean? What's happened?"

She tells him quickly what Anthony is doing. It's the abridged version, but it's enough. It's all that Jeffrey needs to know.

"Where's he gone? Where exactly?" Jeffrey says.

"I don't know whereabouts for sure," Stacey says, "but it's Second City Skulls territory – that's south. But they have a lot of territory. He could be anywhere – you need to call him, talk to him, get him to turn around and come back! You can help him, right? You can help him?"

Jeffrey pulls out his phone, but he's not dialing Anthony. "I've been trying to call Anthony the last few days," Jeffrey says. "I don't expect to get an answer this time."

27

"Looks like she let him in at least," Cindy says, leaning forward and looking up at the windows of the building. She points at one with a dim light, as if it's lit by a lamp and nothing else. "I think she's that one."

Tom doesn't get a chance to say anything back. His phone starts to ring, and he sees that it's his father. He frowns, not understanding. Jeffrey just got inside a few minutes ago. As he answers, Jeffrey cuts him off before he can even say hello.

"Anthony's in trouble," he says. "Immediate trouble. He's gone to rip off a stash house – Stacey says it's in a rival gang's territory, but she doesn't know where exactly. Go get him, Tom. Bring him back before he gets himself killed."

Tom starts the engine, motioning for Cindy to climb up front and to bring her laptop with her. "Any details?" Tom says, keeping it brief.

"Gang name – Second City Skulls."

"Location?"

"South."

"Text any information you've got to Cindy." Tom hangs up and pulls away from the curb, heading south.

Cindy's phone buzzes, and she pulls it from her pocket, checking what Jeffrey has sent her. "Second City Skulls," she says out loud, turning on her laptop. "I can find territory with that, that's good." She's still looking at her phone. "Ah, but this is better. Apparently your brother and some other guy called Connor left about two hours ago – I can search around the timeframe, maybe find them that way, track them down to exactly where they've gone."

Tom doesn't answer. In his head, though, he thinks how two hours is a long time. If Anthony has any sense, he's been using that time for surveillance, but he can't guarantee that his brother has done what is sensible. Tom cuts through the Chicago traffic, heading blindly south for now until Cindy can give him directions. He trusts Cindy. She knows what she's doing. He waits for her to tell him where to go.

28

A nthony and Connor pull on their balaclavas, and they move in.

They've watched the stash house for two hours now, from their same spot on top of the garage on the street slightly elevated from the one with the stash house. It's grown dark around them. They've watched through their binoculars and made sure nothing unexpected has transpired. Everything at the stash house looks the same as it did the last time they were here.

They stick to the shadows as they move in closer, and at first it feels like the other night, when they struck the corner. Except this time, instead of staying close to buildings, they're crossing over lawns and doing their best to make sure they're not seen by anyone inside the houses, too. No doubt everyone here is Skulls-affiliated, whether they're a member of the gang or not. They're too close to have a choice in the matter. It's a choice of either Skulls, or get the fuck out of here.

Anthony squeezes his Glock tight, leading the way. He

breathes hard and feels the mouth area around his mask getting warm and moist. He thinks only of the stash house. Only of what is in front of him. Only of the task in hand. Only of this. There is nothing else. There is no after. There is only right now.

He reaches the corner opposite the house and ducks behind a bush. Connor sticks close to him. They peer at the house through the bushes. There are lights on inside. Anthony can see three men moving around, but he's sure there are likely to be more in there. The three he can see are standing and laughing about something. They smoke blunts and drink alcohol from the bottle. The curtains aren't drawn. They're brazen. They don't expect anyone to come up on them like this, especially not in their own territory.

"Soon as they answer the door, we stick a gun in their face," Anthony says. "We're not gonna be able to lure them all out. We gotta grab the first guy who comes to the door, use him as a shield, and keep the rest of them covered. It's gotta be *fast*."

Connor nods. "In and out."

Anthony slips around the bush and crosses the road, bent double, gun raised. Connor is behind him. They both move quietly. They duck low so the men at the window can't see them. Anthony gets into position at the door and waits until Connor is behind him and has him covered, Glock raised and held in both hands. Anthony and Connor exchange glances and nods, and then Anthony knocks. Three short, sharp pounds with the side of his left fist, and then his left hand promptly returns to the gun handle with his right.

Anthony waits. He can hear music playing inside, but it's not so loud that they wouldn't hear him knocking. He scrapes his teeth over his bottom lip and then knocks again, harder this time.

"Who that?"

The voice is so close and so sudden on the other side of the door that Anthony gives a start. He isn't sure what to do, so he knocks again, pretending he hasn't heard.

"Who's out there? What you want?"

Anthony doesn't want to speak. If whoever is on the other side hears his voice, they're going to know he shouldn't be here. Anthony isn't going to attempt to deepen his voice and use slang like some kind of racist caricature. They'd see right through that.

Before Anthony can make a decision how to proceed, before he can knock again or do anything else, gunshots erupt and tear through the door.

Anthony throws himself back. Connor drops to the ground. Anthony doesn't think any of them hit him. A moment later, Connor rolls to the side, away from the door. The gunfire has stopped. The door swings open. Anthony raises his Glock toward the man in the door. He spots Anthony and raises his own weapon in turn. They both fire and pull back. Anthony's bullet hits the wall behind where the man previously stood, and the man's bullet bounces off the sidewalk behind Anthony.

As Anthony throws himself to the side, closer to Connor, he catches a glimpse inside the house, down the hallway. Other men are already coming, and they're carrying heavy weaponry. Assault rifles.

"*Fuck*," Anthony says. They can't get in there. They can't fight their way through that. If they don't move right now, they're dead.

He grabs Connor and hauls him to his feet. Their

priority has now changed. Their one point of focus is to get away. To stay alive.

At the sounds of the gunfire, the street has come alive. The houses have lit up. Anthony can hear doors starting to open. He tries to drag Connor away. "We got to go," he says.

Connor is twisting back, firing at the house, at the men piling out of it.

"Connor, we've gotta *go!*"

Connor finally turns and moves with Anthony, running with him. They head for the dark houses off to their left, the buildings that haven't lit up with all the noise. Anthony hears gunshots from behind and feels them cut through the air around them. Chunks are torn out of the road and sidewalk. Some of the fire is from handguns, but some of it comes from the assault rifles.

Connor cries out and goes down to a knee. Anthony thinks he's done, he's dead. His mind is racing. He's holding Connor by the collar, and he can't let go. Anthony sees blood on the ground, but it's come from low down.

Connor doesn't fall all the way. He keeps hold of Anthony's arm and uses it to pull himself up, favoring his right leg. Something caught him in the back of his right thigh. Anthony thinks it must be either a fragment from something else, perhaps bouncing up from the ground, or else it came directly from a handgun. It's not assault-rifle fire, he's sure of that. If it were, Connor's leg would be hanging off.

Anthony supports his weight, and they disappear into the shadows, running down the back of a house. The house is still in darkness. Anthony doesn't think there's anyone inside. He forces Connor into the porch, and they press themselves up against the wall. Anthony pushes the balaclava up from his face and wipes sweat from his top lip and brow and out of his eye sockets. He peers back around the corner, expecting a heavily armed man to come into view. He sees a couple run by, searching, but they don't come down here where Anthony and Connor are hiding out.

Connor has his back pressed up against the wall, grimacing as he squeezes his right thigh. "Ah, *fuck*," he says. Blood drips from the back of his leg onto the porch floor's tiles. It's not a gusher, though. *That's good*, Anthony thinks. It means nothing serious has been hit.

Anthony pulls off Connor's mask to cool him off and to use it to apply pressure to the wound. He pulls off his own belt and uses it as a makeshift tourniquet and to hold the balaclava in place. "Can you put weight on it?"

"I have to," Connor says.

"We've gotta get out of here," Anthony says, straightening back up and peering out from around the porch again. "Come on, the way's clear." He takes Connor's arm, and they head round to the back of the house, sticking to the shadows. They continue on down the back lane. Anthony glances down between houses as they go. There's a lot of people out on the street, and they all look armed.

It's a long way to get back to the car. Anthony isn't sure they have a clear way out. Up ahead, he sees someone step into view, about to come down the way they're running. He hasn't spotted them in the dark yet. Anthony and Connor slip down the side of the nearest house and press themselves up against the wall, as flat as they can. The man gets closer. Anthony can hear his footsteps. He's jogging. Anthony squeezes the Glock and braces himself to use it.

The man doesn't stop. He keeps going. Doesn't glance down the alleyway where they are. Anthony doesn't allow himself to feel relief at this. They need to keep moving.

There are too many people around, and if they stay still, it's just a matter of time before they're found.

Then, as they start to move again, they hear a voice shouting from the street. From near to the stash house. A loud voice. An authoritative voice. The kind of voice everyone on the street, everyone in the whole neighborhood, can hear and is going to pay heed to.

"Looks like we got a couple of dumb fucks here in these streets!" the voice announces. Anthony and Connor look at each other. "We got a couple of white boys running wild, thinking they can rip us off. Everyone hear? I want them found and brought to me – dead or alive, I don't give a shit. Yo, dumb-fucks, I know you can hear me. My voice *carries* through these motherfucking streets. These streets are *mine*. You ain't gonna get far." His voice lowers, talking to people closer to him, but he's still loud enough to be heard. "Go get them – anyone white is game. I don't care. I ain't taking chances."

Anthony looks down through the houses toward the main street, and he sees how they're swarming. He isn't sure how they're going to get clear without being seen. The car is too far away. He grits his teeth. "Come on – we've gotta do something."

They keep moving, sticking to the backs and sides of the houses that are in darkness, avoiding streetlamps. Anthony can hear engines starting up. Cars are going to be roaming the roads, searching for them. All ground is going to be covered. Every inch will be searched. He feels his heart rate increasing. His mouth is dry. Sweat is pouring down his back.

"Anthony," Connor says, slumping against the side of a building while Anthony peers around the corner. Anthony quickly pulls back from the corner when he spots a group of four armed men huddled together under a streetlamp. They were looking up and down the road, but he doesn't think they saw him.

"*Anthony*," Connor says again.

"What is it?"

Connor reaches into his pocket and holds something up. Anthony knows what it is as soon as he sees it. Connor never mentioned he was bringing it. The grenade.

"We can use it," Connor says. "Cause a distraction. Slip away."

Anthony swallows. Connor is right. Anthony nods and holds his hand out for it. He looks around, deciding where best to put it. He peers out around the corner again, hoping the four men are gone. They're still there, but they've moved down a little, searching between every house, but going in the other direction.

Anthony turns to the left. There are others there, too. Two men and a woman. The men have automatic rifles, and the woman is carrying a shotgun. They're not looking this way. They're searching down the sides of the buildings, too. Behind them, a car crawls along slowly, men leaning out the back of it on either side. Anthony can hear hooting and hollering. He can hear maniacal laughter coming from seemingly all around. Before long, the car will be closing in. It's already getting nearer. Anthony needs to do something soon.

On the other side of the road is a parked car. Anthony thinks about rolling the grenade under it. The explosion will bring everyone running. *Or* he could wait until the approaching car gets closer, closer, close enough – and he could roll the grenade under *that*.

Anthony pulls the stiff pin, still not decided where he's going to throw it, but knowing he needs to make a decision. He keeps tight hold of the strike lever. He knows that when he releases this, he has about three or four seconds before the grenade will explode. He doesn't intend to be holding it when that happens.

To the left, the car is getting closer. Anthony has made his decision. If he hits the car with the people inside, he might wound them. If the men inside are hurt, that will bring others running to help them – at least, he hopes. Anthony pulls his arm back, getting ready to throw.

A hand grabs him by the forearm, a vise like iron holding him still, and another hand wraps around his, squeezing the grenade, making sure he can't release the lever.

Anthony's stomach sinks. He never heard anyone approach, and now this is it. It's over. They're dead men. He turns and looks to see who has captured them, but it's not the black face of a Second City Skull he's expecting to see looking back at him. It's white. It's familiar.

It's his brother.

It's Tom Rollins.

29

"Give me the pin," Tom says.

Anthony hands it over. Tom pushes it back into the grenade and takes it from Anthony. He slowly releases the lever. It stays in place. The grenade is an M67. Army issue. Tom is familiar with them. He hands it back to Anthony. "Keep hold of this," he says, reaching down and scooping up the wounded other man – Connor, he assumes – throwing him over his shoulder. "And don't throw it. Follow me."

Tom doesn't hang around long enough to see the look on his brother's face. Anthony follows, but Tom is sure it's begrudgingly. He doesn't have any other choice.

Tom heads back the way he crept in, moving through back alleys and over yards, sticking close to the sides of houses. He's cautious as he goes, listening to the sounds of engines and the shouting. He heard the earlier announcement from the man he assumes runs things around here. Tom knows that if they're seen, it's going to be a case of *shoot first*. They can't afford to be seen.

They stop at a house, and Tom checks the road ahead. "Uh," Anthony says.

Tom turns back and looks where Anthony is looking. The window directly above them, there are two small children looking right back at them. A boy and a girl. For the longest moment, no one moves. Tom presses a finger to his lips. The boy giggles and shakes his head. The girl turns and bolts from the window, racing deeper into the house, no doubt raising the alarm.

"Move, move!" Tom says.

They start running as the door to the house bursts open behind them. There's gunfire. It sounds loud, like a cannon. Tom dives to the side, using the yard's fence as cover. Anthony dives in after him. Tom hears running footsteps. He dumps Connor and tackles the man as he comes around the corner.

The man hits the ground hard, the air knocked out of him. His gun is a .44 Magnum. Tom grabs his wrist and forces the gun away, then drops all of his weight through his elbow, across the man's face. It doesn't knock him out, but it incapacitates him as much as Tom needs. He takes the Magnum and looks up. Others are coming, drawn by the sounds of gunfire. There are two bullets left in the gun. Tom fires them both, causing the people coming to scatter and dive into cover. Tom isn't aiming. He isn't trying to hit anyone. He just wants to slow them down and scare them off.

He returns to Anthony and Connor and scoops Connor back onto his shoulder. Connor cries out, clutching at his right leg. It's dark, but Tom can see how it looks wet and shiny with blood soaking through the makeshift tourniquet. Tom runs, and Anthony follows. Tom still has the Magnum.

Someone steps out on them a few houses down, but Tom doesn't slow. He strikes them across the face with the barrel of the gun, and they go straight down. Anthony has to jump over the fallen body.

The route Tom took on his way in is covered. The people here are too spread out. He throws Connor over a fence and then climbs over, dropping low into a dark backyard. Anthony follows. Tom stays close to the fence so he can see out, watching as feet race past, looking for them. Tom reaches into his pocket and pulls out his phone. It's already on a call. Cindy.

"We're covered," he says, keeping his voice low. "We're going to have to find an alternate route out of the neighbourhood."

Cindy is in the car. She's been waiting for his call. "I'm in the next neighborhood," she says. "I noticed it was elevated, so I've come up here to look out. I've got a good vantage. Tell me where you are, and I'll tell you if I can see a way out."

"Central," Tom says.

"The north is a no-go," Cindy says. "I think they're expecting you to try to go that way. They've got it all blocked off. South is covered, too. Which way are you facing right now?"

"West."

"West, that's good. Head west, that's where there's the least people. There's a chain-link fence, but there's a road on the other side of it – get there, and I can pick you up."

"How far are we talking?"

"About three houses."

Tom looks ahead through the fence. He can't see the chain-link fence, but he can see the first house. It's not too far, but that doesn't make it any less dangerous. "Got it," he says. "Head there now. We'll be there soon." Tom hangs up, then turns to his brother. "That way," he says, pointing straight. "Over the fence, to the road."

Anthony nods.

Tom hauls Connor back up, but doesn't put him over his shoulder yet. He supports his weight for now. They don't go back over the top of the fence. They go to its gate. Anthony heads out first and is promptly tackled to the ground. There are two men. One of them is on Anthony. The other has a knife. Tom drops Connor and goes for the one still standing. He avoids his swipe with the knife, which passes inches from the tip of his nose. Before the knifeman can recover, Tom drives a knee into his midsection, then takes the knife from him and throws it away into the darkness. He grabs the knifeman by the side of the head and pushes him up against the fence. He drives a fist into his throat, and he falls to the ground, gasping for air.

He turns and sees that Connor has thrown himself onto the man pinning Anthony. He's wrapped an arm around his jaw to keep him from calling out. Tom is glad to see this. He strides up to the side and kicks the attacker in the face, busting his nose and mouth. Connor drags him off. Anthony scrambles to his feet and kicks the fallen man twice in the ribs. Tom hauls him away and sees why he's so annoyed – his nose has been bloodied, and his cheek is swollen.

Tom sees a car coming down the road from the right. There are people there, too, heading this way. To the left, he sees someone running their way, and he thinks he's seen them. Behind, he can hear shouts, and they're getting closer. Everything is getting closer. Tom throws Connor over his shoulder again and turns to his brother. "Just *run*."

They burst from the alley and run over the road and

down the side of the house opposite. Everyone sees them. They shout and come running. The car's engine roars, and it screeches to a stop behind them, unable to come any further. The men inside jump out and pursue on foot.

Tom doesn't keep to a straight line. The men behind will have guns. They need to put objects between them. Tom veers to the right and circles around the house. Anthony gets the idea and goes to the left. Tom continues straight on, feeling the weight of Connor bearing down on him, getting heavier and heavier with each step.

Tom circles around another house and almost runs into someone. A man. He's unarmed, and Tom can't guarantee he's a threat, but he can't take any risks. He barrels through the person, knocks him flat, and keeps going. The fence is in sight. He spots Anthony already climbing over it. Tom doesn't slow. He throws himself into the chain-links to stop, and lifts Connor over. Anthony catches him on the other side. Tom can see people coming for them, getting close. They have guns. They'll start shooting soon.

On the road, Cindy catches up to them. She spots them and slams the brakes on. Tom hauls himself over the fence. He and Anthony each take one of Connor's arms and half-carry, half-drag him to the car. They throw him inside and dive in themselves as the guns open up behind them. Tom can see some people climbing the fence after them.

Cindy can see them, too. She can hear the gunfire. She doesn't need to be told what to do next. She slams her foot down on the accelerator and tears off down the road, away from the neighborhood and the people coming for their blood.

30

Cindy didn't drive straight back to Stacey's. They swung around to the same neighborhood where she had found a better vantage point so that Anthony could pick up his car. He followed them back. She and Tom kept Connor in the car with them, not wanting to move him unnecessarily before Tom had a chance to fully assess his wound. They didn't have Anthony in the car with them for long, but for how brief it was, it was incredibly uncomfortable. The only thing Tom said to his brother was, "Keep pressure on the wound," while motioning to Connor's leg.

Cindy could feel the tension in the air between the two brothers. She was glad when Anthony got out to get his own car.

Connor occasionally moaned in pain, but he didn't make too much noise. Tom watched the mirrors. "They haven't come after us," he said. "I think once we were out of their neighborhood, they stopped caring."

"How'd you sneak up on us like that?" Connor said. "How'd you even find us?"

"Cindy tracked you until the security footage ran out," Tom said. "She also looked into Second City Skulls territory, and the security footage happened to run out right on the outskirts of one of their neighborhoods."

"What security footage?"

"General CCTV. Businesses, traffic stops – the kind of cameras you find all over the city."

"How'd you – how'd you get access to that? Did you – did you hack it?" Connor sounded impressed.

"She did, and she led us to *you*," Tom said. "Once we were close enough to hear all the shouting and shooting, we knew we were in the right place."

"But how did you find us, in the streets?"

"I got lucky," Tom said. "I was moving around like the two of you were, in the shadows, and I saw you cross the road, and I followed you from there."

When they reached Stacey's building, Anthony wouldn't let Tom carry Connor up. He got Connor out of the back of the car himself and supported his weight, carrying him inside and into the elevator. He didn't wait for Tom and Cindy to join them before he hit the button and closed the doors in their face.

"He seems happy to see you," Cindy said.

Tom didn't reply. They waited for the elevator to come back down.

They're all in Stacey's apartment now. Tom and Jeffrey are tending to Connor's leg. They're in the living room. Cindy stands to one side, close to the kitchen. Anthony is opposite from her, by the window. She notices how he looks down into the street from time to time. Stacey is with her son in his bedroom, making sure he's sleeping through what is happening in here.

"The bullet's in deep," Jeffrey says.

Tom grunts in agreement. They have a lamp angled down over them so they can see what they're doing. "It's a 9mm, possibly just a fragmentation of one," Tom says. "We leave it in."

"That's what I was thinking," Jeffrey says.

"What the fuck?" Connor says, twisting to look at them back over his shoulder. "You're gonna leave it *in*?"

"Keep your voice down," Jeffrey says. "And mind your language. There's a child next door, and he's trying to sleep."

"The bullet can't do any further damage," Tom says. "It's lodged in deep. We'd do more damage trying to get it out."

"But – but what about – what about infection?"

"It's not going to infect you."

Connor bites his lip. "I mean – if you're sure…"

"We know what we're doing," Jeffrey says. He turns back to Tom. "Let's clean it and close him up."

Billy's bedroom door opens, and Stacey steps out. She carefully closes the door behind her, then steps up next to Cindy.

"Is he sleeping?" Cindy says.

Stacey nods. "I just heard Connor's outburst, and it didn't wake Billy, so I figure if he can sleep through that, then he should be good." She looks around the room, taking everything in. She sees Anthony by the window, but he won't meet her eye.

Cindy looks to Anthony, too. When he's not checking out the window, he's glaring at Tom. She senses the same tension she felt in the car, and she's glad it's not in such suffocating close quarters anymore.

Stacey leans in close to Cindy. Cindy gets the impression she wants to say something quietly, so no one else will hear, and she puts her ear close to her mouth. "Is that Anthony's brother?" she says.

Cindy nods. "Tom, yeah," she says, matching her whisper.

"*Full* brother?"

"Uh, I think so. I mean, that's their dad, and I'm pretty sure they had the same mom."

"Anthony never told me he has a brother," Stacey says. "And I've asked. I asked if he had siblings. He flat-out denied it." Her brow furrows, confused, like she can't understand why he would lie about such a thing.

"Yeah, they're, uh – they're not close," Cindy says. "I just recently found out the particulars of this family dynamic myself."

"Yeah? How long have you and Tom been together?"

"Oh, we're not together. We're friends. We've known each other a few years."

"Oh, right, okay," Stacey says.

"Hayley is back in New Mexico," Cindy says. "His girl-friend, I mean."

Tom and Jeffrey finish up with Connor. They've disin-fected the wound and sewn it shut. They've wrapped it in bandaging. Stacey had a first aid kit in her kitchen. It had never been used before.

"How's that feel?" Jeffrey says.

"Sore," Connor says.

"You'll live," Jeffrey says, patting his shoulder. "It could've been worse. It's not like you're gonna lose the leg."

Tom doesn't say anything. He goes to the kitchen sink and washes the blood from his hands. He dries them on a towel and then returns to the living room. Anthony has straightened. He's looking right back at Tom. Neither of them says a word.

"Anthony," Jeffrey says. "Tom." His voice is stern, warning them both to back down.

His sons don't listen to him. They don't move. The tension between them permeates the apartment. Cindy can feel it thick in her throat, and she can tell that Stacey, beside her, feels it too.

Stacey clears her throat. "Anthony," she says.

Anthony steps closer to his brother, making no indication that he's heard her.

Everyone present, apart from Connor, who remains convalescing on the sofa, has straightened. Cindy sees how both Anthony and Tom are staring into each other's eyes. Their jaws are set. She can see a vein pulsing in Anthony's temple. His jaw starts to work. He's grinding his teeth. Tom is steadfast. The similarities between the brothers are apparent, yet their differences are jarring. Anthony is thinner than Tom. They both have stubble, but Tom's hair is cut shorter. His features are coarser, leaner, but there is more of a thickness about his body. He stands firm, calm, while Anthony looks like he's shaking.

"Tom," Cindy says. "Tom, why don't you come over here with me, huh? And Anthony, why don't you go be with Stacey, and we can all talk about what happens next –"

Anthony hits Tom.

31

The punch draws blood at the corner of Tom's mouth, but it doesn't knock him down. It doesn't knock him off balance. Tom stands his ground. He stares back at Anthony, defiant. "Did that make you feel better?" He knows the question is antagonistic, but he can't help himself.

Anthony hits him again, catching him on the corner of his left eyebrow. It bursts, and Tom feels blood running down the side of his face.

"Anthony, stop it!" It's Stacey's voice. She sounds horrified.

Again, Tom does not falter. He puts his arms behind him and stands his ground. Anthony hits him again and again, bruising his left cheek and rattling his jaw. Tom can see his blood on Anthony's knuckles.

"The two of you, cut it out!" Jeffrey says.

"Tom, just walk away!" It's Cindy. "Just walk away – stop letting him hit you, for Christ's sake!"

Tom doesn't turn away from his brother. He spits blood. "How about now?" he says. "Do you feel better?"

Anthony looks like he's going to hit him again, but he doesn't this time. He holds up both of his balled fists, and they're trembling. "Fuck you! What the hell are you doing here? I don't want you here, Tom, get the fuck out of here!"

"I didn't come for you," Tom says. His blood drips to the ground below. He keeps his hands clasped behind himself. He won't back down to Anthony. He nods toward their father. "I came for him."

Anthony bares his teeth, then glances back at Jeffrey.

"Please, Anthony," Jeffrey says now he has his attention. "Just calm down, okay? I know you're hurting, and I know you're upset, but this isn't the way to go about it. Let's just talk. Let's just sit down and talk."

"What the hell is going on here?" Connor says, pushing himself up on the sofa, gritting his teeth and holding his leg. "What's the problem? Anthony, your brother just saved our asses back there. Why are you hitting him?" He looks around the room, to Tom and Cindy and Stacey, then up to Jeffrey, who is closest to him. "Have I missed something?"

Anthony spins back to Tom and catches him by surprise. The left hook knocks Tom back a step. It dazes him. The room spins. Tom shakes his head, trying to clear his vision and his thoughts. When he can think again, he hears Anthony. "Where the fuck are they?" He's screaming. He grabs Tom by the lapels of his jacket with both hands, pushing his face into his. Their foreheads are touching. "What did you do with them? *Where are they?*"

Tom's blood is on Anthony's face now. Jeffrey has stepped in, and Cindy and Stacey. They're separating them. Jeffrey and Stacey have Anthony, and they're pulling him away.

Cindy wraps her arms around Tom and forces him back. Some of his blood gets into her hair and onto her face. Tom wipes it away. She looks up at him. "Stop provoking him," she says.

Tom knows she's right. He already knew he shouldn't. He pats Cindy, and she lets go of him. Before he can speak, a door opens, and everyone turns to it.

"Mom?" The child is rubbing his eyes. He looks scared and confused. His eyes scan the room, and he sees all of these strange new people. He sees the blood.

"Billy," Stacey says, letting go of Anthony and rushing to her son. She scoops him up in her arms and turns him away from the scene.

Anthony shrugs his father off and goes to them, saying, "Billy, buddy, it's all right, it's just –" but Stacey gives him a look so fierce, he freezes where he is.

"They're just playing," she says, rocking her son from side to side. "Anthony and his brother are just playing, and they got a little too loud and a little carried away."

Billy tries to turn back around. "I didn't know Anthony has a brother."

Stacey won't let him turn. "Neither did I," she says, again shooting Anthony the same fierce look. "The two of you need to sort this out, or else get the hell out of my home. My son was *sleeping*."

When she looks his way, Tom nods apologetically. Anthony does the same. "I'm sorry," he says to Stacey, and glares at Tom. His fists are balled by his sides.

Stacey puts Billy back down. "Get into bed and stay there," she says. "I'll be through in a minute. I want to make sure everyone here is going to behave."

Billy reluctantly does as she says, and Stacey closes the

door after him. She wheels on Anthony and Tom. "Who are *they*?" she says.

"I told you what happened to Alejandra," Anthony says, his eyes never leaving Tom's. "To Alejandra, and to our *child*. But I never told you what happened to her ashes."

"They're in Mexico," Tom says. "Guaymas. It's what she wanted."

"No, it's what *you* wanted, you piece of shit," Anthony says.

"Calm down," Stacey warns him.

Anthony doesn't listen. "What about what *I* wanted? What about what I fucking *needed*? You took them away from me. They were my *family*..."

Tom feels Cindy place her hand on his lower back in support.

Anthony turns away from Tom, waving his hands at him, dismissive. He's tired of looking at him. Of talking to him. He faces the wall with his hands on his hips and takes a deep breath. He turns back around, and again he talks to Tom, as if there's no one else here. "Why are you here?" His tone isn't so aggressive anymore. He sounds tired. He's worn himself out.

Jeffrey answers. "We came for you," he says. "To help you."

Anthony tears himself away from Tom to face their father. "To *help* me? What do you mean?"

"I got your messages," Jeffrey says.

"What messages?"

"Maybe you don't remember sending them," Jeffrey says. "It seemed like you were drunk when you sent them."

Anthony is confused. "I never sent you any messages."

Jeffrey pulls out his phone and brings them up. Anthony

takes it from him and reads them. His forehead is creased. He shakes his head. "I never sent these. This isn't even my number."

"You never gave me your new number after you left," Jeffrey says. "I assumed this was it. These weren't you? You're certain?"

"Of course I'm certain. I don't know this number at all."

Jeffrey and Tom exchange looks. "He doesn't need us," Tom says. "Let's go."

"Something's going on here, Tom," Jeffrey says.

"Wrong number."

"I doubt that."

Tom doubts it too, but Anthony has made it very clear he doesn't want them here. Or, at least, he doesn't want Tom here.

"Whatever all *this* is about," Jeffrey says, shaking his phone, "the fact is that *you*," he looks at Anthony, "are clearly in trouble. I'm not going anywhere while you're in danger."

Anthony holds up his hands. "You can stay," he says. "If that'll make you feel better. At least for tonight. Hell, *she* can stay, whoever she is." He points at Cindy. "But *you*" – he turns the finger on Tom – "are out. I don't care where the fuck you go, but you're not staying here."

"Now, hold on a minute," Stacey says, "this is my place, and I'm not comfortable with you kicking your own brother out onto the street –"

"It's fine," Tom says. "I can find somewhere, but thank you." He turns to Jeffrey. "I'll still be in Chicago. If you need me, call."

Jeffrey nods and then crosses the room to be closer. He studies Tom's face, sees the damage that Anthony has done to it. Jeffrey looks pained, as if the wounds are his own. "I'll keep an eye on things here."

Tom lowers his voice. "Are you going to tell him?" He raises his eyebrows, meaning the cancer.

Jeffrey nods. "I'll tell him tonight. Later. I'll get the two of us some privacy first."

Tom prepares to leave.

"I'm coming with you," Cindy says.

Tom nods appreciatively, and together they leave the apartment. Out of the corner of his eye, he can see Anthony. He's watching them go. He stares at Tom all the while, and Tom can feel his eyes burning into the back of his head even long after they've left the apartment.

32

Tom and Cindy check into a hotel. Cindy goes to the front desk to pay and get the keys. Tom hasn't had a chance to tidy up yet. He's still covered in blood. He sneaks through the lobby once Cindy waves him inside.

In the room, he takes a shower and washes away all of the blood. He watches it swirl pink down the drain.

Cindy sits up on one of the beds, her back against the headboard. She's on her laptop. "I'm just checking if there's any chatter about what happened back in the Skulls' neighborhood," she says.

Tom doubts there will be, but he says, "Is there?"

"No, nothing." She closes her laptop and comes closer to him. She sits on the edge of the bed and looks his face over. "Doesn't look so bad now that all the blood is gone," she says. "Though you've got some nasty bruising on both cheeks."

"It won't look so bad come the morning," Tom says. "I've always healed fast."

"I'm sure that's very lucky for you," Cindy says. "But you don't need to always try to push the limits, you know?"

Tom takes a seat in the chair by the window. There are two beds in the room. Cindy has already claimed her own, but is now sitting on his. She crosses her legs and pulls them up under herself. She looks like she wants to say something. Tom doesn't hurry her. He looks out the window at the Chicago lights. He can see part of the El down below, but it's too late for a train in this part of the city.

Cindy clears her throat. "Back – back there, at Stacey's apartment, were you letting Anthony hit you because... Was it some kind of penitence thing? Because you took the ashes?"

"I don't know," Tom says. "Maybe. Maybe that's part of the reason, from somewhere deep down inside." He sighs. "My brother and I have fought before. I've hit him back plenty of times. But this time... I couldn't. I knew I couldn't. I knew I had a receipt coming. Because of what I'd done. So, yeah, I guess you're right. That's the reason. I didn't look at it as being penitence or redemptive or anything like that, but I think that's why."

"You were goading him," Cindy says, raising an eyebrow.

Tom looks to the side.

"Why were you doing that? Did you think he wasn't hitting you hard enough or something? Was it self-destructive?"

Tom shakes his head slowly. "No."

Cindy waits, but he doesn't offer anything further. "Tom, you know you can talk to me."

Tom sighs. "I didn't want to hit him back," he says, "but I wanted to *hurt* him. Not physically. Mentally, emotionally. I wanted him to know that he couldn't hurt *me*."

"Why?"

Tom grits his teeth. His jaw aches. "He hates me for taking Alejandra's ashes," he says. "But I..."

"What? Tom, what? You can tell me. You know you can."

"But it's his fault she's dead in the first place," Tom says, looking at her. "And I hate *him* for that."

"You blame him for Alejandra's death."

"Her death is on him," Tom says. "He caused it. It's his fault. It's his responsibility. He can be angry at me for taking her ashes, but it's on him that she was in that urn in the first place."

"Tom, he – he probably knows that already. Maybe – maybe lashing out at you, holding you responsible for some part of it, maybe that's a way for him to cope."

"I'm sure it is," Tom says. "But no matter how hard we hate each other, we can't bring her back." He checks the time and wonders if Hayley is still awake. "I'm going to have to call home," he says, pulling out his phone.

"I'll give you some privacy," Cindy says, stepping off the bed. "I need a shower anyway."

She disappears into the bathroom, and Tom calls Hayley. "I hope I haven't woke you," he says when she answers.

"No, I wasn't sleeping," she says. Tom hears Cindy start the shower and get under the water. "I was hoping I'd hear from you tonight. How's it going?"

"Well, that's mostly what I'm calling about. We found Anthony." He doesn't go into details. He moves promptly on. "Listen, I want to get home as soon as I can, but I think we're going to be stuck here a few more days. It might even be longer."

"How come?"

"I don't think my dad's going to want to leave so easily, and I can't go without him."

"I see," Hayley says. "How's he doing?"

"He seems all right, for the most part." Tom pokes at the scab at the corner of his eyebrow and tongues the cut in the corner of his lip. He can hear Cindy turning off the shower and getting out. "How's Sylvia?"

"She's better. She's just worried about your dad. He called her this morning, though, and I think that helped a lot."

"I'm glad he did that. He never mentioned that he had."

"Yeah. Okay, well, you stay safe out there, Tom. I miss you."

"I miss you too."

"I hope you can come back soon." She pauses, then says, "I love you, Tom."

The bathroom door opens, and Cindy steps back through. She's wrapped in a towel. Her hair is slicked back, and the ends of it are dripping. She smiles at him and then raises her eyebrows, seeing that he's still on the phone, and then creeps past on her way to her side of the room and her things.

"Tom?" Hayley says.

"I love you too," he says, turning away from Cindy. "I'll see you soon."

33

Stacey has kicked Anthony out of the bedroom. "Not after tonight," she said. "I'm not sharing my bed with – with whoever *that* guy was."

Anthony didn't protest. He can understand where she was coming from. Despite her knowing what he does for a living, she's never seen him like that before. Stacey has taken Billy into the bedroom with her, and Connor is sleeping in Billy's bed, under strict instructions not to get blood all over the sheets. Anthony is in the living room with his father.

He's given Jeffrey the sofa. Anthony is on the floor. The apartment is very quiet. The blinds are open, and there is light from the moon and the stars that illuminate the room and casts deeper shadows where they don't reach.

Anthony and Jeffrey haven't spoken, but Anthony knows it's just a matter of time. He knows his father is still awake. Anthony lies flat on his back and stares at the ceiling. He thinks about what his father told him earlier. About his cancer. They haven't spoken since then. Anthony is processing. He tries to listen to his father's breathing. It sounds fine. There are no wheezes or rattles. It sounds normal.

Jeffrey clears his throat and rolls onto his side. "You still awake, Anthony?"

"Yeah."

"You wanna talk about earlier?"

"No."

Jeffrey sighs. "I do."

"Then talk," Anthony says. "I'm not going to stop you."

"You never answered Tom."

"I thought you meant did I want to talk about the cancer," Anthony says. "I don't want to talk about Tom, either."

Jeffrey continues like he hasn't heard. "When he asked you if hitting him made you feel better..." Jeffrey waits a beat. "Did it?"

Anthony laces his fingers across his sternum. He takes a deep breath, then sighs it all out. "No," he says. He takes another breath. "But I don't know if that's because hitting him couldn't ever make me feel better, or if I just didn't hit him enough." He grits his teeth. Out of the corner of his eye, he thinks he can see Jeffrey wince.

"Tom knows he made a mistake, Anthony," Jeffrey says.

"I've never heard him say that. Have *you*? Or are you just making an assumption?"

"He came all the way here to help you."

"He came for *you*," Anthony says.

"Maybe he presents it that way, but deep down, he came for you. He might never admit it to anyone, not even himself, but it's the truth. He's your brother, and he loves you. He came here for you."

"He doesn't show it."

"Tom doesn't show much of anything. He never has. He's stoic. He's always been this way, ever since – ever since your mother died. Do you think he tells me he loves me? Or Sylvia? No, he doesn't, but he shows it. We know he loves us. We know that if we need him, he'll come running. He's *done* that, Anthony. He's done it for us, and he's done it for you. He's doing it for you right now."

Anthony pushes himself up on an elbow and turns to his father. "Why are you pushing this so hard?"

"I'm not pushing anything. I just want you to understand how things are."

"I know how things are."

"Anthony, I'm dying," Jeffrey says. "It might not happen anytime soon, but it's going to happen. It's coming. It's on its fucking way. I can almost feel it bearing down on me, Anthony. I know it's close enough that it's got me in its sights, and soon everyone else is going to be able to see it clinging to me, too."

They look at each other through the moonlight.

"I don't expect anything to change today or tomorrow," Jeffrey says. "But if I'm going to die soon, I hope I don't go knowing that my sons can't stand to be anywhere near each other. I hope that when the time comes, the two of you have made some kind of peace."

Anthony wants to tell him not to hold his breath, but it feels wrong in light of everything Jeffrey is saying. So Anthony doesn't say anything. He can't make that promise to his father. He lies flat and turns back to the ceiling. "It's been a long night," he says. "I'm going to try to get some sleep."

Jeffrey stays turned, watching him for a while. Anthony doesn't look back at him. He stares at the ceiling until Jeffrey finally rolls over, and then Anthony closes his eyes.

34

It's morning. Tom and Cindy return to Stacey's apartment after Jeffrey messaged, asking them to come.

Stacey is leaving as they arrive. She's taking Billy with her. "We need groceries," she says, passing Tom and Cindy out in the hall. She looks at Cindy and says, "Maybe you want to come with us?"

"I think it's best I stay here," Cindy says. The two women exchange knowing looks.

It's obvious to Tom that Stacey doesn't want to be around when he comes face-to-face with his brother again. She doesn't want her son to be present in case things get heated like they did last night.

In the apartment, Connor is lying on the sofa with his leg elevated over its arm. Jeffrey is sitting in a chair, but Anthony is standing by the window again with his arms folded. He stares at Tom as he enters, and smirks at the cuts and bruises on his face.

Tom faces Jeffrey. "You asked us to come," he says. "Here

we are."

Jeffrey nods. "Two of you wanna take a seat?"

"I'm good," Tom says, and Cindy stays by his side. He notices how she eyes Anthony warily, fretful he's going to come on the attack again.

"Suit yourself," Jeffrey says. He coughs, then clears his throat. He takes a deep breath, checking to make sure he's not about to have a fit.

"Hey, man, listen," Connor says, getting Tom's attention. "You and your brother might not be on good terms or whatever, but I appreciate what you did for us last night, getting us out of there. You hadn't shown up when you did, the two of us were dead men. Thank you."

Tom looks at Anthony. Anthony looks away at this, and Tom can see how he's grinding his teeth.

"All right, let's talk about what we're doing next," Jeffrey says. "Anthony and I spoke this morning, and while he didn't send me those messages and he doesn't know who did, turns out he *is* in trouble."

"I think we could guess that from last night," Cindy says. Anthony shoots her a look.

"Don't look at her like that," Tom says.

Cindy places a hand on his arm. "Tom, it's fine."

Jeffrey lowers his hands, urging everyone to remain calm. "Come on now, we're all friends here."

Tom talks to his father, knowing he won't get a straight answer out of his brother. "So what kind of trouble's he in?"

Jeffrey tells him.

Tom absorbs this information. He looks around the apartment. Stacey's home. Billy's home. He looks at Anthony. "You're in a gang?" he says.

Anthony doesn't nod, doesn't say anything. Just stares.

Tom turns to Connor. "And you're in it too? What're they called?"

"We're the South Side Street Kings," Connor says.

"Uh-huh," Tom says, turning back to Anthony. "The South Side Street Kings." He doesn't sound impressed. "So not only are you running around getting yourself in trouble with rival gangs, you're also in trouble with your own?"

"That wasn't our fault –" Connor says, but Tom cuts him off.

"I'm talking to him now." He stares back at his brother. He's aware that the same kind of tension that filled the room last night has permeated the air again. "Judging by the two of you, white as the driven snow, and the fact you were trying to rip off a black gang last night, I'm guessing the South Side Street Kings are white?"

Anthony remains silent, but he bristles. He knows what Tom is getting at.

Tom's eyes narrow. He's bristling, too. "That's answer enough," he says. "You're running around with a bunch of fucking Nazis?"

"Whoa, man, hold up –" Connor says, but this time it's Anthony who cuts him off.

"They're not Nazis," Anthony says. "They hate Nazis. They're a group of dirty white boys, looking out for each other, sticking together, getting by. Race doesn't come into it. They're *not* Nazis. Are you insane? Do you really think I'd join up with a bunch of fucking peckerwoods?"

"I don't have any idea *what* you might do," Tom says.

Anthony takes a step forward, but he stops himself when Jeffrey glances up at him.

Anthony looks like he has a bad taste in his mouth. Looks like he wants to spit. "You're an asshole, Tom. You're a goddamn asshole. That you would even *think* such a thing –!"

"Let's put that to one side, Anthony," Tom says. He *does* take a step forward, and he doesn't back up when Jeffrey looks at him. Cindy holds onto his arm, though, and he doesn't shrug her off. "They're not Nazis, fine. I was mistaken. But how about *this* – what the hell are you thinking getting involved with Stacey and Billy when you're running around with a gang and shooting off guns in the street? *Well?* What are you thinking? You're not just putting yourself in danger, you're putting *them* in danger, too. You're just the same selfish idiot asshole you've always been. You've never grown up."

"Fuck you."

"Fuck *you*, Anthony. What are you trying to do? You trying to turn another mother and child to ash?"

Tom hears Cindy suck air sharply through her teeth. The room goes very still. Anthony's eyes blaze. He's about to charge Tom, but Tom is ready for him.

Jeffrey stands, holding out his hands. "That's *enough!*" He glares at his two sons in turn. "That's *more* than enough. I should never have let this go on so long." He coughs and grits his teeth, forcing himself not to erupt in a fit. He swallows. "Everyone just calm down and *listen*. This isn't getting us anywhere, and I'm sick to death of seeing the two of you at each other's throats. Tom, I know you're still upset about Alejandra, but you can't say things like that. You can't say that, son. We're all hurting for her, but no matter what you believe, no one is hurting more than Anthony. And Anthony, listen – I don't agree with how he said it, but Tom is right. If you're in danger, Stacey and Billy are in danger. You understand that, don't you? Yeah? All right, so let's all stay calm and talk about what we're going to do to get you *all* out of danger."

Tom and Anthony continue to stare at each other. They are not calm. No one can calm them.

"We can just leave Chicago," Jeffrey says. "No one will ever know. We can just sneak right on out."

Anthony shakes his head.

"Now listen, don't shoot it down so fast," Jeffrey says. "I mean *all* of us – all of *you*. You, Stacey, Billy, even Connor – we can get you all out, and you don't have to think about what's happening here or the danger you're in –"

"No," Anthony says. "I'm not doing that." He tears his eyes away from Tom long enough to glance at his father. "This is my home now. This is *our* home, all of ours. I don't need to ask her. I *know* Stacey wouldn't agree to this. *I* don't agree to it. I'm not running away. I won't run away again. I didn't ask any of you to come. *I* will deal with my problems. I can't make that any clearer than I have already. These are my battles, and I'll resolve them. You all might as well just leave right now. I'm not going with you."

"You heard him," Tom says.

"We're not going anywhere," Jeffrey says.

"You can't help me!" Anthony says. "I don't need your damn help!" He wheels on Tom, jabbing a finger toward him. "I especially don't want anything to do with *you*!"

"We're on the same page on this one," Tom says. "It's him you need to convince." He nods at their father.

"You know what, man? Fuck this." Anthony strides across the room toward Tom. Tom feels Cindy stiffen beside him. He puts an arm across her to move her back out of harm's way. Anthony gets close to Tom. "You're gonna leave. You're gonna leave if I have to kick your ass all the way out of Chicago myself."

Tom looks into his eyes and silently dares him.

Anthony lowers his voice. "What you said about Alejandra," he says, and shakes his head. "I won't ever let anything like that happen again. And I won't let you get away with saying it."

"I said it because it's true," Tom says, and he can't keep himself from sneering. "Alejandra is dead because of *you*, and I won't pretend otherwise anymore."

They're close to blows again, Tom knows. He can see how Anthony trembles and how he balls his fists.

"I'm done holding back, Anthony," Tom says. "You take another swing at me, I'm swinging right back."

There's a pause. Everyone in the room around them is holding their breath.

And then Anthony throws a punch.

35

Tom blocks Anthony's swing, then throws one of his own and puts Anthony down. The blow landed on Anthony's cheek, and Tom can see it redden. If it had connected with his jaw, it would have knocked him out. Tom wasn't trying to knock him out. He wanted to put him on his ass.

Anthony jumps straight back to his feet. He throws another punch, but Tom ducks it and buries his own fist into Anthony's midsection. Anthony crumples down to his knees, coughing, making noises like he's about to throw up.

"Tom, that's enough!" Jeffrey says.

"That's up to him," Tom says.

Anthony snorts, trying to catch his breath, then forces himself back to his feet. He throws another punch, but Tom easily blocks it. He returns the punch, landing it on Anthony's nose and mouth. Tom feels warm blood splash the back of his hand. Anthony doesn't go down this time. He stumbles back a couple of paces.

"Anthony, leave it, man, come on," Connor says.

"Just stop," Jeffrey says, to both of them.

Anthony roars and charges this time. Tom raises a boot and kicks him in the chest, knocking him down flat onto his back. Anthony coughs and groans, but he doesn't stay down. He rolls over and forces himself up.

"Tom, he's had enough," Cindy says.

"I haven't had enough!" Anthony says, getting his legs under him. Blood runs down his mouth and chin. He raises his weak arms. He can barely make a fist.

Tom knows he's going to attack again. He can see it in the way Anthony rocks from side to side and the way his eyes flicker over Tom, trying to work out where to attack this time. When he does move, he swings a left, but Tom easily catches it. Anthony is too weary and too slow now. Tom hits him with a left of his own, catching his right cheek and splitting it open. Anthony hits the ground. He lies like a turtle on his back for a moment, straining, struggling to get up. He manages to get an elbow under him, and starts to push himself back up. His whole body is shaking. Blood drips from his nose to the floor. He gets back to his feet, but he sways where he stands. He can't raise his arms. He's defenseless.

"I'm not staying down," Anthony says.

Tom steps in close. "You don't need to stay down," he says, his voice low. "You just need to know that every time you've ever landed a hit on me, it's because I *let* you."

Jeffrey gets between them and pulls them apart. "Is that enough?" he says. "Are we done here? Is it finally out of your fucking systems? You're like goddamn children!"

Cindy holds onto Tom's arm. She isn't trying to hold him back. It's for support, though Tom isn't sure if it's for him or for her.

Connor has gotten to his feet. He's hopped over, and he's supporting Anthony's weight, and he's looking at Tom like he sees him in a new light. Like he regrets thanking him earlier.

Jeffrey stands in between them all, keeping them separate. "This has to be it," he says. "No more fighting. We're not enemies here – we're all on the same side, damn it! Now, if the two of you are done, it's time for us to work out what we do next, and how we deal with this trouble –"

"I'm done here," Tom says. Everyone looks at him. "I'm done getting him out of his own mess, over and over and over again. I've had enough. I've had a lifetime of it. He doesn't want us here, well, now he can have what he wants." He faces his father. "And when you've had enough, you know how to reach me. I'll still be in town, but I'm done with all of this." He leaves the apartment, and Cindy follows him. Jeffrey calls after them, but Tom doesn't answer.

They take the elevator down. Tom breathes deep, calming himself internally. "I'll take you home," he says. "Something tells me I'll have time to make the drive."

"And then what will you do?" Cindy says.

"Then I'll come back here, check into the hotel, and wait until my dad gets tired of trying to help someone who doesn't want it."

"Then I'm staying here with you," she says.

"You don't need to do that."

"We're a team," Cindy says. "I'm not going to leave you here by yourself."

The elevator reaches the bottom, and they step out. They leave the building, and on the way out, they pass Stacey and Billy. Stacey is carrying a grocery bag in one arm and holding Billy's hand with her other.

"Tom," she says. "Cindy."

They stop with her, and Tom wipes off the blood from the back of his hand on his jeans, hoping she doesn't notice.

"I'm guessing from the fact that the two of you are alone that things didn't go well up there," she says.

Cindy looks purposefully at Billy and then says, "You should probably give them some time. Twenty minutes maybe, half an hour."

Stacey bites her lip. She looks up the front of her building, then sighs through her nose. "Listen," she says, looking at them both. "Can we talk?"

36

Harlan sits in his car, and he watches Stacey's apartment building. He can see Stacey. Can see her talking to a couple of people who have just left her building. Even at this distance, Harlan can see the resemblance between Anthony and his brother. There are differences, sure, but there are enough similarities. Harlan goes on his phone and checks the image he has saved of Tom Rollins in his Army uniform, but he didn't have to bother. It's definitely him.

Harlan doesn't know who the woman with Tom is. She turned up with Tom earlier. Harlan saw them arrive. Knows the car they're in and where it's parked. The woman is dressed all in black and wearing the T-shirt of a band Harlan has never heard of. She doesn't matter, though. Tom is here. *That's* what matters.

Tom and the woman walk away with Stacey and Billy. Harlan watches them go off together. He grins to himself. Everything, finally, is falling into place. All it took was a little patience.

37

Tom and Cindy take Stacey and Billy to a nearby diner. They get Billy a milkshake. Stacey and Cindy drink coffee. Tom has water.

Stacey puts sugar into her coffee, and she keeps stirring it and stirring it, staring into the swirling darkness. Tom lets her take her time. Billy drinks his chocolate milkshake through a straw. He stares out the nearby window. He's quiet and shy around the two strangers.

Stacey snaps out of her trance and stops stirring. She puts the spoon down. "I love Anthony," she says finally, looking at Tom. "And I'm worried about him."

"Seems like everyone is," Tom says.

Stacey doesn't respond to this. "We've been together a couple of years now. I don't suppose he told you how we met? No, I didn't think you would have had a chance to talk about anything like that. Doesn't seem like you've wanted to talk at all, neither of you. But he was working in the club where I dance, and he wasn't like the rest of the Street Kings who would work security. He was so much more sweet and charming. I could hold an actual conversation with him and not feel like he was talking to me just so he had a closer view to ogle my –" She pauses and glances at Billy. He smiles back at her, his teeth coated brown with the milkshake. "To ogle *me*," she says. "It had been a long time since someone would just *talk* to me like that."

She takes a drink of coffee, holding the cup in both hands. She looks to the side, remembering. "He's started...*changing* since we first met. It feels like the longer he's a Street King, the more poison just keeps seeping into him. He's not the same person anymore. He's always stressed, and he's always on edge. He hasn't...he hasn't ever taken any of it out on me, but sometimes I wonder if it's coming. If he'll start losing patience with me and raising his voice, or maybe staying away for days at a time and never telling me where he is. Although, that last one, he's getting closer and closer to that already."

She reaches over to Billy and strokes the back of his neck. He giggles and squirms, trying to pull away from her

"He's good with Billy," she says. "He's like a father to him. He's more like a father than his actual father." She scrapes her teeth over her bottom lip. "I don't want him to get hurt. And right now, this money he owes to the Street Kings – if he doesn't pay them off, they're going to kill him."

"We can't help him if he doesn't want us to," Tom says.

Stacey watches her son. He's sipping on his milkshake again and staring out the window, watching people walking by on the sidewalk. "It's strange that he never said he has a brother," she says. "We talked about our pasts. About our families. He never mentioned a brother. Are you his *only* brother?"

Tom nods. "No sisters."

"See, that makes me wonder if he's kept any other secrets from me."

"I'm not surprised he didn't tell you about me," Tom says. "I'm not going around telling people about him."

"I can see that," Stacey says. "The two of you need to sit down and talk to each other sometime. *Really* talk, I mean. None of this macho bullshit posturing, all up in each other's faces and throwing punches. Don't think I missed that blood on your hands, Tom. I know he's gonna be as marked up as you are when I see him later."

"In fairness," Cindy says, "Tom warned him."

Stacey holds up her hands. "I'm not interested in that. I'm not picking sides. Look, I wanted to talk to you both because I'm worried – I think I've made that clear. What I haven't done is ask you for your help. Not for Anthony this time – for *me*. I want my Anthony back, but the way he's going, he's going to be dead before that can ever happen. I don't want him to get hurt. Just – Tom, take him away. Get him out of here. Out of Chicago. He can't stay here. He thinks he can deal with all of this, but he can't. The Street Kings, the Skulls, it's all too much, and that's not even *all* of it. Just get him out."

"Our father already suggested that," Tom says. "Anthony refused. He won't leave you. I don't think he'll leave, full stop. He has something to prove."

"It's not proving anything if he's *dead*," Stacey says. "Tom, I'd rather he was gone and I never saw him again but I knew he was *alive*, than not know he's lying dead somewhere in this city."

"What are you suggesting?" Tom says. "That we tie him up, bundle him in the trunk of our car and get him out of here that way?"

"If that's what it takes." Stacey reaches across the table and places her hand on Tom's forearm. She squeezes. "Tom, I love your brother. Billy loves your brother. We don't want anything to happen to him. I don't know you, but when I spoke to your father last night, when you were saving Anthony from the Skulls, he made it clear he certainly seems to think you're the only person who can help Anthony. I'm asking you if you will."

Tom takes a deep breath. He looks down at her hand. "What about you?" he says. "What do you want?"

"What do you mean?" She takes her hand back and wraps both of them around the coffee like she's cold.

"Anthony said you won't leave Chicago. Is that true?"

She considers this. "It's my home," she says. "But no, there's nothing tying me here. If we had the opportunity, Billy and I could start over anywhere. We just don't have the finances for that."

"*You* could get Anthony out of here," Tom says. "If you said you wanted to go, there wouldn't be any need for bundling him into the trunk and smuggling him out."

"If Anthony said that, he was using me as an excuse," Stacey says. "I've never given him the impression I'd refuse to leave. For whatever reason, *he* doesn't want to leave."

"You know why that is?"

Stacey doesn't. "Do *you*?"

Tom considers this. "Maybe he doesn't want to feel like a failure," Tom says. "Could be he has younger-brother syndrome. He feels like he needs to prove something, even if he gets himself hurt doing it. He's refusing to leave, to give up, because that would be something else he hasn't finished."

They all sit in silence for a while. Stacey stares down into her coffee. Billy has finished his milkshake. He plays with the straw, scraping the remaining creamy bubbles from the inside of the glass.

"The reasons don't matter," Stacey finally says. "Will you get him out?"

Tom looks at her and then at Billy. "You don't have to stay behind," he says. "If there's nothing holding you here, you can come with."

Stacey smiles a little. "Does that mean you'll do it?"

"I'll do it for you and for Billy," Tom says. "Because I know Anthony's sure as hell not going to thank me for it."

38

Tom and Cindy take Stacey and Billy back to the apartment, only to find that Anthony is not there.

"He went for a walk," Jeffrey says. "We figured it was best to let him go. Let him cool off."

Jeffrey stands. Connor remains on the sofa. He makes space for Billy to sit next to him. Tom notices that Anthony's blood has been cleaned from the floor.

"How was he when he left?" Stacey says.

"He was fine," Jeffrey says. "His pride was just bruised, was all."

"How long's he been gone?" Tom says.

"Not long." Jeffrey checks the time. "A half hour." He looks at Tom. "I'm surprised to see you back."

"We got talking to Stacey," Tom says.

"Yeah? And what came of that?"

Tom looks at Cindy by his side, then back at his father. "We're going to help you get Anthony out."

Jeffrey looks pleased, but also cautious. "You got ideas on how to do that?"

"With force," Tom says.

"He's making it sound worse than it'll be," Cindy says. "This is actually Stacey's idea. She agrees it's unlikely Anthony will leave of his own accord. He's determined to see things through here, for whatever reason that might be. So what we're going to do is get him in the car and drive him away. If we have to bind him and gag him, then so be it."

"And this is Stacey's idea?" Jeffrey says, looking to her for confirmation.

She nods.

"But what about the two of you?" Jeffrey says, indicating her and Billy.

"We're going to come with," Stacey says. "Maybe it'll work out, maybe it won't, but I'd rather take a chance than wait around here for something bad to happen."

Jeffrey tilts his head. "But Anthony said –"

"Anthony lied," Tom says.

"He made excuses," Cindy says, trying to soften some of Tom's word choices.

Jeffrey nods. "Well, listen, if you're on board, why don't we try to find him right now? He can't have gotten too far."

"No time like the present," Tom says, thinking of Hayley and of Hopper Creek. The sooner they deal with Anthony, the sooner he can go home. Once they get him out of Chicago, whatever comes next is down to Jeffrey and Stacey. Tom will have played his part. He'll have done more than he ever intended to.

"We need to find him first," Jeffrey says. He turns to Stacey, Billy, and Connor. "You three stay here. If he gets back before we do, call us. If we find him first, we'll call you, and we'll all meet out front. Tom, listen – I'm glad you're on board, but let me *talk* to him first, all right? Don't go trying to kidnap him straight off the bat."

"You're not tired of trying to talk to him yet?" Tom says.

"*Tom.*"

"Fine. You can talk to him first. But when he doesn't listen, he's going in the trunk."

39

Anthony didn't leave the apartment to take a walk. He left because he'd been summoned.

Anthony has to walk six blocks to get to Harlan's car. He's not sure why he's parked so far away. He gets into the passenger seat and says, "I don't have any money on me."

Harlan grins. "If I wanted you to bring money, I would've told you in advance." He looks Anthony over. "Been fighting? That looks fresh, buddy."

"It's nothing," he says. "If you don't want money, what'd you call me here for?" Anthony thinks of the botched raid last night. Wonders if Harlan has called him here to gloat about it. No doubt he's aware of it and all the noise it caused.

"How are your money troubles?" Harlan says, and Anthony thinks his theory is likely correct. "You any closer to paying off Ezra and saving your skin?"

Anthony chooses not to respond.

"Suit yourself. I heard about last night."

Bingo, Anthony thinks. He isn't sure why Harlan would

bring him all the way here just to gloat. Anthony shifts in his seat. realizes he's probably going to try to recruit him for his 'big money' job again. He braces himself for the pitch. He's sick of hearing it by now. He doesn't want any more to do with Harlan than he already does. If he can keep putting Harlan off until his trial, if he can keep him at arm's length, then if he gets lucky, he might not hear from him again. From what Anthony has heard, because of the footage, Harlan is likely to get in a lot of trouble. Losing his job on the force is almost guaranteed. He could even be looking at prison time.

"From what I hear, I assume it didn't go in your favor," Harlan says. "There was a lot of noise, apparently. You're lucky you're still alive. That *was* you, wasn't it?"

"Sounds like you already know the answer."

"I like to be sure, you know," Harlan says. "That's a detective's job, after all."

"Oh, really? The way you go on, I thought it was to beat up minorities."

Harlan laughs. "Oh, man, you really like to push your luck, don't you?"

Anthony folds his arms. His stomach aches from Tom's fist.

"Listen, Anthony, do you know your Bible stories?" Harlan says.

Anthony frowns, not understanding.

"You know the stories of Jesus, right? You remember the one about how he tells Peter, tells him he'll deny him three times. You remember that?"

"Vaguely," Anthony says, waiting for Harlan to make his point.

"Well, Anthony buddy, I've come to you twice already

with an offer of work," Harlan says. "And you've denied me twice. I'm coming to you now a third time, offering you part of a job, offering you an end to all your money woes – are you going to deny me a third time?"

"I'd hate to meet anyone who would compare you to Jesus."

Harlan laughs. "What do you say, Anthony? Wanna be my disciple?"

"No, Harlan. No, I don't. You need to stop asking. My answer isn't going to change."

"Well, suit yourself," Harlan says. "Just remember, I gave you three opportunities to come on board, and you turned me down three times."

Anthony is tense. He knows Harlan doesn't like to hear the word no. He's taken it surprisingly well the last two times. This could be when he finally erupts. This could be when Anthony feels fists for the second time today.

"It'll be going forward soon," Harlan says. "So don't expect me to ask you again. It's a real shame it had to go down like this, Anthony." Harlan looks at him for a long time. He's smiling, but there's no warmth in it. Not for the first time, Harlan reminds Anthony of a shark. "You might as well get on out of the car now, buddy. Doesn't seem like we have anything here left to talk about. You've made up your mind."

Anthony gets out of the car cautiously. He closes the door, and Harlan waves at him through the glass, and then he drives away. Anthony watches him go, not sure what the purpose of that was. Sometimes it feels like Harlan just likes to mess with him. He rubs the back of his neck and then starts walking again. He's got a distance to go before he gets back to the apartment.

40

Harlan speeds ahead, gets back to Stacey's apartment building. He checks the area. Tom Rollins's car is no longer parked nearby. Harlan scratches the corner of his mouth and wonders where he could have gone. Out looking for Anthony, perhaps? Or maybe he and the woman he's with got back from wherever they went with Stacey and her kid and he's just left. Whatever the answer, it doesn't matter right now. Harlan will find out soon enough. He pulls his own car forward and parks in front of the entrance to the building.

He pulls out his handgun and quickly checks it over. He carries a 9mm Luger. He keeps it concealed as he gets out of the car and enters the building. He doesn't need to get buzzed in. He found out the code a long time ago, from another resident. It didn't take much for the guy to give up the code to Harlan and his detective ID.

He takes the elevator up, wondering how far away Anthony still is. Probably five blocks, he'd guess. Harlan has plenty of time. He goes to Stacey's apartment and knocks on the door.

It takes a while before anyone answers, though Harlan can hear movement inside. Can hear voices, too, though it's not clear what they're saying to each other. Connor opens the door. He's favoring his right leg. He blinks when he sees Harlan.

Harlan doesn't give him much more of a chance to react. He whips him across the bridge of the nose with his pistol, then grabs him by the front of his shirt and pushes him back into the apartment, ready to use him as a human shield.

The shield isn't necessary. The only other people present are Stacey and her child. Harlan pushes Connor away, and his leg buckles under him. He drops hard, crying out as he goes. Harlan keeps the gun raised. "Just the three of you, huh? I was expecting more of a party." He smiles at Stacey and Billy cowering together on the sofa. Stacey has her arms wrapped around the boy, staring at Harlan and the gun. She holds him close. "Oh, well. We don't need to worry. This still works."

41

Tom drives around the block, looking for Anthony. Cindy is in the back on her computer, trying to track him via security cameras. Jeffrey sits up front, trying to get in touch with him on his phone.

"That's the right number this time?" Tom says.

"He gave it to me this morning," Jeffrey says. He holds up a hand to silence Tom, then speaks into the phone. "Anthony," he says, "I've tried calling you a few times. Where are you? Well, you've been gone a while, and I started to get worried. Listen, tell me where you are, and I'll come and pick you up." Jeffrey shoots Tom a look out of the corner of his eye. "No, no, Tom's not here. It's just me." He coughs, as if lying to his youngest son has pained him. "Okay, got it. Wait right there. I'll not be long." He hangs up the phone. "He's not far. Take the next right and then straight on. He said he'll wait for me on a bench."

"He might bolt when he sees me," Tom says.

"I don't think he will," Jeffrey says. "Not straight away. He'll hang around long enough for me to try to talk to him."

In the back, Cindy puts her laptop away now that they know where he is.

Tom takes the corner and drives straight on, and soon enough they spot Anthony on the bench. He doesn't look up as they approach. He's on his phone. Tom pulls up in front of him, but the passenger side is closest to Anthony. When he looks up, he'll see Jeffrey.

Tom can see the look on his brother's face, though. He's concerned. Something is wrong. He looks up and sees the car, and without hesitation, he runs to it. He's shoving his phone back into his pocket. He dives into the back, next to Cindy.

"Drive!" he says, not registering or reacting to Tom's being here. It's clear that something far more pressing is plaguing him. He's frantic, waving his arms. "Go back to the apartment – someone's taken Stacey and Billy!"

42

They get back to the apartment to find the door wide open. Connor is on the floor with his back up against the wall. Blood is running down his face from the bridge of his nose and under his left eye. His hand is pressed to his forehead, his left knee bent, but his wounded right leg is stretched out in front of him.

Anthony hurries to him, sliding across the ground. "What happened?"

"I'll try to find them," Cindy says, pulling out her laptop as she sits down on the living room's chair.

"It was that guy, the cop," Connor says, wiping blood from his mouth. "The one who came to us in the bar."

"Harlan?" Anthony says.

"Who's Harlan?" Jeffrey says. He stands by the door with Tom. Tom has checked the door over. There's no sign of forced entry.

"He's a cop," Connor says. "He's been leaning on Anthony – extorting him."

Anthony can't answer. He looks shell-shocked.

Tom doesn't say anything, but he feels this is something they should have been told about sooner. He remembers Stacey saying, not so long ago, that Anthony had other problems than the Street Kings and the Skulls.

"Harlan who?" Cindy says. "What's his full name? Did you say he's a cop?"

"I don't know," Connor says.

"Ross," Anthony says. "Harlan Ross."

"Got it," Cindy says.

"How long ago did he take them?" Tom says.

"I called you as soon as I came to and realized they were gone," Connor says. "What's that? How long's that been?"

"About twenty minutes," Jeffrey says.

Anthony gives a start, like he's been shocked. He snatches at his pocket and pulls out his phone. It's ringing. "It's him," he says, reading the screen. "It's Harlan."

"Put it on speaker," Tom says.

Anthony answers and does as Tom says. "Where the hell are you?" Anthony says. "What have you done?"

"Now, now, Anthony," comes the voice on the other end. "I gave you three chances. I want you to remember that."

"Where are Stacey and Billy?" Anthony says. "Bring them back here right now."

"Anthony, you're not in any position to make demands," Harlan says. "I've told you to watch your tone so many times now, haven't I? Now, are you going to calm down?"

Anthony breathes hard and says nothing.

"That's better," Harlan says. "Do you have me on speaker right now, Anthony? It's fine if you do. I want your little party to hear this. Now then, you know I have Stacey, and you know I have Billy, so I'm sure you're about to listen to me very closely."

Harlan pauses, and it's clear Anthony feels like he has to say something. "I'm listening."

"Good. Is your brother there, Anthony?"

Tom and Anthony look at each other.

"Well?" Harlan says. "Is he? Tom Rollins, can you hear me? Are you there?"

"He's here," Anthony says.

"Good," Harlan says. "Anthony, in one hour I'm going to text you an address. It's my address. You're going to come here, Anthony, and you're going to bring your brother, Tom. Just the two of you. In one hour. You got that?"

"I've got it," Anthony says.

"One hour," Harlan says. "Just the two of you. We're all going to be waiting here, just me and your sweet little family." Harlan hangs up.

43

There is no question. Anthony doesn't have to ask. Stacey and Billy are in danger. Tom agrees to go with him.

The hour that Harlan demanded they wait was excruciating. Cindy tried to find him via security footage, but she came up empty. When the hour is up, Harlan texts Anthony his home address.

Tom drives. On the way, Anthony explains to him who Harlan Ross is. A cop, a detective, on suspension. Anthony tells him what he did. Tom grimaces. "How did you get involved with someone like him?"

"It's not like I had much say in it," Anthony says. "He picked me up and leaned on me for money. Do I need to explain anything else? I didn't want anything to do with him, but here we fucking are. And listen, Tom, I don't wanna hear any 'I told you so' – this is beyond –"

Tom holds up a hand. "We don't have time for that. Just tell me where we're going."

They reach Harlan's suburb. It's in the north of the city. It's a pleasant neighborhood, middle class, but it's not too upmarket. It looks exactly the kind of place Tom would expect a cop's salary to afford.

He parks the car, but neither of them gets straight out. Anthony is counting up door numbers, working out which is Harlan's. "Will he be alone?" Tom says.

"I've never known him to work with anyone else," Anthony says.

"Is he married? Does he have a family?"

"I don't think so. He doesn't wear a ring." Anthony points. "That's his house."

Tom looks. It's on the opposite side of the road from them and four doors down. Like all the rest, it's a single floor. There's a basement window. The curtains on the main floor are open. Tom can see someone standing at the window, but only the outline of them. The shape waves and then walks away.

"He's seen us," Tom says.

They get out of the car and go up to the house. They ring the bell and knock on the door, but there's no answer. Tom tries the handle. It's unlocked. Tom holds an arm across Anthony's chest to stop him from walking straight in. He checks the hall, searching for signs of traps or an ambush.

"Come straight in," Harlan calls. "I'm in the kitchen."

Tom doesn't let Anthony go. Anthony strains against him, wanting to know what the wait is. "Stacey and Billy are there, man," Anthony says.

"You don't need to worry," Harlan says, his voice raised to be heard. "You don't have anything to be concerned about. I figured you might be a cautious man, Tom. Come on through. Nothing's gonna bite."

Tom steps into the house, but he doesn't take Harlan at his word. He's cautious, and he ensures that Anthony is the same.

Harlan is in the kitchen. He sits at the table, his chair turned out and facing the door. Stacey is with him. She's on her knees beside him, a leash around her neck and a ball gag in her mouth. Harlan holds the end of the leash in his left hand. His right is concealed beneath the table. Tom imagines he's armed. Stacey is breathing hard through her nose, and her eyeliner is smudged and running. There's no sign of Billy.

At the sight of Stacey, Anthony attempts to rush forward, but Harlan raises a gun, a 9mm Luger, and points it at her. "Uh-uh," he says. "You just stay right where you are, Anthony. Let's not go getting carried away."

Anthony has to stop himself, but he's shaking. Tom places a hand on his shoulder and pulls him back a step. Anthony shrugs him off. Harlan keeps the gun pointed at Stacey.

"Where's Billy?" Anthony says. His voice cracks.

"He's somewhere safe," Harlan says. "Don't worry about him right now. He's insurance, to make sure you all do as you're told."

"Damn it, *where is he?*"

"Anthony, calm yourself," Harlan says sternly, with a faux-serious expression. He starts grinning again. Despite what he's done, he's not taking this seriously. "We're not going to get anywhere if you keep losing your temper."

Tom places a hand on Anthony's shoulder again and holds him still. "What do you want?" Tom says to the detective.

"Ah, there we go," Harlan says. "Y'know, I've been

working with Anthony for a long time now, and I know what his moods are like. I had a feeling you might be the more levelheaded brother, Tom. You are the oldest, after all, isn't that right?"

Anthony tries to shrug Tom off again, but Tom doesn't let him. He tightens his grip.

"Just tell us what you want," Anthony says, spitting the words.

Harlan tugs on the leash, choking Stacey. Anthony stiffens, but Tom holds him steady. Harlan smirks. He was trying to get a reaction. Tom has prevented this.

"All right," Harlan says. He looks at Tom while he speaks. "I'm sure your brother has filled you in on some of my extracurricular activities. Now, one that he doesn't know about is the work I do for the Mob here in Chicago. I work security in one of their money man's apartments. It's an easy job. Easy money. No one ever tries to raid the place, but the Mob knows it's better to be safe than sorry.

"Now, I've worked for these men for a good few years now. They know me. They trust me. They trust me enough to keep guard of the million dollars that's held in that safe at any given time. And *because* they know me, and *because* they trust me, they don't suspect that I'm going to rob them."

"Good for you," Tom says. "What's that got to do with us?" He notices, however, that Anthony has a look of realization on his face.

"This is the job," he says. "This is the one you've kept trying to get me to help you with."

"And you turned me down three times," Harlan says.

"So you take Stacey and Billy?" Anthony says.

Harlan shrugs. "Whatever it takes."

"You want us to rob them for you," Tom says, understanding.

"*Ding-ding-ding*," Harlan says. "You got it. Anthony, if you'd agreed to help out before now, when I asked you so nicely, I would have given you a cut. You could have paid off the Street Kings. You'd be on easy street. But you turned me down *three times*. Because of that, you know what your cut will be this time? It'll be Stacey and Billy. You'll get them back, unharmed, once I have the money. I owe you that much at least. After all, this whole idea came to me thanks to *you*."

Anthony frowns. "What are you talking about? I didn't know anything about this apartment until now."

"No, you didn't, that's true. But do you remember a few months ago, that night I didn't feel like drinking alone and I took you along with me? You're a lightweight, Anthony. You got drunk *fast*. And you're a bitter drunk too, aren't you? Once you had a few drinks in you, you started telling me all about your ex-Army, Black Ops big brother who was always pulling you out of scrapes, and how you resented him for it."

Tom and Anthony look at each other. Anthony's face shows that he doesn't remember any of this.

"Now, admittedly," Harlan says, "I *may* have slipped a little something extra into your drinks, just to ensure your tongue was plenty loosened up. Once you told me all about your brother here, my mind started to race. I got to thinking. *How* could I use this specialist brother of yours to *my* advantage? After you'd passed out, I went through your phone. I couldn't find a number for Tom here, but I could find your father's. That was good enough. You'd told me enough about *him*, too, and I figured he could prove useful, too. And from what you'd told me, *he* was usually the one who pulled Tom in to help you out."

"You sent the messages," Anthony says.

"Guilty," Harlan says. He starts giggling and leans forward in his chair. He puts his mouth close to Stacey's ear, but looks at the brothers while he speaks. Stacey flinches from him, but he holds her close. "Do you think I should tell him what else I did? He's not going to like it." He straightens up, still giggling.

"What did you do?" Anthony says.

Harlan smiles, self-satisfied. He leans back in his chair. "*I* ripped you off, Anthony. *I* hit the stash house you were guarding."

Anthony's jaw is working, like he wants to speak but can't find the words.

"Yeah, I'm afraid it was *me* who got you in all this trouble with Ezra. But I gave you an out, didn't I? The way I saw it, you'd agree to help me – maybe not the first time I asked, admittedly, but probably the second – and after you were locked in, your father and your brother would show up, and they'd be locked in, too. But as you can see, I was prepared for the eventuality that you'd remain stubborn." He tugs on Stacey's leash to prove his point. "I know how stubborn you can be. I'm a realist, Anthony. I have to be. Why do you think I'm doing all of this? With that footage, they're going to try to send me to prison. I can't go to prison, Anthony, Tom, not as a cop. I won't go to that hell. Too many devils are waiting for me. Once I have the money, I'm not staying in Chicago. I'll be gone. In the wind.

"Now, I'm not unreasonable, you know I'm not. When I grabbed your family here, I could have killed Connor, but I didn't. That was a sign of good faith. We're partners now. We're a team. And, as another sign of good faith, I don't expect you to heist this apartment blind. I have details for you. I have information on the security features. Hell, I even have pictures."

Tom weighs up their options. He measures the distance between himself and Harlan. Sure, he could reach him, but not before Harlan can put a bullet through Stacey's head. And then what about Billy? Harlan is the only one who knows where he is, and Tom doubts he's close by. Cindy could potentially track him down, but they don't know how long that would take, and her being able to find him isn't guaranteed. Tom could torture Harlan, try to get him to talk, but he looks so maniacal that Tom doubts he could make him speak. He'd be more likely to turn the gun on himself before telling them where the boy is.

Their options are clear. They only have one. They have to do as he says. They have to help him. They have to rob the Mob.

"All right," Tom says. "You want us to steal the money. It looks like we don't have any other choice."

"Good," Harlan says, grinning from ear to ear. "I knew I could make you see reason."

"What's our timeframe?"

"I don't expect you to rush into anything," Harlan says. "But you need to remember, little Billy is all alone right now. I've left him with some food and water, but he's a child. Who knows if he'll measure it out correctly?"

"How much did you give him?" Tom says.

Harlan wriggles his eyebrows, but he doesn't give an answer.

"You son of a bitch," Anthony says.

Harlan laughs. "I've been called worse. If you want to play it safe, you should stick to a reasonable timeframe – I wouldn't take any longer than three days. More than that, I can't guarantee he'll still be alive."

"You're sick," Anthony says.

"My back's against the wall, Anthony," Harlan says. "Just like yours. We're all running out of time here."

"What are you going to do with Stacey?" Anthony says.

"She'll be staying here with me. I have very comfortable accommodations for her down in the basement. It's a cage, but it's plenty roomy." He winks.

Tom can't be sure if he's serious or not, but judging from the fact he has a leash and a ball gag handy, he doesn't doubt that there's a cage down there.

"You'd better get a move on now," Harlan says. "I think we've said everything we need to say here, and time's a-ticking. I'll message you all the details soon, Anthony. All the pictures. Be sure to pass them around. Oh, and I expect to be kept abreast of all progress. When you're going to move in, I want to know about it. I'm going to be patched in, boys, so no funny business." He reaches under the table, and while he's turned away, Tom thinks he could charge him. Harlan is too fast, though. He turns back and dumps a bag on the table. "This is for you to take with you now. Cameras and earpieces. When you go in, I'll be patched in. I'll see and hear everything. I'm not an idiot. I'm not leaving anything to risk." He throws the bag to Anthony. "Now, the two of you'd better get a move on, hadn't you? Give me and Stacey some time to better get to know each other." He strokes her hair.

Tom has to restrain his brother. "We need to go," Tom says.

Anthony clenches his jaw, staring at Stacey. He knows Tom is right, though. They need to think about Billy, all alone wherever Harlan has hidden him. They turn and leave the house.

44

By the time they get back to Stacey's building and the others waiting for them, Harlan has sent Anthony the details of the apartment they're to raid. Tom tells everyone what Harlan has done, and what he wants, and Anthony forwards them the details and the pictures he's received.

"I'm going to go there now," Tom says. "I want to start surveillance immediately. For Billy's sake, we don't have any time to waste. Cindy, you're with me."

Cindy nods and stands, her laptop already packed and ready to move.

"I'm coming too," Anthony says.

Tom holds up a hand. "We need some distance right now."

"Like hell –"

"Anthony, this is on you." Tom looks at him. "I had no intention of saying I told you so, but here we are. You got drunk, and you ran your mouth –"

"You heard what he said – the motherfucker drugged me!"

"I don't care. I expect better from you, Anthony. I've always expected better, and you've always let me down. And now Stacey and Billy are held captive, they're in danger – the *exact* damn thing I said could happen has happened. For now, I need you to stay here. I need to be away from you."

Anthony bristles, but he doesn't push things. He backs down. "Fine," he says, but he's biting his lip, and it's already bloody. "I'll sit this out *for now*. But this is my city, this is my *life*, and they're *my* family. I'm not letting you do this alone, not again. I won't wait this out like I had to with Alejandra. When you make your move, I'm fucking *right there* beside you."

Tom doesn't say anything. He prepares to leave.

"Do you need anything from me?" Jeffrey says.

"Not right now," Tom says, but he tilts his head imperceptibly, just enough for his father to see, toward his brother. Jeffrey nods. He understands what Tom wants. He wants him to keep an eye on Anthony. "I'll let you know if and when that changes."

Tom looks at Cindy, and she nods, ready. They leave the apartment and head to the Mob building.

45

Harlan whistles on his way down into the basement. He carries Chinese takeout. He left Stacey here while he went out. He didn't believe Anthony and his brother would be stupid enough to try to come here and get her while he was gone, especially not while he has Billy imprisoned somewhere else, but, regardless, he has a camera in his basement. A speaker there, too. Had they turned up, he would have received an alert through his phone. He would have been able to tell them he was watching them, and that if they didn't leave immediately, they would never see Billy again.

It didn't come to that. They weren't stupid.

"I don't know what you like," Harlan says, hitting the lights and illuminating the room. "But I got you some noodles."

Stacey cowers in the corner of the cage. Her hands are cuffed behind her back, and she's still wearing the ball gag. He couldn't run the risk of her screaming the place down while he was out.

The walls of the basement are adorned with S&M paraphernalia. There are gimp masks and gimp suits. Strap-ons. Whips and leashes, studded collars, ribbed dildoes. He notices how, in the light, Stacey's eyes study these items. She looks simultaneously concerned and appalled.

The cage is pressed up against the wall, directly beneath a window so if anyone looks in, they can't see it. He put a mattress on the ground in the cage, along with a couple of blankets. There's a chair close to it. The chair has straps for the wrists and ankles, but they're hanging loose right now. Harlan puts the takeout on the chair for now. He pulls a key from his pocket.

"Turn around," he says. "Roll over." Stacey does, and he removes the cuffs from her. He takes the ball gag from her too, and she rubs her cheeks and stretches her jaw once it's off, moving it like she can feel and hear it clicking. Harlan drops a carton of noodles in for her, but he doesn't give her chopsticks or a fork. He takes a seat. "While I'm home, you don't have to wear the ball gag so long as you behave yourself. I expect you to be as quiet as a mouse while you're down here. But if you *sneeze* too loud, it goes straight back on. That clear?"

She doesn't answer. She doesn't touch the noodles. Instead, she says, "Where's my son?"

"He's safe."

"*Where is he?*"

Harlan kicks the side of the cage, and she shrieks. "Calm down," he says. "Your tone was very demanding, Stacey, and you're not in any position to be making demands. Now, I asked you a question."

She chews her lip and nods her head. She forces herself

to look at him. "*Please*," she says. "Where did you take him? Just tell me where he is."

"Nope." Harlan got noodles for himself, too. He opens the carton and uses the chopsticks to get some out. He slurps them up like spaghetti. "If I wanted you to know, I wouldn't have left you here in this cage, now, would I? He's my insurance policy, Stacey. You understand how that works, right? *No one* knows where he is until I say so. That goes for you. If anything happens to me, you'll never know. Is this making sense now? *No one* gets to know where he is. If something happens to me, well, that's too bad. You'll never see him again."

Stacey draws her knees up to her chest and rocks back and forth. She shakes.

"Come on, now," Harlan says. "I've told you he's safe. Isn't that enough?"

"You're a monster," she says. When she raises her face a little, Harlan can see that her mouth is bloody. Whether that's from chewing her lip, or from the ball gag, he isn't sure.

Harlan shrugs and eats more noodles. "Believe me when I say I've been called worse." He nods toward her own carton of noodles. "You should eat while the bulbs are on. When I leave, I'm turning the light back off, and I'll be cuffing you to the cage."

Stacey stares at the noodles, but she doesn't touch them. "I'm not hungry."

"Suit yourself," Harlan says. "I'm sure that'll change in time." He sits back and eats, not paying her any attention. He looks to the walls. To his toys. There are posters, too. Naked women in bondage gear. He grins to himself. He's spent many pleasant hours down here.

When he finishes eating, he turns back to Stacey. "I

noticed you admiring the walls when I first turned the lights on," he says.

Stacey continues to sit with her legs drawn up, her face pushed into her knees.

"I'm sure you're probably wondering about that cage you're currently in," Harlan says. "It belonged to an old girl-friend. She was a submissive. She liked being locked up and tied up, that sort of thing. My cuffs came in very handy back then, believe me." He chuckles, remembering. "She moved in for a little while. It wasn't long. Six months, tops. Maybe I should've said she *thought* she liked being tied up. I think my tastes got to be a little more extreme than hers, over time. But anyway, she brought the cage with her. She was about your size. Little cramped, isn't it? That's how she liked it. You're gonna be stiff when you get out, Stacey. I know from experience. Not *my* experience, of course. But just think about all those pins and needles you're going to have in your legs and your feet. You won't be able to stand without support. Anyway, she left, but the cage stayed. I didn't mind. I've grown quite fond of this cage. I've gotten plenty of use out of it since she went. As you can tell from your current occupation, it's proved to be multipurpose."

Stacey doesn't move. Doesn't look at him. The noodles remain untouched. They'll be cold and congealing by now. Harlan leaves them in the cage with her. They're her problem now.

"All right," he says, slapping his thighs and getting to his feet. He pulls the key back out. "You right-handed? Give me your right arm." She does, knowing she doesn't have any other choice. Harlan cuffs her to the cage. "No noise," he says, kneeling down so his face is level with hers. "The gag is always close, and I'll happily put it back on you." He straightens. "It certainly has been pleasant talking with you this evening, Stacey. I hope you have a wonderful night down here. And remember, if you get hungry, you've got the noodles. Try not to make too much mess. You're the one who's gotta sleep in it."

He turns and exits the basement. He kills the light and leaves her alone in darkness.

46

It's late. Tom and Cindy are parked outside the building, on the other side of the road. The El runs right in front of it. Tom has been watching the trains go by, monitoring their schedules. Every detail needs to be noted, no matter how small or seemingly inconsequential.

There's nothing much to see of the building itself. They know the apartment is on the twelfth floor, but all they can see from down here are the windows. Even if someone were standing right there and looking back down at them, they wouldn't know.

Harlan also provided information on the men who will be inside. Matt Rossi and Al Bruno and the men whom Harlan is usually on guard duty with. He only gave names, but Cindy has been able to find images of them online. Tom has committed their faces to memory. He's seen a couple of them come and a couple more go. A changing of the guard.

While Tom watches, Cindy has been trying to find Billy. She's going through all the security footage she can find, tracking Harlan's car and his face through the city from when he first took Stacey and her son.

"He takes Stacey straight back to the house," she says. "Did you say he's keeping her in a cage?" She shakes her head. "That's disgusting. Anyway, he must leave her there. I'm guessing that's when he called Anthony and told you to come to his in an hour. During that hour is when he's hiding Billy, wherever he took him. He goes half an hour one way and then half an hour back."

"And there's no chance of pinpointing where he took him?" Tom says.

Cindy shakes her head. "I'm still trying, but it's not looking like I will. For twenty minutes, he's in a black hole. He knew what he was doing, no doubt. He was avoiding security footage. He wasn't taking any chances. Wherever Billy is being held, he's within those twenty minutes of black hole."

"I assume that's going to be too much for us to search."

"Needle in a haystack," Cindy says. "What are you thinking? Are we just going to have to go through with what this Harlan piece of shit wants us to do, and then hope he sticks to his word?"

"I don't expect him to keep his word," Tom says, looking the building over all the while they talk. Checking all points of entry and exit. Watching the main entrance, and studying the people who come and go. A lot of people come and go. Other residents. They are Tom's biggest concern. A variable it's going to be very hard to plan and prepare for. "Right now, our best option for keeping Stacey and Billy unharmed is to do as he says, and to rip off the Mob."

"How do you feel about that?"

"Not great, but it's not like we have any other options. But at the same time, we need to be making alternate plans for what comes next."

"How do you mean?"

Tom turns back to face her. "For Harlan. Like I said, I don't trust him to keep his word. I don't think any of us do. With that in mind, we need to be prepared for when he inevitably breaks it. Our priority is saving Stacey and Billy. We need to figure out how to do that."

"You got any ideas yet?"

"Not yet." Tom turns back to the building. "Not fully. I've got the germ of an idea. I'm still working on it."

47

It's getting late. It's already after midnight. Anthony sits by the window and looks down at the street below, wondering when Tom and Cindy are going to come back. Wondering *if* they're going to come back tonight, or if they'll maintain surveillance at the building overnight.

Connor is in Billy's bed again, resting. Anthony gave him a couple of painkillers and helped him into the bedroom. He doesn't know if Connor's sleeping or not. He hasn't checked in on him. Jeffrey is on the sofa. He has the television on. Anthony knows his father is trying to keep him distracted, but Anthony isn't paying it any attention. He watches the road, wondering if each passing car is Tom.

"Anthony," Jeffrey says.

Anthony tears himself away from the window to face him.

"I know things must feel pretty dark right now," Jeffrey says, "but Tom *will* help Stacey and Billy. He knows what he's doing. He'll get them back."

Anthony shakes his head. He sits forward. "*I* will save

them," he says, unblinking, holding his father's gaze. "How many times do I have to say this before you all understand it?"

"Anthony, relax," Jeffrey says, raising his hands in a placating gesture. "I just don't want you to worry, that's all."

"Until I get them back, I'm going to be worried," Anthony says. He pushes himself to his feet and starts pacing the floor. He runs his hands back through his hair and laces his fingers atop his head. He stares out the window. He lets his arms drop and turns back to his father. "I'm not useless," he says.

"Son, I know you're not."

"I know what everyone believes, but it's not true. I'm not useless. I don't always need Tom to get me out of trouble. It's been three years since I saw him last, and I've been doing just fine since then."

Jeffrey doesn't say anything.

Anthony starts pacing again.

After a moment of silence, Jeffrey's phone begins to buzz. It's Tom. Jeffrey holds the phone up so Anthony can see who's calling him. "I'm going to put it on loudspeaker," he says.

Anthony shrugs.

"Tom, I'm here," Jeffrey says, answering. "I've got you so Anthony can hear."

"I need you to find me a rifle," Tom says.

"Tom, I've got weapons in my car."

"You don't have this weapon."

Jeffrey raises an eyebrow. "What is it?"

"A Springfield Armory 2020 Waypoint .308."

"That's very specific. You're right, I don't have it in my car. It needs to be that *exact* rifle?"

"I'd rather it was that rifle."

"Okay. Are you going to tell us what you want it for?"

"Not right now," Tom says. "Not over the phone."

Anthony frowns, curious.

"I'm not sure I'll be able to find one at this time of night," Jeffrey says. "I'm starting from zero here. I don't know anyone around here, but I'll make a start. I'm sure I'll be able to find the right kind of people to ask. I always do."

"Okay," Tom says. "As with everything right now, the sooner the better."

"Got it."

Tom hangs up.

"What the hell does he want with that?" Anthony says.

"You heard as much as I did," Jeffrey says. "I'm sure he has a reason, and I'm sure it's a good one."

"Something to do with the heist?"

"Anthony, I told you – you know as much as I do."

Anthony nods, forcing himself not to ask anything further. He wants to know what Tom is planning. It kills him not having more information. "Are you going now?"

Jeffrey nods. "Like I told your brother, I doubt I'm going to find one at this time of night, but I can at least make a start looking. He was right – sooner the better. And for what we're about to do, I don't think we need to wait until a gun store opens. I have a feeling we're not going to want any record of where we got this gun from." Jeffrey gets to his feet.

"You want me to come with?" Anthony says.

Jeffrey shakes his head. "You stay here. Hold down the fort. And if Connor's sleeping, we don't want him to wake up and wonder where everyone's gone."

"I know people in this city," Anthony says.

"I know you do, and that's all the more reason for you to *not* be the one asking them about this rifle."

Anthony accepts this.

Jeffrey squeezes his shoulder on his way past. He pauses and turns fully to his son. He pulls him in, hugging him tight. "We'll get them back," he says into his ear. He pats him on the back and lets go of him. "I don't know how long I'll be out. It'll be a while. Get in touch if anything comes up."

Jeffrey leaves, and Anthony goes and stands by the window, looking down. He's not tired. He knows he won't be able to sleep.

He goes into the bedroom he shares with Stacey and stands in the dark. He breathes in. The air here smells like her. He closes his eyes. He takes another deep breath, and then he has to leave the room. It's too overwhelming. It makes him sick with fear, imagining her down in Harlan's basement, locked up in a cage, likely still leashed and gagged.

He goes to Billy's room and knocks on the door. Connor is still awake. "Yo," he says. "Come on in."

This room smells like Billy, but it's mixed with the scent of Connor and not so overwhelming.

"What's up, man?" Connor says. "You look like hell."

"I feel like hell," Anthony says, taking a seat on the end of the bed. "You been awake this whole time?"

"Can't sleep."

"I know the feeling. You hear everything we said out there?"

Connor nods.

Anthony leans forward, resting his elbows on his thighs. He laces his fingers together. He doesn't say anything for a while. He stares into the corner of the room, where the baseboards meet. One of Billy's toys is lying near there. A super-hero action figure. Spider-Man. Anthony closes his eyes tight until he sees stars.

When he opens them, he doesn't turn back to Connor. He stares at the wall directly in front of him. "All my life," he says, "I've been expected to match up to Tom. My big brother. The Army veteran. The CIA Black Ops specialist. Tom fucking Rollins. He's been on the news, you know that? More than once now, probably. He saved some senator's life. I don't know what it had to do with Alejandra's death, but it was around the same time."

He trails off, pulling on his fingers and popping his joints. "All my life, when people have looked at me, they've wondered why I'm not more like *him*. But you know why? Because I don't *want* to be. That's not what I want. Some regimented, lonely life serving the country, or a government agency, or criss-crossing the country. Why the hell would I want anything like that? No one ever seems to be able to understand that I want *my* life. Something of my own. Yeah, maybe I've fucked it up along the way, but so what? Every-thing's not supposed to be perfect. It's supposed to be messy. You're supposed to make mistakes. I'm *allowed* to make mistakes, for Christ's sake."

Anthony falls silent again. Connor doesn't prompt him. He lets him speak.

Anthony takes deep breaths. He turns to Connor now. "Everyone wants me to be like *him*," he says. "Tom is bigger than me. He's stronger than me. Hell, I can admit that he's smarter than me. Tom is better than me in every way. Tom can be meaner than me. He's got a hell of a nasty streak in him – I've seen that firsthand, more than once. He can be nasty, but do you know what I can do better? You know what

I can be that Tom can't? I can be *nastier*. I can go further than he can. He has this stringent moral code that keeps him in check? Fine. I don't need to abide by that. *I* can be better than Tom. I can be better than him by being worse. All those lines he won't cross, *I* can. I *will*. All those things Tom can't be..." Anthony trails off. He sees how Connor is looking at him. His face is pinched, and his eyes are unblinking. It's almost as if he's scared. Anthony is undeterred. He sets his jaw, and he makes his point. "All those things that Tom can't be – *I'm* going to be them."

48

In the morning, Anthony is summoned to Ezra to check in. Connor is summoned too, but Anthony tells him to stay at the apartment.

Tom and Cindy didn't come back last night. Jeffrey is still out, presumably looking for the rifle Tom has asked for.

Anthony goes to The Cauldron. It's too early in the day for the door to be unlocked. Anthony doesn't have a key. He pounds on the door around the back. Ethan Hardy answers. He scowls at Anthony and lets him in. There are bruises on his neck, and Anthony wonders what has happened to him, and why he's staring at him like it's his fault.

There is music playing. It's too loud for Anthony to hear anyone speaking. Ezra sits in his chair and nods his head along. His head is hanging down. It's hard to tell if he knows Anthony has arrived. It's so loud it takes Anthony a moment to realize what he's listening to. Rude Boi, by King Louie. He stands and waits. Stewie Norton stands to the left of Ezra, leaning against the wall. He looks bruised up, too. He stares at Anthony just like Ethan does, like he had something to do with it.

The song ends, and Ezra raises his head, waving his arm for the music to be turned off. "All right," he says, looking Anthony up and down. He spots the cuts and bruises on his face. "What you got for me?"

"Nothing yet," Anthony says. "But I'm working on it. Soon."

"Uh-huh," Ezra says. He leans forward, running a thumb along the edge of his jaw, stopping when he reaches the bottom tip of his scar. He presses his thumb into it. "What happened to your face?"

"Nothing," Anthony says.

"Doesn't look like nothing."

Anthony doesn't respond.

Ezra leans back, holding his tongue down flat over his front teeth. "I'm sure it ain't none of my business. However, the lack of cash you're putting into my hand *is* my business. It's a lot of money you owe me, Anthony, and I'm yet to see penny one."

Again, Anthony has nothing to say to this.

Ezra drums his fingertips together. "I heard some shit went down with the Skulls a couple of nights ago," he says. "That you?"

"No," Anthony says. He's not going to admit to such a failure.

"I sure hope not. Where's Connor right now?"

"He's busy. We're always working, Ezra. Always trying to get your money."

"Uh-huh. He's not hurt?"

"No. Why would he be?"

"Why are you? I mean, your face?"

"What's up with the two of them?" Anthony points at Stewie and Ethan. "They look worse than I do."

"Well, Anthony, interestingly enough, they were watching *your* house, and someone who was paying a lot of attention to it got the drop on them."

Anthony thinks of Tom. He plays it dumb. "What are you talking about? Who was at my house?"

"Looked like you," Stewie says.

"Well, it wasn't me."

"I know that," Stewie says, sneering.

Ezra waves a hand in the air to silence them both. "Here's the thing, Anthony. Right now, I've got a lot of problems, and they're all revolving around you. Some guy who looks like you beat up two of my men, who were just doing their job and making sure you're not trying to skip out on us. Maybe that's just a coincidence, but maybe it ain't. And then I hear about a raid going wrong in rival territory – Skulls territory, no fucking less – and maybe that has nothing to do with you, but maybe it does. And if it does, maybe the Skulls find that out for themselves. And then I've got a fucking war on my hands. You understand what I'm saying, Anthony?"

"I understand what you're saying, but I already told you – none of this has anything to do with me."

"Maybe if the Skulls bullshit *did* have something to do with you, I'd feel better thinking you were actually trying to get me my fucking money."

"I'm working on getting you your money," Anthony says, lying through his teeth. All he can think about right now is Stacey and Billy – and Harlan. Fucking Harlan. But he needs to keep Ezra off his back. Ezra and the Street Kings are a problem for another day. Right now, he needs to buy himself some time. "And I'm working on it in a way that isn't going to drag us into a war with another gang. Connor's out there right now, chasing down leads, and once I'm done here, I'm gonna get right back out there with him."

"Two of you are really hoping for some last-minute heroics, huh?" Ezra says.

"Nothing last minute about it. We've still got time."

"That what you think? Less and less every day."

Anthony is aware of this. It feels like time is against him. It feels like the whole damn world is against him. "You need me for anything else?"

Ezra strokes his scar. "I think you need some encouragement, Anthony," he says. "And a reminder – a reminder for you and Connor – of how little time you've got left. And a reminder of what's waiting for you when that time's up."

Ezra nods, and Stewie and Ethan move in. They grab either side of Anthony and drag him over to a table.

"Damn it, what are you doing?" Anthony says. He looks back at Ezra over his shoulder. Ezra is getting to his feet and slowly following them over. "I ain't got time for this!"

"Oh, I know that, Anthony," Ezra says. "Like I said, I'm gonna give you a reminder."

There's a toolbox on the ground by the table. Anthony feels his blood run cold. Ezra leans over and reaches into the box. He pulls out a ball-peen hammer. He flips it so it does a somersault in the air, then catches it by its wooden handle. "Remind me," he says. "You're right-handed, ain't you?"

Anthony swallows. "Ezra, come on, please don't do this –"

"Wish I didn't have to," Ezra says, flipping the hammer and catching it again. "He didn't answer, boys, but I'm pretty sure he's right-handed."

Stewie is on Anthony's left. He grips his left arm tight

and forces his hand down flat, splaying his fingers. Anthony strains his arm, trying to pull back, but Ethan hits him in the kidneys until he's compliant.

"I don't wanna slow you down too much," Ezra says. "But you *do* need to be taught a lesson in time management." He reaches across the table with his free hand and presses weight down on Anthony's left wrist, helping Stewie to hold the hand into place. "Don't worry," Ezra says, their faces close. "It's not going to be one of the important ones." He brings the hammer down, its heavy head smashing into Anthony's left pinky.

Anthony screams. His finger feels like it has burst, and he can't bring himself to look at it. Ezra is laughing. Anthony feels like he might throw up. The finger is on fire. Stewie and Ethan let go of him.

"You should go and get that set," Ezra says. "If you ain't careful, it's gonna heal funny."

Anthony forces himself to look. The pinky is mangled at the joint, twisted and pointing the wrong way. The skin has burst, though not as badly as he feared. Blood has splashed onto the table.

"Get out of here, Anthony," Ezra says, and Stewie gives him a shove. "You got your reminder. Don't you forget it."

Anthony flees The Cauldron, taking the back door out again and clutching his bleeding and broken finger to his chest. It throbs. He squeezes his palm below the finger, hoping this will ease the pain, but it doesn't. Outside, he hears the music start up again. He presses his back up against the wall beside the door. His chest feels tight. He struggles for breath. The Street Kings. Ezra. Harlan. The Mob. Stacey and Billy. It's all too much. It's all weighing him down.

He closes his eyes and takes deep breaths. Steels himself as best he can. The pain makes it hard to think straight. He remembers what he told Connor last night. He has to be better. To *do* better, even if he has to do worse to accomplish that. He has to find a way. He looks back at The Cauldron. He pictures the men inside. They'll pay for this. They'll pay for what they've done to him. He needs to figure out how to deal with them. He needs a plan. He needs something that will make all of his problems go away.

49

After the first full day, after his successful hunt for the rifle Tom requested, Jeffrey met Tom and Cindy outside the Mob building. He's watched it with them. Anthony has been left in the apartment with Connor. It's no doubt driving him crazy, Tom is sure. How Anthony feels isn't important. Getting the job done, getting Stacey and Billy back safely, is what's important.

While watching, Tom has been thinking. Planning. Harlan is going to double-cross them, he's certain of this. They need to be prepared for its inevitability.

They return to the apartment at the end of the second day. Anthony is on his feet, pacing the floor. Connor is on the sofa. He forces himself to sit up as they enter. Anthony stops pacing and looks at the three of them, waiting. He looks like he's about to burst. "*Well?*" he says. Tom spots his left hand, his pinky and ring fingers bound together and heavily bandaged. Anthony tries to keep it hidden.

"What happened to your hand?" Tom says.

"It doesn't matter," Anthony says.

"Jesus," Jeffrey says. "It *looks* like it matters."

"Ezra broke it," Connor says, and Anthony shoots him a look. Connor shrugs, like he doesn't understand why it should be a secret.

"What the hell did he do?" Jeffrey says.

Anthony sighs. "He hit it with a hammer. Look, let's not get into it right now. We need to think about Stacey and Billy. What have you all been doing?"

"We've been watching," Jeffrey says, rolling his neck to work out a kink, but staring at Anthony's hand with concern while he does so. They've taken turns sleeping in the back of the car, always two of them on watch. When not resting, Cindy was usually on her laptop, getting into the cameras inside the building, inside the apartment, as well as the cameras outside in the surrounding area. Jeffrey and Tom kept notes on who came and who went. Jotted down their timing. They did the same for the public transport that passed by, too – the trains on the El pulling into the nearby station, as well as the ones pulling out of it in the opposite direction, and the buses on the road below stopping just down the block. They've studied and memorized these schedules, just in case. Every detail could prove important.

"*And?*" Anthony says. "I've been sitting in this apartment with my thumb up my ass. You need to give me more information than that. This is taking too long."

"We were never going to rush into anything," Tom says. "If we rushed straight in, we'd end up dead, and then Stacey and Billy are as good as dead, too. We need to be careful, always. Harlan said we have three days, and we've needed to use that."

"Those three days are almost up," Anthony says. "And he said three days for the supplies he left with Billy – who knows if that was accurate? Billy is a child. Harlan said it himself. He doesn't know if Billy will ration out what he's left him. We need to make it sooner than later. We need to get them back, both of them."

"That's why we move in tomorrow," Tom says.

Anthony opens his mouth as if Tom has said something contrary, and then stops. "Tomorrow?" he says.

Jeffrey steps forward. "That's right," he says. "But before we do that, we need to talk. We have a plan."

"I'd better figure into that plan," Anthony says. "Because I made it clear I'm not sitting on the sidelines."

"We know that," Jeffrey says. "You're in this plan."

"But you need to stick to it," Cindy says. "No deviations. No complaints. No bullshit."

Anthony looks at her and then at Tom. Tom hasn't said anything. This is by design. Tom knows Anthony is more likely to listen to anyone other than him. For Anthony to understand the severity of what they're doing, and what they need to do, it needs to come from someone other than his brother.

Anthony turns back to Jeffrey. "All right," he says, intrigued. "I'm listening."

"To the letter, Anthony," Jeffrey says. "This goes down *exactly* how we've planned it. We've tried to prepare for every outcome. We need to keep our margins of error low, and that means you do exactly as we say."

Anthony opens his mouth, but stops. Closes it. Tom wonders if he was going to say something argumentative. Accuse them of thinking he can't follow simple instructions.

When he speaks, he's not belligerent. He looks the three of them over, then glances over his shoulder to Connor, who's watching them all intently. Anthony turns back to them and nods. "All right," he says. "Tell me this plan."

50

It's the next morning. The morning of the heist. Anthony has barely slept. He lay in the bed he usually shares with Stacey and stared at the ceiling. He could smell her on the sheets and in the air. He's breathed her scent deep all through the night. She's on his mind. She and Billy. He swallowed hard and tried not to be sick and waited for the sun to come up.

Connor slept in Billy's room again. Tom, Cindy, and Jeffrey slept in the living room. Cindy had the sofa. Tom and Jeffrey were on the floor. Anthony doesn't know how they slept. Wonders if they rested well, or if they struggled, as he did. He heard them moving around at some points. Going into the kitchen for a drink. Going to the bathroom. Standing by the window, perhaps, though he can't be sure of this latter.

Anthony sits on the edge of the bed with his head in his hands. Next door, he can hear the others moving around. Getting ready. He needs to call Harlan. To let him know they're going in soon. Tom chose midday. Harlan's intel and their own surveillance told them that Matt Rossi and Al Bruno usually go out at eleven. Cindy tracked them via security footage. They head to an accounting office with Matt's name above the door. It's not too far away from the apartment building. The amount of time they stay there is variable, but it at least means they'll be gone a couple of hours. Two fewer bodies in the apartment to worry about. The traffic is busier around that time, too. People on their lunch breaks. The traffic provides them more cover for their escape. A stream of vehicles they can disappear into.

Harlan answers the phone. "Anthony!" he says. "I was beginning to wonder when I would hear from you. It's getting to be that time."

Anthony takes a deep breath. "That's what I'm calling for."

"Is today the day?"

"Yeah," Anthony says. He looks down at his left hand, at his broken finger. The bandaging is tight. He did it himself. He bends his other fingers around it. "I wanna talk to Stacey."

"You can talk to her very soon. Face-to-face."

"I want to talk to her now."

There's a pause. Harlan is thinking about it. "All right," he says. "Since you can't be patient. Bear with me, buddy." Anthony can hear him moving, heading through the house and down into the basement. "She's been a wonderful house guest, Anthony. She's been very well behaved. Is she so quiet at home? I've never had to gag her. She's understood what's happening here. I've been very impressed."

Anthony doesn't say anything.

"All right, here we are," Harlan says. He hands the phone

over. Anthony can hear him telling Stacey who it is on the other end.

"Anthony?" she says warily, like she's cautious of this being a cruel trick. Her voice is croaky, parched.

"It's me," Anthony says. "How are you doing? Is he feeding you? You sound thirsty."

"Anthony, where's Billy?" she says.

"I'm working on it, baby, I'm working on it," Anthony says, feeling a pain in his chest. "You'll have him back soon, okay? Real soon. Just a few more hours, that's all. End of today, max."

Harlan comes back on the line. "All right, you've spoken to her," he says. "I'm sure you said some very reassuring things, but now it's time for us to talk business."

"She sounds thirsty," Anthony says. "Are you giving her water? Are you feeding her?"

"That's on her," Harlan says. "I've been taking care of her, Anthony. What kind of host do you think I am? Whether she eats and drinks what I give her, well, that's up to her."

Anthony grits his teeth. It doesn't sound like Harlan has started moving again. He's still down in the basement with Stacey.

"When's it happening?" Harlan says.

"Soon."

"I want a time."

Anthony checks the time on his phone. "Three hours. Midday."

"I want plugged in before then."

"I figured you would."

"Before you're in the car. An hour before."

"Got it."

"And remember, Anthony – you won't be able to hear

me, but I can hear all of you. I'll be watching and listening to every single thing you all say and do, and if I see or hear anything I don't like, I'll kill them. Have you got that? I'll kill Stacey and Billy."

Anthony swallows. "I know that."

"Good. Call me when you're hooking yourselves up. I want to make sure everything's clear and good to go."

"Okay."

"This is exciting, Anthony! Try to sound more pleased! You're going to get your little family back very soon. Ah, I get it. I get the tone. The disappointment. It's because you're never going to see me again, isn't it? You're going to miss me. I'm moved, Anthony, I really am. I'd like to say we'll keep in touch, but I'm afraid I'm going to disappear completely. You really will never see me again. Ah, well. We had our time. It's been emotional. Oh, but of course – the Street Kings! I suppose you'll still have to deal with them, won't you? And no doubt the time's running out on paying Ezra back, I suppose. Such a shame."

"I just want Stacey and Billy back," Anthony says. "Nothing else matters."

Harlan laughs. "Did you hear that, Stacey? It's really very sweet. I'll tell you later. And Anthony, I'll see *you* later. I'll see all of you later." Harlan hangs up.

Anthony realizes his heart is hammering. He presses a hand to the wall and breathes deep, calming himself. Today is a big day. In so many ways. In more ways than the people in this apartment even realize.

He gets to his feet and dresses. All black. He goes into the living room. Tom and Jeffrey are all in black, too. The bag containing the cameras and earpieces Harlan gave them is on a counter in the kitchen. They're micro cameras, and they'll be clipped onto the front of everyone's shirts, just below their collars. The microphones will be right beside them. They'll be practically invisible against their dark clothing. Tom and Jeffrey turn to Anthony. Cindy is behind them, sitting on the sofa, tapping at her laptop. She's all in black, but Anthony has never seen her in anything else.

"You ready?" Jeffrey says.

Anthony nods.

"You've spoken to Harlan?" Tom says.

"Yeah. He wants us hooked up an hour before we leave."

Tom checks the time. "Then I'll go and park the car and come back. That should take us up to then."

Tom leaves the apartment. Anthony watches him go. Once again, he finds himself needing to rely on his older brother. He doesn't like it, but it's necessary.

It's always fucking necessary.

"I'm just gonna check in with Connor," Anthony says.

Jeffrey nods. Cindy doesn't look up.

Anthony slips into Billy's room. Connor is awake. He's sitting up in the bed. Anthony told him not to leave the room this morning. To stay here until after the rest of them have left. Connor is staying behind because of his injury.

"After I'm gone, we can't be in touch," Anthony says.

Connor nods. He understands.

"Do you know what you're doing? You have the timings?"

"I know what I'm doing," Connor says. "It's all I'm thinking about." He forces a smile, but it's brief. He looks at Anthony, and it's the most serious Anthony has ever seen him. "Are you sure about this?"

"I'm sure," Anthony says.

"It's going to be dangerous. It's going to make today more dangerous than it already is."

"I know that."

The muscles in Connor's cheeks twitch. He's worried. Anthony can't tell him not to worry. He just needs him to do what he's been told.

Connor reaches down the side of the bed. "Take this," he says. It's the grenade. He sees how Anthony looks at it. "It might come in handy."

"How'd you get this back?" Anthony says.

"I found where your brother hid it."

"Where'd he hide it?"

"In his backpack."

Anthony raises his eyebrows. "He hasn't noticed you went through his stuff?"

"He's been gone most of the time since then. I don't think *he's* been through his stuff."

"He won't be happy if he realizes."

Connor waves his arm, pushing the grenade toward him. "Just take it. I don't care if he's not happy. It might not matter later."

Anthony takes it. He hides it, knowing he can't let Jeffrey and Cindy see it. It will raise questions. "Just keep an eye on the time," Anthony says. "And keep an eye on the news, too, just in case. Stay in here until we're gone. I don't want Tom to see you. He won't get anything out of me, but he might see through you. He has a knack for that."

Connor nods. He doesn't try to protest. He trusts Anthony. "Be careful out there."

They look at each other for a long time. They both know what they need to do. They both understand what they're about to do, and what it means. What it means for their futures. What it could mean for their lives. Finally, Anthony leaves the room and prepares for what is coming next.

51

"I'm gonna start carrying these around in my pocket," Cindy says, handing out earpieces of their own for them to keep in touch. "Because every time I see you, Tom, I need to buy new ones."

They're already hooked up to Harlan's equipment. They did that first, with him on the line, so he couldn't complain if they'd affixed their own gear first.

Tom got back ten minutes before they called Harlan. He parked Jeffrey's car. It's around the corner from the Mob apartment, a couple of blocks away and well out of view. It's not on their route to the building, Tom has made sure of this in case Harlan knows what Jeffrey's vehicle is, in case he recognizes its make and model and plates. They don't want to pick it up on the cameras as they make their way there. They don't want Harlan to spot it and become suspicious.

"Okay," Anthony says, to Harlan on the phone. "We're wearing your cameras and your microphones. You satisfied?"

Harlan is on loudspeaker. He wanted everyone to be able to hear him. He pauses a moment, no doubt examining his laptop and all of their individual cameras. He's already made each of them speak into their microphones to make sure he can hear them.

"Yeah," Harlan says finally. "I'm satisfied. Remember, I see *any*thing I don't like, the mother and the kid are dead. I'm not fucking around. Bring me my fucking money." He hangs up.

Tom, Cindy, Jeffrey, and Anthony are standing around the kitchen table, looking down at the phone. They exchange glances. Tom and Jeffrey have balaclavas with them, ready for when they move into the apartment. They have their own cameras, too, so Cindy can see them when they're inside. They're taking Tom's car to the building. They have weapons in the trunk. They transferred them from Jeffrey's car. Assault rifles that he'd brought along, all the way from his commune to Tom and Hayley's house in Hopper Creek and up to Chicago, in case anything was going down with Anthony and he needed to get heavy. Tom also carries his Beretta and his KA-BAR. Jeffrey and Anthony both have Glocks. Cindy is unarmed.

"You heard the man," Tom says, knowing that Harlan is watching, that he's listening. "Let's go."

52

They get to the apartment building half an hour before midday. Tom parks in what has become his regular spot over the road. They watch the building. Nothing is out of place. It looks how it always does. Gradually, the traffic begins to pick up. There's a café nearby, and the seats outside are filling. Through the glass, they look busy at the counter with orders.

Tom and Jeffrey are in the front of the car. Anthony and Cindy are in the back. They'll be staying behind while Tom and Jeffrey go inside. Cindy's on her laptop. "I'm in," she says. She's hacked into the security cameras inside the building. When the time comes, she'll kill the feed.

"Are they gone?" Tom says.

"Matt and Al are gone," she says. "The security in there are sitting around in their surveillance room. One of them has his coat on already."

Tom looks down the block, waiting for the replacement security to arrive. Eventually, Tom spots two faces he recognizes. Leo DeLuca and Peter Fanelli. They approach the building together. Wordlessly, Tom and Jeffrey get out of the car and go to the trunk. There's a sport bag inside. It contains a couple of M4s, plastic ties, balaclavas, and some plastic explosive. Tom slings it over his shoulder.

They've tested their microphones and speakers already, but Tom checks them again. "You hear me?"

"Loud and clear," Cindy says.

"Same here," Anthony says.

"Testing," Jeffrey says.

"We got you," Cindy says.

Tom and Jeffrey cross the road and follow Leo and Peter into the lobby of the building. They're heading for the elevator. Peter is laughing about something Leo has said. Tom scans the lobby. It's clear.

Jeffrey pulls out his Glock. Tom drops the bag and moves up on Peter on the right while Jeffrey takes Leo on the left. Jeffrey strikes Leo hard across the back of the skull with the handle of his Glock. Leo stumbles forward, caught by surprise, but Jeffrey clasps him by a shoulder and forces him down to his knees, hitting him again and again until he's limp.

While his father is doing this, Tom hooks Peter's right arm behind his back and holds onto his skull, slamming his forehead into the wall next to the elevator. Once he's stunned, Tom spins him around and punches him in the corner of his jaw, knocking him out cold.

"Tom, shit, look behind you," Cindy says into his ear.

Tom wheels around, expecting an ambush, but that isn't what he finds. Instead, he sees a young lady stepping into the lobby from the street. Her eyes go wide, taking in the sight before her. She starts to blink, working out what has happened, even if it doesn't make sense to her.

"Tom, what are you doing?" Anthony says. "Dad? Do something! Deal with her, for Christ's sake!"

They're not going to do anything like that. She's not part of the Mob. She's a civilian. This was always a risk in an apartment building like this. The biggest risk Tom has been aware of from the get-go. The one thing they couldn't prepare for, or take any real steps to prevent, was people coming and going to and from their homes.

She turns and she runs.

"*Shit!*" Anthony says.

"Anthony, calm down," Tom says. "Harlan, I know you're listening. This isn't anything to worry about. We have plenty of time. No one needs to get themselves worked up or carried away. We're continuing as planned." He looks at his father, and together they reach down and grab Leo and Peter under their armpits. They drag them through the lobby to the door leading to the boiler room. They break the door open and stash the men inside. They take plastic ties from the bag and bind their wrists. Tom nods toward the stairwell, and he and his father head up. They're not taking the elevator. Too much risk of being ambushed on the other side. With the stairs, they can see their way ahead. Tom wasn't sure Jeffrey could manage this part of it, but Jeffrey maintained he could. Already, he can hear his father breathing hard, pressing his shoulder into the wall and using it for support. He doesn't slow, though. He pushes himself. Tom doesn't slow for him. Doesn't hold back. Jeffrey will catch up.

Out in the car, Tom imagines Cindy is calming Anthony down, reminding him that Harlan can hear everything they say and do, and they don't want to alarm him by acting like they're losing control.

Tom wonders about the lady who walked in on them.

She probably lives in the building or else was visiting someone who does. What else does she know about the building? Does she know about the Mob presence? Does she know who Leo DeLuca and Peter Fanelli are? If she does, she could know others. She could get in contact with Matt or Al, or anyone else who works in the apartment or for the Mob. She could let them know something is happening. If there's a million dollars in the apartment safe, as Harlan says there is, they'll no doubt come running.

Whatever the lady does next, it's out of their hands. Tom pushes on, Jeffrey only a few paces behind him. As they near the twelfth floor, Tom takes their balaclavas from the bag and hands one to his father. He and Jeffrey pull them down over their heads, covering their faces. In and out. No one needs to get seriously hurt. They get in and out and continue on their way, and without knowledge of their faces, the Mob never knows who is to blame.

Next, Tom pulls out the M4s. They pause a moment, checking them over, though they already did this before they packed them into the sport bag. They're not taking any chances. They hold them ready and continue on their way.

53

Harlan sits in the basement with Stacey. He's popped up a folding table and positioned the laptop so she can see the screen from her cage.

"Isn't this fun?" he says. "You can see how your fate and your son's play out in real time."

Stacey swallows. Her hair lies lank and clings to the side of her face. She looks too scared to watch the screen, but too terrified to turn away.

"Believe me, I'm rooting for you," Harlan says. He watches the screen intently. He knows how she feels, but he doesn't let it show. He has almost as much to lose as she does if this goes wrong.

Next to the laptop is his Luger. He wants her to see this, too. Wants her to know that if it all goes to hell, he'll shoot her instantly.

He doesn't want it to come to that. He wants Tom and Anthony and the rest to get the money and to get out. Right now, he's calm. His breathing and heart rate are all even. Nothing has spooked him. It looks to be proceeding according to the plan they filled him in on this morning while they hooked his equipment up to themselves – or at least *mostly* according to plan. He could hear the worry in their voices as the woman walked in off the street and saw them in the lobby, and they begged him not to overreact.

Harlan wasn't anywhere close to overreacting. He's prepared for small things to go awry. It's unlikely the heist will happen *exactly* as planned. All that matters to him is that he gets the money. How that happens is up to the people in the field. Harlan won't start panicking unless they can't get the money. Or if they get the money and they lose it. Or if they try to pull a fast one. *That's* when he'll start shooting.

Harlan has to admit, he enjoyed watching Leo get pistol-whipped. He's wanted to beat down the miserable mother-fucker himself on more than one occasion. Seeing the back of his skull split open as he was beaten unconscious, that was satisfying. Harlan is thinking he might keep that footage to watch again at later dates. Hell, provided this all goes well, he might watch the whole thing.

He glances at Stacey. "Are you having as good a time as I am?"

She doesn't answer him. She stares at the screen.

54

Cindy watches the progress on her laptop. Beside her, Anthony keeps an eye on the surrounding area. They both watched the woman who fled from the lobby. Watched her run from view down the block, pulling out her phone as she went.

On the screen, Cindy can see as Tom and Jeffrey reach the twelfth floor. "I'm ready to kill the feed," she says. "Just give the word."

"What's this?" Anthony says, straightening.

A Mercedes screeches to a halt in front of the building, and two men jump out. They both look familiar to Cindy. She's studied their faces in the images she found online and on previous days via the cameras she's hacked into in the apartment. Matt Rossi and Al Bruno. They're running into the building. Al Bruno is carrying a shotgun. "Shit, Tom, listen – Matt and Al are here, and they're armed and in a rush. Looks like the lady knew them and she's called them, and they got here *fast* – if they weren't already nearby." She checks the feed in the apartment. She can see the two guards leaping to their feet. "They've called ahead – the guards are ready for you. Repeat, the guards are ready for you."

Tom's voice is calm. "We stick to the plan," he says. "Kill the feed."

55

Tom and Jeffrey leave the stairwell and move in on the apartment. One of the guards is coming to the door, getting ready for them. Cindy is already telling them where he is, step by step. Tom raises the M4 and, as the guard pokes his head out the door, slams the stock of the rifle into the center of his face, knocking him down. He's not unconscious, but he is dazed. Tom grabs him and pulls him out the rest of the way, dumps him in the hall and leaves him for Jeffrey to finish subduing. Tom continues into the apartment.

"Next one's in the guard room," Cindy says. "He's on the phone – he's gotta be calling in reinforcements. The room is down the hall, second on the right. He's armed, but he's right behind the door, and it's not locked. Hit it hard enough, you're gonna knock him down."

Tom does as she says, throwing his weight into the door and into the man beyond it. The guard hits the ground, and his phone goes skittering. Tom keeps his feet. He stomps the fallen guard in the face, cracking the back of his head on the ground. He takes the handgun from him and dismantles it, then shatters the dropped phone with the heel of his boot.

Jeffrey drags the other guard into the room. They tie the two of them up, back-to-back on the floor with the plastic ties, and leave them where they are. On the way out, Tom spots the bank of screens on the walls and sees how they're all blank.

They've memorized the route through the apartment from Harlan's pictures and from Cindy's hacking of the security. They go to Matt's office and to the painting of a ship on stormy waters on the wall behind his desk. From Harlan's picture, they know the make and model of the safe. They know that the fastest way to get it open is to blow it. Tom takes the plastic explosive from the bag and molds it into place around the lock. Jeffrey stands guard by the door, M4 raised and pointing down the hall.

"You're looking good," Cindy says. "All clear for now. Matt and Al are in the elevator."

Tom leaves the office, and he and Jeffrey take cover behind the walls on either side of the door. The plastic explodes. Tom heads back into the room, and Jeffrey resumes his guard. The safe's door is hanging off the hinges. Tom transfers the money from the safe into the sport bag. He doesn't bother counting it. Harlan can see well enough that he's packing everything that's inside. Tom guesses it *is* a million, though. There's certainly plenty of it. When he has it all, he slings the bag onto his back. Jeffrey leads the way. He covers the hall. Tom steps out, heading for the stairwell again.

They hear the elevator door open. Matt Rossi and Al Bruno step out. They're hurrying, but they pause as they look down the hallway, seeing Tom and Jeffrey with their rifles and their masks.

Al Bruno doesn't hesitate. He's carrying the shotgun Cindy warned them about. A Remington Model 870. He opens fire.

Tom grabs his father and pulls him into the stairwell. The shotgun blows chunks out of the wall. It blasts a hole in the door as father and son start running down the stairwell.

56

"What the hell...?" Anthony says, sitting up.

Cindy raises her face from her laptop and checks the area. A black van pulls to a stop near the front of the building. "The van?" she says. "What about it? What do you see?"

"I think I recognized the driver," Anthony says.

The back doors and side door of the van open, and half a dozen men get out. Cindy can see that they're armed. Some of them have handguns tucked down the backs of their jeans, covered with their shirts, but some have assault rifles that they keep concealed between their bodies. Someone is at the back of the van, leaning in to work at something, and Cindy has a feeling there is more weaponry back there.

Anthony lowers himself in the seat. "That's Ezra," he says, nodding towards one of the men standing at the rear of the others, arching his back to look up the front of the building.

"Ezra?" Cindy says. "Who broke your finger? This is your gang?"

"It's the South Side Street Kings," Anthony says, nodding. He chews his lip, staying low.

"What are they doing here?"

"How the hell should I know?" Anthony says.

A couple of the Street Kings move down the side of the building. Cindy accesses cameras near to where they've gone. They're covering the rear exit.

"*Shit*," Anthony says, looking the area over. He ducks down lower when Ezra glances his way. "Tell Tom," he says. "They need to know what's happening out here."

57

Cindy tells Tom and Jeffrey about the Street Kings' arrival outside. Tom and Jeffrey continue to descend the stairwell. They don't have any other option. Al Bruno is in pursuit. His shotgun can carry between three and seven rounds, and so far he's only fired it twice. Tom imagines, from the fact he hasn't heard him reload it, that it likely holds the higher end of that number. Al hasn't fired at them again. He's waiting for a clearer shot. They can hear his heavy footsteps pounding down behind them.

There's only a few more levels to go before they reach the ground floor. Tom's mind races. Their exits are covered. If the Street Kings are here, there's more than likely going to be trouble. There's a chance they're going to have to leave the building shooting.

Tom thinks about the Street Kings, wondering what they're doing here. How do they know about the building? Do they know what's happening in here? About the heist?

Tom and Cindy weren't being followed while they observed the building. Tom made sure of that. He circled the block on foot to check. There was no one watching them.

"Shit, Tom, we've got more bad news," Cindy says. "More Mob guys have just turned up – a couple of full carloads of them. They got here *fast*."

"What's happening?" Tom says.

"Nothing yet," she says. "They're eyeing the Street Kings, and the Street Kings are eyeing them right back. I can see guns though, Tom. There's a lot of firepower out here."

"Do you see an alternate way out for us?" Tom checks, but he knows it's unlikely. He's studied this building closely the last few days.

"No, I don't, but listen," she says. Tom can hear her moving. "I'm going to turn the car around and pull up in front of the building, like I haven't noticed them and like I'm waiting to pick someone up. You just keep coming down. When you get here, dive in the back. Anthony's coming up front with me, so you're gonna have space. Just dive in the back, and I'll start driving. At the sight of you, the Mob and the Street Kings might start shooting, but I think they'll get too distracted with each other to be able to catch up to us. Listen, it's not much of a plan, but it's the only one we've got right now."

"We're not far," Tom says. Beside him, he can hear his father breathing hard, sounding like he might keel over, but Jeffrey keeps on pushing. He doesn't falter. He doesn't complain. No doubt his adrenalin is forcing him on right now.

Behind, he can hear Al Bruno, still in pursuit. He's not gaining. They're faster than he is.

"We've got one floor to go," Tom says.

"We're in position," Cindy says. "I'm gonna throw open the back door as soon as I see you."

Tom jumps to clear the last few steps, the bag of money bouncing against him. He holds the door open for his father. Jeffrey rushes into the lobby, and Tom is right behind him. He pulls the bag's strap tight. He can't lose the money.

They don't slow. They don't hesitate. They burst out onto the street. There's a pause as both sides – the Mob on their right, and the Street Kings on their left – watch them go, taking a moment to realize who they are, and then the gunfire erupts from both sides.

Jeffrey and Tom dive into the backseat of the car. Tom drags the door shut behind him. Cindy hits the accelerator. They're in the middle of the shoot-out. The rear window shatters. Glass showers down over Tom and Jeffrey. The windshield cracks. The window above Tom caves inward, and a bullet tears a chunk out of the driver's seat headrest.

They're caught in the crossfire.

Bullets thud into the side of the car. Tires burst. Cindy slams her foot down on the accelerator and gets them out from in the middle of it. She doesn't get them far. The car hits a support strut of the El, but they're not going fast enough to do any real damage.

Anthony is in a ball in the passenger seat, covering himself with his arms. He was already ducking before the shooting started, to avoid being seen by the Street Kings. Cindy is screaming. A piece of broken glass cuts her cheek. Tom grabs her and drags her into the back, covering her with his body. Not all of the gunfire is aimed at the car. The Mob and the Street Kings are concentrating most of their fire on each other, but the occasional shot comes their way, just to make sure they can't go anywhere.

"We're pinned," Jeffrey says, looking at Tom as bullets whizz through the air above them and glass sprinkles down over them. He shakes his head. "They've got us pinned."

58

Harlan stands up straight. They haven't lost the money, but he's starting to panic now.

He paces the floor, a hand over his mouth. "Oh, fuck," he says. "*Fuck!*" He kicks the side of Stacey's cage, and she whimpers, but she's still cuffed to it, and she can't back away from him.

Her eyes never leave the laptop, though. She stares, scared of what might happen next.

Pacing is no good. It doesn't help. Harlan sits back down. He stares at the screen, leaning closer to it, blocking Stacey's view. "Come on, you sons of bitches," he says, wiping sweat from his top lip with the back of his hand and willing them to do something, *anything*, to somehow get themselves free of their predicament. "Get out of there. *Come on.*"

59

L ying low, looking up through the shattered rear window, Tom sees a train approaching. It's going slow, approaching the station. Tom checks the time, remembers the schedule. The train will pull into the station and be there for five minutes. At the speed it's going now, on its approach, they have about seven minutes. Tom formulates an escape plan. He doesn't think the train will be disrupted by the shoot-out below. They won't be able to see or hear it from up there.

Tom is still wearing the balaclava. He notices Jeffrey has pulled his off. Tom does the same. There's no point wearing it now. They're going to have to fight their way out, and people are going to die. Cindy and Anthony were maskless already. Providing they all get out, Cindy can wipe the security footage in the area, clear their faces from it.

Blood runs down his face from where shards of glass have cut through the balaclava's fabric. He wipes some from his brow to make sure it doesn't get into his eyes. Cindy is still beneath him, covered. There's glass in her hair. He feels her flinching. He notices she's clutching her laptop to her chest. She probably doesn't realize she's doing this.

Jeffrey is to his side. Jeffrey and Tom lock eyes. The look in his eyes, on his face, is clear – he thinks they're going to die. He's holding Tom's arm. He squeezes it.

In the front, Anthony is covering his head and forcing himself down as low as he can get.

Tom raises his head a little. A new Mob car has arrived. Slowly, it approaches them, the windows down on the passenger side. On the driver's side, the rear passenger is leaning out, firing on the Street Kings. Tom notices how the shooting on their own car eases. This new arrival has diverted some of it.

The passengers are coming for the money. They won't ask for it nicely. They're going to kill them all before they take it.

"Listen to me," Tom says to the team while there's a lull enough in the crossfire for him to be heard. He shrugs the bag of money off his back and passes it to Jeffrey. "Get to the train station! Get on the train! I'll hold them off and catch up with you. Either on the train or somewhere down the line, we'll meet back up."

Anthony raises his head. They lock eyes. Neither of them nods, they don't say anything – they can't, not with Harlan watching – but Anthony understands. He knows what to do.

Anthony reaches back and pulls something out. "I have this," he says.

He hands over the M67. The grenade. Tom doesn't ask why he has it. There's no time, and it doesn't matter now. He takes it. The approaching Mob car is almost upon them. Tom pulls the pin and holds down the lever. "Get ready to run," he says.

Tom gets off Cindy. She looks up at him, scared for him. Jeffrey slings the bag of money onto his back. He takes off the M4 and leaves it for Tom, placing it between them. He takes out his Glock and nods at his son.

Everyone stays low. Tom can see the roof of the Mob car. He can hear the fierce firefight between the Mob and the Street Kings in front of the apartment building. He wonders, briefly, where Al Bruno is. If he was taken out in the cross-fire, as they almost were.

The Mob car pulls alongside them. Tom sits up. He releases the lever and throws the grenade into the back of the car, through the open rear window. The mobsters begin to panic, scrabbling for the grenade.

"*Go!*"

Anthony, Cindy, and Jeffrey get out of the car on the other side. Tom is right behind them. He slings Jeffrey's M4 onto his back and raises his own.

The grenade explodes in the Mob car.

The sound draws the attention of the Mob and Street Kings alike. They turn toward the sound, surprised by it. There's a momentary lull in the firefight.

Tom opens fire on the Mob. They're closest to Jeffrey, Cindy, and Anthony's escape route. He mows them down and gets their attention, draws their fire. He ducks for cover behind the incapacitated Mob car. Overhead, the train is gone. It has pulled into the station. Tom needs to remain aware of the time.

He notices, as he fires, that the streets have cleared of civilians. A couple of cars whose drivers don't realize what is happening speed by on the other side of the road, desperate to get clear of the gunfire. The pedestrians have all fled or dived into the nearest buildings and businesses for shelter and cover.

In the distance, over the gunfire, he can hear sirens. Police. They're faint right now. Far away. They won't get here in time.

As he fires, Tom glances down the road. He sees his father and brother and Cindy running. Jeffrey and Anthony keep Cindy between them. They stop at cars, ducking behind cover and looking back to check they're clear before they continue on. One of the Mob heavies has gotten clear of the shoot-out, and he's going after them, gaining on them, his handgun raised. Jeffrey spots him and guns him down with his Glock. He takes him off his feet with three shots into his chest, then puts two more into his side when he's on the ground. The heavy isn't moving. The group runs on. They're not far from the station.

Tom spots Al Bruno. He's crouching in the building's lobby, but he's staring straight at Tom. Further down from him, at the corner of the building, he can see one of the Street Kings barking orders to the others. Tom guesses this must be Ezra. Tom sees how he's looking down the road, too, and he thinks he's spotted Anthony. Not for the first time, Tom wonders what the Street Kings are doing here.

Tom picks off a couple of Street Kings poking their heads out from behind their van. He notices the tires have already been blown out. The van isn't going anywhere. He turns to his left and guns down one of the Mob. He looks to the station and sees his group running up the stairs, waving back the people who have got off the train and are trying to come down into the neighborhood. They don't take much persuading. Once they realize what's happening, they all quickly turn around.

The train won't be there for much longer. Tom lays down suppressing fire until the magazine runs empty. He dumps the M4 as he gets to his feet and starts running for the station, swinging his father's rifle from his back and into his hands.

Gunshots ricochet around him, flying through the air, striking nearby buildings and cars, ricocheting off the El's framework, and hitting the ground. Tom takes cover behind one of the El's support struts. He hears a couple of bullets rattle against the metal. He fires back blindly and then races across the road to a parked car, diving in front of it. Instantly, he hears its windows shatter. He lies flat and looks back under the bottom of the car. He sees four Mob guys still standing, not including Al Bruno or Matt Rossi. There are three Street Kings, including Ezra. Dead and wounded bodies lie strewn across the road. They continue to take potshots at each other, but they're starting to realize that their true objective – the money – is getting away. Tom thinks that because they've been so distracted with each other, they haven't been able to fully concentrate on him and his team. Whatever brought the Street Kings here, it seems to have worked in their favor against the Mob, at least.

The Mob are closer to where Tom is. He aims low under the car and blasts out a pair of kneecaps. A heavy goes down screaming. The others near him dive to the side, alarmed. Tom sees one of them shot through the side of the head as he tries to escape, taken out by a Street King.

Tom hears the police sirens getting closer. They sound like they're coming from all directions now. He needs to move. The train will be leaving soon. The next vehicle parked down from him is a truck with a high body. Tom crawls backward, staying on his stomach so he can look back up the road. He gets under the truck and to the other side.

The door to the lobby is kicked open, and Al Bruno steps out. He blasts the nearest Street King with his shotgun. Blood explodes from the man's torso. The impact almost tears him in half. He flies back through the air almost six feet, and his body skids across the ground. Tom sees Ezra run around the front of the van, out of view of him, but Al Bruno turns away from the Street Kings. He fires on the car where Tom was previously sheltered. The whole car rocks with the impact. More glass shatters.

The train is going to pull away at any second. Tom needs to get moving.

He rises from the front of the truck and empties his magazine in the direction of the Mob. He sees one of them fall, strafed by his fire, but Al Bruno dives behind a car. He drops his shotgun as he goes.

Tom dumps the emptied M4 and starts running. There is pursuing gunfire again, but not as much. A few rounds fly wide or fall short. There aren't enough men left, and Tom can hear what is left of the Mob and the Street Kings continuing to shoot at each other.

Tom runs. He doesn't go for the steps leading up to the station. He runs beyond the station. Tom is counting off the minutes in his head, and he knows the train will be starting to roll now. He needs to get ahead of it. He needs to put distance between himself and anyone who might be following on foot.

He dives onto a support pillar, and he starts to climb. The jagged metal cuts into his hands. Tom pushes up, ignoring it. The train moves slowly, setting off. It passes by overhead. Up here, the whole frame trembles and shakes. Tom continues to climb. He reaches the top as the train goes by. Tom hauls himself onto the tracks. A bullet whizzes by, barely missing him as he pulls himself over. He glances down at the road. It's Al Bruno in pursuit, firing with a handgun now. He starts to climb. Behind him, following but holding back, ducking from cover to cover, Tom sees Ezra. Al has not noticed him.

Tom gets to his feet and starts running down the tracks, chasing after the train. He doesn't look back. He has no idea what kind of speed Al Bruno possesses. He wasn't able to catch up to them in the stairwell, but this isn't a stairwell. Al's a big guy, but he could be fast on a straight. Tom can't afford to look back, to slow. He's gaining on the train. There's a ninety-degree bend around a building up ahead, and the train is slowing for it. He can see passengers at the back, looking out with wide, shocked faces. Tom gets close enough to jump. He lands on the back of the train, grabbing at the door handle, trying to get it open.

There's a gunshot behind him. The bullet embeds itself in the train door. Tom glances back. Al Bruno is in pursuit, and he's getting close. He's fast. His gun is raised, but he's moving so fast he can't get a clear shot. Al knows this. He lowers the gun and presses on. Further back down the track, Tom sees Ezra raise his head over the top. Ezra is lithe and looks faster than Al. With the train slowing, Tom thinks he'll be able to catch up. They might both be able to catch up unless he gets lucky and they kill each other on the tracks.

Tom turns back around, and he climbs, pulling himself up to the top of the train.

60

Most of the people who got off the train at the station promptly got back on when they saw the shoot-out. The carriages are packed tight, and people are breathing hard, trying to calm themselves, knowing that they're moving away now.

Cindy was pressed up against a window, looking down, watching out for Tom. Jeffrey and Anthony were beside her. Tom didn't reach the station. They spotted him below, running past as the train began to move.

"I think he's climbing up onto the tracks," Anthony said.

"We need to get to the back of the train," Cindy said.

They're three cars from the rear. They push through the tightly packed bodies. Jeffrey leads the way. He has the bag with the money strapped tight to his back. He holds the strap. They can't afford to lose it, not now, not after everything. Cindy sticks close to him. Anthony pushes her along from behind.

They reach the final car and hear a commotion coming from the back. The bodies here surge against them, pushing in the other direction, trying to get away, to escape through into the other cars.

"He's got a gun!" someone says.

"He's shooting!" shouts someone else, right beside Cindy's ear.

They feel themselves carried back by the fleeing mass. They try to push through, but they're separated and carried away on the wave.

61

The train is around the bend and picking up speed. Tom struggles to keep his balance. He moves along the top of the car. He'll drop down at the end, get inside.

He hears pounding footsteps on the roof behind him and feels himself tackled onto the roof. Tom turns with the momentum. Al Bruno is on top of him, snarling and grabbing at his face. He doesn't say a word. He's not here for conversation. He has murder in his eyes.

Tom bites at his fingertips as they come near his mouth. Al grunts and hits him in the side of the face with his other hand. Al pushes off and rises to his feet, aiming a stomp for Tom's head. Tom rolls to the side, but Al kicks him, and Tom keeps rolling. He grabs the edge of the train's roof and keeps himself from falling. He can see Chicago down below him. It's passing by fast, in a blur. Falling from here is death.

Tom rolls back from the edge and scrambles to his feet. Al closes in on him. Al doesn't look concerned about their speed or how high up they are. There's nothing in his face.

He's blank. Fearless. He moves on Tom and lands a punch to his chest. Tom gasps. It felt like getting hit with a brick. Al swings for him, but Tom catches his arm this time and head-butts him. Al bleeds, but he doesn't seem to register the blow. Tom slams an elbow across his jaw. Al grimaces at this and spits blood. He grabs the back of Tom's head. He shows his teeth. There's blood on them. He's pulling Tom in close. His mouth is getting wide, and his face is lowering. He's aiming for Tom's throat. He's going to tear it out with his teeth.

Al's legs are spread and braced for purchase. So far, he hasn't reacted to Tom's strikes. Tom has a feeling this one will be different.

He brings up his leg and buries his shin into Al's crotch. Al's teeth gnash together, and he cries out, his body compressing. His legs are still wide, and Tom kicks him there again. Al's grip on the back of his head loosens. Tom keeps hold of his arm. He brings up a knee into Al's midsection, driving the air out of him, then grabs him with both hands by the back of his neck and the back of his trousers and throws him off the side of the train. Al flies through the air and is instantly snatched from view.

Tom falls flat on the roof, feeling an ache in the back of his neck where Al was pulling on him. He looks down the length of the train. The wind whistles in his ears. There's a tunnel in distant view. Tom knows the route. There's a station through it, on the other side.

Tom is struck across the back of the head with some-thing hard, and his forehead bounces off the roof. Dazed, he's rolled over onto his back, and a gun is jammed into his neck.

It's Ezra. He caught up with them. Likely he held back

and stayed out of view while Tom and Al battled.

"Where's Anthony?" Ezra says, pushing the barrel of the gun in hard, his face close to Tom's. "Where's the money? That motherfucker isn't getting away from me! He owes me! I'll fucking kill him for trying to skip out on me!"

Tom makes like he can't speak. Like he's choked off. He's killing time. He doesn't think Ezra has noticed they're approaching a tunnel. If he had, he'd be thinking about ducking low right now, or trying to get off the roof. Every second, they get closer and closer.

Ezra eases the gun from Tom's throat, just a little. *"Where's the money?"*

Tom motions Ezra closer.

Ezra is cautious. He lowers himself, but he takes his time. He keeps his grip tight on the gun. Tom waits until he's close enough. He wants to check how close they are to the tunnel, but he can't risk flicking his eyes upward and having Ezra notice.

"Speak to me," Ezra says. He has to raise his voice to be heard.

"The money," Tom says, making himself sound choked.

Ezra pushes his face in closer. "Where is it?"

Tom speaks clearly. "It's *inside* the train, you fucking idiot."

Tom gets his arms under Ezra and pushes up on his chest. They reach the tunnel. It tears Ezra's head off.

Tom pushes the body away, which is gushing blood from the stump where its head should be. He lies as flat as he can, bracing himself. The roof of the tunnel feels close, like it could scrape his face off.

The train is slowing. It's leaving the tunnel. It's pulling into the station.

62

The train rolls into the station, and Anthony, Cindy, and Jeffrey rush off, along with everyone else. No one knows what has happened on the roof of the train. The passengers flee, not wanting to hang around if there's more shooting. They warn others waiting in the station of the gunfire, and they turn and flee too. The station is in chaos.

Jeffrey looks toward the roof. "Where's Tom? Is he still up there?"

"Tom?" Cindy says, trying to contact him through his earpiece. "There's no answer. He could have lost it in the chase, or if they were fighting, or –" She's starting to look panicked.

Anthony presses a hand to his father's chest, holding him back. "Get out of here," he says. "You and Cindy, go. Take the money. Make sure Stacey and Billy are freed. I'll stay for Tom."

"There could be others still up there," Cindy says.

"I know," Anthony says, pulling out his handgun. "That's

why you need to get clear. All that matters is that Stacey and Billy are safe." He locks eyes with his father, and Jeffrey nods. Jeffrey takes Cindy by the arm, and together they turn and head out of the station.

Anthony watches them go. Most of the station has emptied out. From behind, he hears movement. He turns. It's Tom. He rolls to the edge of the train's roof, then lowers himself down. Anthony helps him. "Is there anyone else up there?" he says.

"No," Tom says. "Just me. Where's Cindy? Where's Dad?"

"They're running," Anthony says. "I said I'd catch up." Anthony looks around the station. There's no one else here. He and Tom are the only two left.

"Then let's go," Tom says.

"I said *I'd* catch them up," Anthony says. He raises the gun.

Tom turns to him. He looks at the gun and then at his brother. He raises an eyebrow. "What are you doing?" he says.

Anthony holds his arm steady, pointing the gun at Tom's chest. At his heart.

"Put the gun down," Tom says. "We don't have time for this."

Anthony takes a deep breath. "You're right about that."

"Anthony –"

Anthony fires the gun into Tom's chest. He squeezes the trigger three times. The gunshots echo loudly around the empty train station.

Tom stumbles backward with the impact. He falls off the edge of the platform and onto the tracks below at the rear of the train.

Anthony looks around and then climbs down off the

platform and crouches over Tom's body. He takes Harlan's camera and microphone from him and speaks into them. Speaks directly to Harlan, knowing he's watching. "We're going to be one short at the meet-up." He throws the electronics to one side, then climbs back up onto the platform and heads out of the station.

Jeffrey and Cindy are at the bottom of the station's steps when Anthony catches up to them. "We need to go," he says.

Cindy looks back up the stairs. "Where's Tom?"

Anthony makes his face solemn. He shakes his head.

"What's happened?" Jeffrey says. "We heard gunshots."

"There was someone still on the roof of the train," Anthony says. "They shot him."

"What?" Cindy says, her eyes wide. "No!" She tries to run back up the stairs, into the station, but Anthony catches her around the waist and stops her.

"There's nothing we can do for him," Anthony says. "I tried already – I checked him. He's... Look, we need to go."

Jeffrey's face is ashen. "Cindy, he... If he's dead, Anthony's right. We need to go."

A car blares its horn, speeding toward them. They all turn to it. Anthony recognizes the car. "It's Connor," he says.

Connor hits the brakes beside them. His window is down. "Get in!"

"What are you doing here?" Jeffrey says.

"You're all over the news!" Connor says. "The radio, too. When I heard what was happening, I came down to see if I could help out." He looks around, checking his mirrors, looking for cops or anyone else who could bring them trouble. "I saw Tom climbing onto the train, so I came to the next station – if you weren't here, I was gonna head on to the next one." He looks around again. "Come on, get in! We can't wait around here!"

Anthony gets into the front with Connor. Jeffrey climbs in the back. Anthony sees how Cindy hesitates, how she looks back at the station, up the stairs, like she expects Tom to appear. Reluctantly, she gets in.

Connor frowns, counting them up. "Where's Tom?" he says.

"Just drive," Anthony says. "I'll tell you later. Get us out of here."

Connor pulls away from the station and disappears them into the traffic. Anthony turns to look back at his father and sees the bag of money stuffed into the space at his feet. Anthony stares at it. A million dollars. The price of Stacey and Billy's lives.

He turns back around. Connor winces as he works the pedals. "If you find somewhere to park," Anthony says, "I can take over driving. I appreciate you getting down here, with your leg how it is."

Connor's lips are pursed. He doesn't say anything. He just nods, once.

Anthony looks straight ahead. On the other side of the road, he can see the traffic building up. The after-effects of the shoot-out. Anthony takes a deep breath. It comes smooth and easy. It fills his lungs. He looks down at his hands. They're not shaking. His heart rate is slightly elevated after all that has just happened, but it's coming down. He thinks about Tom lying there back on the tracks, and what he did to put him there, and he's shocked, after everything, at how calm he feels.

63

Harlan slaps the flat of his hand down on the table and howls with laughter. "God *damn!*" he says, looking back at Stacey.

She saw all the same things he did. Heard them, too. The color is gone from her face. She's frozen in horror.

"You see what he did?" Harlan says, still laughing. "That cold son of a bitch! His own *brother*! Well, shit, he really didn't like him, huh? Little-brother syndrome." Harlan leans back in his chair, shaking his head. His elation is not just at Tom's death. It's relief. They have the money. Despite everything, they're getting away.

Mostly, though, his elation *is* at Tom's death. He turns back to Stacey, glad to have someone to talk to with all these thoughts racing through his head. "Tom, though, he was a fucking *animal*, huh? He was like a machine." He leans forward and clasps his hands, still grinning like a fool. He can't wipe it off his face. He doesn't want to. "You wanna hear a secret?"

Stacey manages to tear her eyes away from the laptop

screen and look at him. She wipes her mouth on her sleeve and looks like she's trying not to be sick.

Harlan laughs at the sight of her. "Oh, your boy's shocked you, hasn't he? You didn't think Anthony had it in him, did you? Hell, I gotta admit, that was a swerve I did *not* see coming! But let me tell you about my little secret, Stacey, because it all ties in. Your potential brother-in-law there, Tom Rollins, he was a dead man walking anyway. You saw what he was like. I wasn't taking a chance on letting him live. You kidding me? I'm planning on living the rest of my life *without* having to look back over my shoulder. No way I'm gonna leave that psychopath on the loose to come try to track me down. No, Anthony has done me a big favor. Bigger than he realizes."

Stacey stares at him blankly. The better part of three days of being locked in the cage, unwashed and hungry and thirsty, and without her son, has weakened and exhausted her. She's pale and looks thinner. Harlan isn't sure how much of what he says is getting through to her.

He bites his lip and leans in a little closer. "You wanna hear my other big secret, Stacey? They're *all* dead. Anthony, his dad, and the little punk girl with them – they're all dead people walking, too. Don't worry, though, you and Billy will be free to go. I don't have anything to worry about from the two of you, do I?"

He notices how her face brightens a little at the mention of her son's name.

"But those three," Harlan says, "well, you can't be too careful, right? You and the boy, you're going to be my shields. Anything happens to the two of you, it's going to be on them. You don't have anything to worry about from me going forward."

Stacey is trying to speak. Harlan has to turn his head to hear her better. "*Billy,*" she's saying.

"Jesus Christ, you're like a broken record." Harlan turns back to the laptop. He stares at the screen that should show Tom's feed. It stares off to the side of the tunnel. Through the microphone, he can hear a train approaching. Tom's body is about to be crushed. Harlan watches until the train pulls into the station, and the screen goes blank.

Harlan claps his hands together. He checks in with the others, but they're still in Connor's car. He closes his laptop. He'll message Anthony soon, tell him that he'll send him the details of where they're going to meet later. He'll be sure to congratulate them all on a job well done, too. Harlan doesn't want to meet up until it's dark. He has just the place in mind. It's not far from where he's stashed Billy. Billy is chained to a radiator in a derelict building. Harlan has paid off a junkie to check in on him and to make sure no one else tries to take him. The junkie has looked in on Billy every few hours and then sent Harlan an update. The last Harlan heard, the kid sounds to be in much the same shape as his mom.

Harlan cracks his knuckles and gets to his feet, twisting side to side to pop his spine. He taps the side of Stacey's cage with his boot to get her attention. Her eyes roll up in her skull to see him. "Look lively," he says. "Not long now. Just a few hours and we'll go and get your son." He sees the hope in her eyes. Some of the life returns to her. Harlan can't help himself. He squats down so his face is right in front of hers. "Or we'll see what the rats have left of him, at least."

The hope goes out of her eyes. She starts to wail. She throws herself weakly against the cage, and with her uncuffed arm she tries to grab at him through the bars. Harlan laughs and stays out of her reach. Stacey's voice has returned to her, he notices. "I'll kill you!" she says. "If he's hurt, I'll fucking kill you! *I'll kill you!*"

Harlan laughs as she descends into heavy sobbing. He leaves the basement. Leaves her all alone with the thought of rats chewing on her boy's body.

64

nthony and the others stay in Connor's car. Anthony is behind the steering wheel. They've parked in a multistory parking garage, and they wait for Harlan to tell them where to go. A couple of hours have already passed since the heist. They keep the cameras and microphones that Harlan gave them on.

They don't speak. Jeffrey, in the back, wraps his arms tightly around the bag of money and stares out the window. Cindy is on her laptop, erasing them from all the security cameras she can find. She sniffs while she works, like she's trying hard not to cry. In the front passenger seat, Connor massages his leg.

Anthony holds the steering wheel with both hands and stares straight ahead. He still feels calm about everything that has happened so far, but he feels a growing concern for Stacey and Billy. It builds in his chest and in the back of his skull. It fills him. It gnaws at him. He grits his teeth and clenches his jaw and squeezes the wheel so his knuckles pop white. He wasn't expecting to be waiting this long. Harlan is probably doing it on purpose. Drawing this whole thing out. Anthony looks at the sky. It's still light, but he has a feeling Harlan is going to wait until it is dark. If so, they still have hours to go. This feeling will build inside him until it feels like it's going to consume him completely.

He swallows, trying to keep it down. Surprisingly, he feels his body grow weary and tired. His eyes flutter, and his head begins to nod. He battles to keep himself awake.

His father notices. "Just sleep," he says, placing a hand on his shoulder. "It's the adrenalin wearing off. We aren't going anywhere. If Harlan gets in touch, we'll wake you. Just rest for now."

Anthony closes his eyes and does as his father says.

When he opens them again, it's dark outside the car. His phone is buzzing. He snatches it from his pocket. A message from Harlan. He's telling them where to meet. A junkyard in the city.

Anthony pushes himself upright and rubs his eyes. "How long was I out?"

"It's been a few hours," Connor says.

"What did he say?" Jeffrey says, nodding at the phone.

Anthony tells them where they need to go, and starts up the engine. He turns the car around and leaves the parking garage. He wants to speed, to race there, but he forces himself to take his time.

"Go slow," Jeffrey says as they approach the junkyard. "We can't rush. Not now. And be careful."

There are crushed and rusted cars piled up higher than the chain-link fence that encloses the junkyard. The main gate is closed, but it's not locked despite the late hour. Connor gets out of the car and limps over to open it. Anthony slowly rolls through and waits for Connor to get back in. "The lock was shot off," he says. "I could see it on the ground off to the side."

They all look around. There's no one around who works here. All the employees are long gone. There's a security camera on the main building, but it's been smashed. They roll slowly through the piles of scrap metal until they can't go any further. "He said he's by the compactor," Anthony says.

They get out of the car. Anthony offers Connor an assist, but Connor waves him off. "I can manage," he says.

Anthony isn't so sure and notices how he uses the walls of cars to support himself as they go, but he understands, too, that it's best for them not to be too close together. They can't weigh each other down.

The compactor comes into view, a metal monstrosity in silhouette against the night sky. The ground here is lit up. Harlan has placed lamps on the ground so he can see their approach. They hear Harlan before they see him.

"There they are!" he says. "My boys and girl of the hour. Come on into the light where I can see you all. You too, Connor, I know you're here."

They do as Harlan says. Anthony sees Stacey and Billy. They look like hell. Harlan has put the ball gag on Stacey again, and the leash. The leash is attached to Harlan's belt. Billy is in his left arm, held off the ground against his chest. A human shield. Harlan's gun is aimed at the side of his head. It's only been a few days since Anthony last saw them, but mother and son look emaciated. Both of their eyes are puffy. They've been crying. Billy is still sobbing. They're both looking at Anthony, they're both begging silently for him to help them, and he feels his heart breaking.

"Nice and easy now, boys and girl," Harlan says. "As you

can see, I expect full care and cooperation. Is that my bag of money?"

Jeffrey holds it up.

"Excellent. Now, that's far enough for all of you. I want to get a good look at you all." He casts his eyes down them, from left to right – Jeffrey, Anthony, Cindy, and Connor. "The old-timer, my old buddy Anthony, the little punk mouse, and the gimp. The gang's *almost* all here. One short." He grins.

There's about ten feet between them. "Let Stacey and Billy go, Harlan," Anthony says.

"A real shame what happened to your brother, isn't it, Anthony?" Harlan is beaming ear to ear, looking like a shark again, peering out at them over Billy's shoulder. "Do your new friends know what happened? Does the old-timer know what happened to his son?"

Anthony feels his father move his feet beside him, shifting his weight. He knows what Harlan is doing. "They know what happened," Anthony says. "We don't have time for this."

"We have as much time as I say we do, buddy," Harlan says. "And something tells me your buddies here know a *version* of what happened back in that train station."

"Let them *go*."

"I don't have my money yet, Anthony."

Jeffrey takes a step forward with the bag, but Harlan stops him. "Uh-uh," he says. "Not you, old-timer. You stay right where you are. You too, Anthony." He looks at Connor and Cindy. "I've got to make a decision. The gimp, or the girl? Hmm." He makes a show of tapping the barrel of his gun against the side of his head, thinking. He grins, showing his teeth. "Girl. Yeah, little mouse, I'm talking to you. Don't look so scared. I'm not gonna bite."

Cindy has left her laptop in the car. Without it, Anthony thinks she looks very small. She steps forward and holds her hand out for the bag of money without hesitation. Her face is firm, determined. Jeffrey hands her the bag. Cindy takes it. She steps forward.

"Not so fast," Harlan says. "Nice and easy. One step at a time, little mouse."

Cindy does as he says.

"Did you tell them the whole story of Tom's ignominious defeat, Anthony?" Harlan says as Cindy approaches. "How his death wasn't so much of a heroic last stand as a sudden and unexpected fall? They weren't watching, were they? Not with their eyes and not with their cameras. They were too busy trying to get away. But I was watching. You know I was. I saw the whole thing. Maybe they'd like me to tell them the story?"

"Anthony?" Jeffrey says. "What's he getting at?"

"Nothing," Anthony says, staring at Harlan.

Halfway to Harlan with the money, Cindy pauses and looks back at him over her shoulder. To his left and his right, his father and Connor are both looking his way. Even Stacey seems to be staring at him with accusation.

"Do you want the damn money?" Anthony says. "Or do you want to do fucking story time?"

Harlan laughs. "Come on, little mouse. Come on to me, that's right."

Cindy tears her eyes away from Anthony and forces herself to continue toward Harlan.

"Maybe I have time for both, Anthony," Harlan says.

"Damn it, stop playing around!" Anthony says, barely able to contain himself. "Just take your money and let them go!"

Cindy has nearly reached him.

"All right, wait right there," Harlan says. "Little mouse, open up that bag. Stacey, now remember? We talked about this? Go and count the money. Little mouse, you stay where you are and hold the bag open for her. Needless to say, everyone, my money had best be all there."

Stacey steps forward as far as the leash will allow her. She starts shifting through the stacks of cash in the bag, counting them up. Harlan is watching all of them closely. "Do it so I can see," he says. Stacey lifts the money higher so he can see the stacks she's counting.

"You don't know how much was in the safe," Anthony says.

"I have enough of an idea," Harlan says.

"You watched as it was packed into the bag."

"I don't take anything for granted."

After a while, Stacey straightens. She turns to Harlan. With the ball gag in her mouth, she can't speak, so she nods.

"You're sure?" Harlan says. "It's all there?"

She nods again.

Harlan pulls on the leash and drags her back to his side. "Close it back up, little mouse. Good, good, just like that. Now, throw it over here. At my feet."

Cindy does. She raises her hands now she's no longer carrying the bag, and she backs away slowly.

"Not so fast," Harlan says. He takes the gun from Billy's head, and he points it at Cindy. He's smiling.

A shot rings out. Anthony watches, wide-eyed, frozen to the spot where he stands. For a moment, nothing happens.

Then Harlan falls back, dragging Billy and Stacey down with him.

Anthony drags his frozen feet free and runs over, dropping to his knees next to them all. He lifts Billy and hoists him from Harlan's body. Cindy is beside him. He hands Billy off to her and then tears the leash from Stacey's neck as she claws at the ball gag to get it out of her mouth. Anthony goes to embrace her, but she pushes him away and hurries to Billy and Cindy. Cindy hands him over, and Stacey squeezes her son tight. They're both crying.

Anthony watches them. He looks down at Harlan's still body. He's dead. The bullet entered his skull between his eyes, through the bridge of his nose. Blood spills from the back of his head. His eyes have rolled back, showing only the whites.

Jeffrey looks down. "Flaccid paralysis," he says.

Anthony looks up at him. "What?"

Jeffrey points at the hole between Harlan's eyes. "The bullet enters the T-box and severs the spinal column on its way out, preventing an involuntary muscle spasm that may have squeezed the trigger and shot Cindy." Jeffrey shakes his head. "Hell of a shot. He didn't learn it from me."

"What happened?" Stacey says, her voice hoarse. She holds onto Billy, pressing his face into her shoulder and refusing to let him go. She spins around. "What happened? Who shot him?"

"Stacey, calm down, it's okay now," Anthony says, standing, holding up his hands. "You're both safe now." He steps toward her.

She steps back. "Keep away from me! I saw what you did!"

"Stacey, wait –"

They hear footsteps approaching, coming through the center of a tunnel of piled-up cars. Cindy is already running toward the sound.

Tom Rollins emerges, the Springfield Armory 2020 Waypoint .308 slung over his shoulder. Cindy throws herself into his arms.

Stacey stares at him like she's seen a ghost, then turns back to Anthony, her mouth agape.

"We'll tell you everything," Anthony says.

65

They knew Harlan would likely try to kill them all. The fact he turned his gun on Cindy after she gave him the money proved this. Luckily, they were prepared.

Anthony used blanks to shoot Tom. It was all for show. Just like when he spoke into the camera and then threw it to one side so it was staring at the tunnel wall. Every detail was important. Once Tom was 'dead' and camera-less, he was free to return to where he'd parked his father's car and use it to get to the meet-up point with Harlan. Of course, they needed to wait until Harlan gave them those details. When they finally came through, Cindy sent them on to Tom, shooting him a blind text without looking at her phone. Again, they couldn't take the risk of Harlan watching them and seeing what she was doing through her camera.

After that, it was a case of taking their time getting there. Allowing Tom a chance to get into position with the rifle. Keeping Harlan distracted. Keeping him talking. Never once breaking character from the belief that Tom was dead, and then showing their shock as Harlan implied Anthony had killed him.

Two days have passed since then. Tom, Cindy, Jeffrey, Connor, and Anthony have been lying low in Anthony's house. Stacey and Billy have not been present. They've been in their apartment. Anthony has messaged a couple of times, but for the most part he's given them their space. They want to be left alone after all that has happened, and he understands. They've been through a lot.

They've watched news reports about the shoot-out. There hasn't been any mention of the heist. Police are theorizing that the battle was a gang dispute.

Cindy has been busy. She already erased the security footage all along their escape route, but she's had more to do. The car that was destroyed and left behind, she's made sure to erase Tom's name from its records. She's changed its details to say that it was off the road and awaiting junking.

Harlan's body is gone. Tom and Jeffrey dealt with it at the scrapyard. They sent Cindy, Anthony, and Connor back to the car with Stacey and Billy to keep them company and comforted. When they were gone, Tom and Jeffrey cut Harlan's body into pieces with an axe they found after picking the lock on the main office. From there, they fired up the incinerator and put his limbs inside. There has been no mention of Harlan on the news.

Tom and Cindy leave the house early in the morning before anyone else has woken. They take the money with them and go to Stacey's building. They make a few stops on the way. Stacey is reluctant to let them up when they buzz her apartment, but she eventually does.

"How are you both doing?" Tom says when they enter

her apartment. They take a seat at the table in the kitchen. Billy is in his room, playing with his toys.

Stacey drinks tea. She takes her time answering. "Terrible," she says. "That's how we're doing. *You* look well though, Tom. For a dead man."

"It wasn't like we had a way of telling you the plan," Tom says.

"I know that." She stares into her cup and takes a deep, shuddering breath. "For a long time that day, I thought Anthony had killed you. And you know what? Not for a second did I doubt he'd done it. After seeing the two of you together, and the way you were constantly at each other's throats – the things you were *saying* to each other – I believed he'd shot you."

Cindy reaches across the table and squeezes Stacey's hand. She looks better than she did the other night. She's showered and in fresh clothes. She's hydrated. She's been eating, though Tom doesn't think she's been eating much.

"How's Billy holding up?" Cindy says.

Stacey shakes her head. "I don't know what to do. He's having nightmares. He barely leaves my side. I think I'm going to have to get him therapy, but I can't afford that. And what's to say it'll work?" She holds her head in her hands.

"Have you spoken to Anthony?"

"A little." Stacey lets her arms drop. They thud against the table. "I don't want to be around him right now. I – I can't. Harlan took us because of him. I thought... I thought I was never going to see Billy again." Her eyes are moist. She wipes them.

"Stacey," Tom says. He waits until she looks at him. "I'm not going to tell you what to do with your life, or what kind of decisions you should make. I love my brother, but he's never been the most reliable. His carelessness has put a lot of lives at risk." Tom places the bag on the table. "There's $250,000 in here. It's more than enough for you and Billy to go somewhere else and start over. You can afford therapy for Billy. And for you. Listen, I said I wasn't going to tell you what to do, and I won't. I understand you might not want to leave, or at least not right away. But you should keep this money. Keep it hidden. Don't let Anthony know about it. It's your get-out clause, if you ever need it."

Stacey stares at the bag. She doesn't know what to say.

"Just think about it," Cindy says, rubbing her arm. "You don't have to rush into anything."

Tom and Cindy stand at the table. Stacey doesn't get up with them. She doesn't see them out. She remains seated, staring at the quarter of a million dollars as they leave.

66

Harlan is dead, and the Street Kings are decimated. Jeffrey feels more comfortable leaving Anthony in Chicago. He did what he came here to do.

It's later that same day, after Tom and Cindy have gotten back from seeing Stacey. They haven't told anyone that's where they went. Tom, Cindy, and Jeffrey are getting their things together, ready to pack them into Jeffrey's car. They're leaving today. It's a long drive back.

Cindy takes Tom to one side. "I've booked a plane ticket," she says. "Can you drop me at the airport?"

Tom cocks his head, surprised. "We can take you back to Texas. We don't mind."

"I know you don't," Cindy says, glancing toward his father. "But I feel like the two of you have a lot to talk about. You haven't had a chance yet. I don't want either of you to feel like you have to hold back just because I'm there."

Tom looks at his father. He's talking to Anthony and Connor. Connor is standing, using the wall for support, but keeping weight on his wounded leg to strengthen it. Jeffrey laughs about something. He turns his head to the side and coughs and then goes on laughing. Tom nods and turns back to Cindy. "I think you're right," he says. "Thank you."

Tom goes to join his father and brother. Jeffrey is talking. "No more of this gang shit," he's imploring. "Get a real job, Anthony. I'm starting treatment soon, and I'm not gonna have the energy to worry about you."

"I will, I will," Anthony says, nodding. "We both will." He taps Connor's chest with the back of his hand.

"I'm not sure what I'm good at," Connor says, "but there's gotta be something where I'm not getting shot at."

"Just don't go falling into bad habits," Jeffrey says. "Promise me, Anthony. I need you to do that."

Anthony looks his father in the eye and nods once. "I promise."

They embrace, and as they separate, Anthony looks up to see Tom waiting for him. "I need to talk to you," he says.

"So talk," Anthony says.

"I think in private."

Anthony shrugs and says, "Sure," and then leads him to the bedroom.

Before he speaks, Tom sees the picture of his mother. The picture of Alejandra. He tears his eyes away from them both to focus on his brother. "Cindy and I have given away the money."

Anthony blinks. "What do you mean?"

"This morning, when we were out, we looked into some places in the city – charities, care homes, things like that – and we shared the money between them. Deposited it anonymously."

Anthony looks like he can't believe what he's hearing.

"Are you kidding me right now? That money – that fucking money could have set us up!"

"Ezra is dead," Tom says. "You don't have to pay the Street Kings back anymore. Harlan is dead. The Mob don't know you had anything to do with it. You don't need that money. And it's Mob money, Anthony. It's dirty. It wouldn't feel right keeping it."

"Speak for yourself."

"Maybe I am, but I'd like to think I could speak for you on this, too."

Anthony starts to respond, but he doesn't. There's no point. The money is gone.

"It's better it goes to do some good," Tom says.

Anthony shrugs and holds out his hands. "Sure," he says. "Whatever."

"Speaking of the Street Kings," Tom says, and this gets Anthony's attention. "Any idea what they were doing there?"

"Not a clue," Anthony says.

"When I was on the roof of the train with Ezra, he was asking for you. He knew you were there. Seemed like he knew what was happening."

"I don't know what to tell you."

"You speak to anyone?"

"You know I'm not that stupid."

"I'm just struggling to see how he could have known what we were doing."

"I dunno – maybe someone was watching us. He had guys following me. You said you saw that for yourself."

"I dealt with them," Tom says. "And there was no one watching *us* while we were watching the Mob."

"You're so sure of that?"

"Yes, I am."

"Then I don't know what to tell you, Tom, and I don't care for what you're insinuating."

Tom looks at his brother, and Anthony holds his eye. Tom is undeterred. "Why'd you bring the grenade?"

"Connor wanted me to take it. In case things went south. I didn't think they would, but I knew it would make him feel better, especially when he couldn't come along with us. And it's a good thing I did, isn't it?"

"Uh-huh. How'd it feel to shoot me, Anthony?"

Anthony smirks. He massages his pinkie finger just below the break. "Not as much fun as I expected it to be. Maybe because they weren't real bullets." He shrugs. "Who can say?"

"The one thing about the Street Kings turning up, the train station was a good place for it to happen. It wasn't supposed to happen there, but it was a better place."

"I thought falling onto the tracks was a nice touch. Looked like it hurt." Anthony grins.

They stare at each other in silence. They're healing, but they both still bear the marks of where they have struck each other, as well as the marks of recent events.

Suddenly, Anthony softens. His shoulders slump. "Listen, Tom," he says. "This isn't easy for me to say...but everything you did, for Stacey and for Billy – and for me, I guess – I appreciate it."

Tom blinks, surprised. He wasn't expecting this.

Anthony forces himself to straighten and to look Tom in the eye. He holds out a hand. "Thank you," he says.

Tom stares at the hand, expecting some kind of follow-up. None comes. Anthony is steadfast. Tom takes the hand. They shake.

67

W hile the brothers talk, Cindy and Jeffrey load the car. Cindy tells Jeffrey she's flying back to Texas.

"That's a real shame," Jeffrey says, leaning against the side of his car. "It's been a pleasure having you along. I was hoping to get to know you a little better, without all of *this* going on around us." He waves a finger in the air.

"I would have liked that," Cindy says. "But I think you and Tom need to talk."

Jeffrey folds his arms and nods. "Yeah, we do. I shouldn't have skipped out on Hopper Creek like I did, but I was worried."

"You don't need to explain yourself to me."

Jeffrey smiles at her gratefully.

Cindy leans against the car next to him, looking toward the house. "What do you think they're talking about in there?"

"Well, I haven't heard any shouting," Jeffrey says. "So I

take that as a good sign. And no one's thrown anyone else out a window yet, so I take that as a *very* good sign."

Cindy laughs.

Jeffrey takes a deep breath. "Cindy..."

"Yeah?"

"I'm under no illusions – I'm gonna die sooner rather than later. Sooner than I ever thought I would." He sighs, staring at the ground. "I thought I'd have more time. More time to see my sons make peace. More time to see Anthony straighten his life out, and for Tom to settle down. Maybe I've gotten lucky, and maybe this is it for Anthony – but as for Tom..."

Cindy frowns. "He has Hayley. They have a home."

Jeffrey grunts. "I'm not so sure Tom will ever settle down. Tom's been running for a long time now. He's never been the same since his mom died."

Cindy watches Jeffrey's face. He looks so morose. She wants to give him a hug, but they don't know each other very well, and she's not sure that's what he wants.

"A point's going to come where he starts moving again," Jeffrey says. "I know it will. I've known Hayley a long time, since she was just a girl. She's sweet, real sweet, and I believe she loves Tom. But I'm not sure that'll ever be enough for him. Tom won't settle. He needs someone who can keep up with him." Jeffrey looks at her.

Cindy frowns.

"You've spent a lot of time with him, haven't you, Cindy?"

"I guess so. What are you getting at?"

"I'm not getting at anything. I'm just pointing out, you're here and Hayley's not."

"It's not like that –"

Jeffrey holds up a hand. "Cindy, I need you to do something for me, after I'm gone."

Cindy waits.

"I need you to take care of him. I need you to look out for him. I don't think there's anyone else who can." Jeffrey looks at her. His face betrays nothing, but his eyes are so earnest. "Will you do that for me?"

Cindy doesn't respond for a long time. She looks back at Jeffrey. She doesn't speak. She nods.

The door of the house opens. Tom comes out, with Anthony by his side. Connor follows to wave them off.

"We've got a long drive," Tom says, reaching them. "I'll take first shift at the wheel." He smiles at Cindy. "And we don't want you to miss your flight." His smile falters as he looks into her face. Behind him, Jeffrey and Anthony are hugging goodbye. "Something wrong?"

Cindy shakes her head. "No," she says. "Nothing."

68

Anthony and Connor watch as the car disappears down the road.

"I wanna ask you something," Connor says, keeping the weight on his right leg and wincing through the pain. "But I should probably ask it inside."

Anthony raises an eyebrow. "Sure," he says. "Let's go."

They go through to the kitchen, and Anthony gets them a couple of beers from the refrigerator. They take seats at the table. Connor eases himself down into his chair. Anthony drinks from his bottle, but Connor does not touch his.

"Well?" Anthony says.

"When the Street Kings turned up," Connor says, "if they'd killed your brother, what then?"

Anthony leans back in his chair, taking another thoughtful sip. "You know, I've thought about that a lot. Especially since the Mob turned up, too – that was unexpected. Ordinarily, I wouldn't have given a shit if they killed him." He bites his lip, staring at the table. "But with Harlan having Stacey and Billy, for the whole plan with the blanks and the sniper rifle... Well, I needed him to survive. That's why I took the grenade when you offered it. In case things got too hairy." He looks at Connor and drinks again. "But if he *had* got himself killed, I would've worked something else out. There wouldn't have been any other choice."

"Then it's a good thing you were the one to kill him."

Anthony laughs. "When you called Ezra, what did you tell him?"

"That you were planning on taking the money and splitting town," Connor says. "And that you'd called in your brother and your dad to help you out."

Anthony grins. "Did he know it was you?"

"I never told him. Never gave him a chance to ask. Gave him all the information he needed and hung up, like you told me."

"Good."

"He obviously believed me," Connor says. "But here's another question. What if Ezra sent some guys along, but he *didn't* go with them?"

"Here's the thing about Tom," Anthony says. "And not many people know this, and not many people want to admit it, but I see it. Tom is not a man. He's fucking *dynamite*. The Street Kings are just a gang. They're not trained. They can't do the things Tom can. He was gonna blow them away no matter who was there – as it turns out, the Mob did most of the work for us. But the point is this, whether Ezra was there or not, the Street Kings were going to be crippled. Without the manpower behind him, what would we have to worry about from Ezra? Hell, we would've just dealt with him ourselves."

Connor frowns. "You mean, like, kill him?"

"These are all hypotheticals," Anthony says. "It didn't happen, so it doesn't matter. Just forget it."

Connor stares at his bottle. He still hasn't taken a drink. He shifts in his seat. His leg is bothering him.

"Ezra is dead," Anthony says. "Harlan is dead. Everything I – *we* – needed. It's a shame about the money, though. It would be nice to still have that."

"What happened to the money?" Connor says.

Anthony tells him. "I suppose I shouldn't be too surprised that Tom would go and give it all away to good causes." He shakes his head. He drains off his bottle, then nods at Connor's. "Are you going to drink that or just stare at it?"

"When I feel like it," Connor says. He's silent for a moment. He opens his mouth a couple of times, but he keeps closing it, almost like he's scared to say whatever is on his mind. Finally, he forces it out. "What now?"

Anthony tilts his empty bottle on its side and spins it, balancing it with the tip of his finger. He does this for a long time. Connor waits for an answer. Anthony places the bottle flat and spins it. He spins it until it points straight back at him.

"Now," he says, staring into the bottle's opening. "Now we rebuild." He raises his eyes and looks at Connor. "And that starts with Stacey."

69

Hayley and Sylvia know that they're coming back. They're waiting at the door as Tom and Jeffrey roll down the road.

It's been a long drive. Tom and his father have had plenty of time to talk. Sometimes, though, they just sat in silence, appreciating the peace of the road.

There was not much to say. Tom knows his father is going to die. While they've been in Chicago, he's seen small signs of its coming. Jeffrey was able to handle himself during the heist and the shoot-out, but Tom knows he will not be able to operate at such a level for much longer. He has not, however, made his peace with the knowledge that Jeffrey is going to die. He's not sure when he will.

Jeffrey squeezed Tom's shoulder comfortingly while he drove, while they talked about it. "I'm scared, Tom," he said. "Of course I am. But it's out of my hands now. All any of us can do is the best that we can do. But Tom, when I'm gone, you don't need to be alone. You know that, don't you? You'll have Sylvia, still. You'll have your brother. You have Cindy."

Tom didn't say anything.

"You don't have to be strong," Jeffrey said. "It's all right to be weak sometimes. It's all right to ask for help. It's all right to lean on people. I didn't realize that until late. I didn't realize that when you and your brother were just young, and I was raising you all by myself. I thought it was better to tell you to be strong. I thought it was better to make it so you weren't weak." Jeffrey sniffed, and Tom realized his father was crying. "I did what I thought was best, I did what I thought was right, but I think I might have been wrong. I wish I'd done better for you boys, I truly do. I wish I'd known what the hell I was doing. I wish...I wish your mother hadn't died."

Tom swallowed.

"I love you, Tom. Never forget that."

"I know you do," Tom said. "I love you too."

"And you're not alone. Never forget that."

Looking into Hayley's smiling face as he gets out of the car, Tom does not feel alone. As she runs into his arms and clasps him tight, he does not feel alone. And he realizes, as he holds her, that when his father was listing names he could turn to for comfort after his death, he never mentioned Hayley. He mentioned Sylvia and Anthony.

And Cindy.

Tom turns a little, Hayley still in his arms, and looks toward his father, but Jeffrey is not looking back. Jeffrey is holding tight to Sylvia, and Sylvia is holding tight to him, and there are tears in her eyes, and they glisten upon her cheeks.

EPILOGUE

Anthony and Connor go to The Cauldron.

They don't go unarmed. They carry their Glocks. They're hoping they don't have to use them, but they're not taking any chances.

Connor is no longer limping. He doesn't wince when he puts weight on his leg. This morning, when Anthony dressed, he looked at himself in the mirror and saw that all of the cuts and the bruises and the markings that were on his face have healed. Only small scars remain in their place.

Anthony and Connor have kept their ears to the ground. They've listened out for news of the South Side Street Kings. They're not gone, not completely, but they've been in disarray since Ezra's death. No one suitable enough has stepped up to take his place. It doesn't seem like anyone can.

It's midday, and The Cauldron is not busy. A couple of regulars prop up the bar. One booth is occupied by a lonely old drunk. The bartender eyes them as they pass, surprised to see them. Anthony strides purposefully through. Connor follows him, carrying a sport bag.

Anthony doesn't bother to knock as he reaches the back room. He steps inside.

Ethan Hardy and Stewie Norton are present, along with a few others. Everyone stiffens as they see who has entered, and Anthony sees a couple of hands go toward guns.

Anthony holds up his empty hands. "Stay cool," he says. "Last thing I'm here looking for is trouble."

"Uh-huh," Ethan says. "Then what is it you *are* looking for? Been weeks since anyone last saw either of you."

"We should just drop the two of you where you stand," Stewie says. "Ezra's dead because of you, motherfuckers."

Anthony motions to himself, faux innocent. "Because of *moi*? I'm positive I have no clue what you're talking about, Stewart." He grins and goes to a table. The same table where Ezra broke his finger with a hammer. The finger is healed now, but it's not as straight as it used to be. It never will be again. "Gather round."

"Who the fuck are you to be telling us what to do?" Stewie says.

Anthony waves him off, not interested in his bravado. "Gather round, and I'll tell you why I'm here."

The Street Kings are wary, but they approach.

Anthony claps his hands together and looks at them each in turn, smiling. Ethan and Stewie glare at him. Anthony is undeterred. There are seven Street Kings present. Anthony is undeterred by this, too. News will spread. Others will come running.

"I'm here to take over," Anthony says. He motions for silence before anyone can react, but a few groans escape. "Hold your applause until the end. I'm here to take over the running of this operation, and I'm going to make us *real* Kings. Not the low-level common street thugs that we were under Ezra. No, now, going forward, we're going to live up to our namesake."

The gathered men look doubtful.

"Uh-huh," Ethan says. "And how are you going to do that?"

"Hell, what makes you think we're even gonna let you walk out of here alive?" Stewie says.

"Because deep down, in your heart of hearts, you know I'm the only one who can do it," Anthony says. "You know I'm the only one who's walked in here since Ezra died and said he's going to rebuild the South Side Street Kings and said it like he's fucking *meant* it. You know that, and you're gonna start to believe it just as much as I do."

They're not all glaring at him now. A lot of them look intrigued. They look willing to be persuaded. Even Ethan and Stewie look curious.

Anthony motions for Connor to put the bag on the table. "This is how we start," Anthony says. "This is my investment in all of our futures." He opens the bag, and they all look in to see what it holds.

$250,000.

ABOUT THE AUTHOR

Did you enjoy *Blood Feud*? Please consider leaving a review on Amazon to help other readers discover the book.

Paul Heatley left school at sixteen, and since then has held a variety of jobs including mechanic, carpet fitter, and book-shop assistant, but his passion has always been for writing. He writes mostly in the genres of crime fiction and thriller, and links to his other titles can be found on his website. He lives in the north east of England.

Want to connect with Paul? Visit him at his website.

www.PaulHeatley.com

ALSO BY PAUL HEATLEY

Blood Line

(A Tom Rollins Thriller Book 1)

Wrong Turn

(A Tom Rollins Thriller Book 2)

Hard to Kill

(A Tom Rollins Thriller Book 3)

Snow Burn

(A Tom Rollins Thriller Book 4)

Road Kill

(A Tom Rollins Thriller Book 5)

No Quarter

(A Tom Rollins Thriller Book 6)

Hard Target

(A Tom Rollins Thriller Book 7)

Last Stand

(A Tom Rollins Thriller Book 8)

Blood Feud

(A Tom Rollins Thriller Book 9)

Made in United States
North Haven, CT
16 July 2023